The Erotic Ghosts Collection

The Erotic Ghosts Collection

Honey Cummings
Urban Legend Erotica Collection

4 Horsemen
Publications, Inc.

Published By: 4 Horsemen Publications, Inc.

4 Horsemen Publications, Inc.
PO Box 417
Sylva, NC 28779
4horsemenpublications.com
info@4horsemenpublications.com

Cover & Typesetting by Valerie Willis

Library of Congress Control Number: 2022949658

Paperback ISBN-13: 978-1-64450-991-3
Audiobook ISBN-13: 978-1-64450-993-7
Ebook ISBN-13: 978-1-64450-994-4

Ghosts

Laying with the Lady in Blue

Honey Cummings

Urban Legend Erotica Collection

TABLE OF CONTENTS

Dedication

To Erik

I had two pieces to the next trio;
Bloody Mary and Woman in White.

Thanks for sharing the alluring ghost story
of the Blue lady from Story, Indiana!

XOXO
Honey Cummings

1

Bed & Breakfast

Jane Story stood in the dark foyer of her old Bed & Breakfast. The building had been built when Story, Indiana, was founded in 1851 as a logging community. Later, hippies purchased the place, then re-assembled the whole town as a tourist attraction. At least, it brought the past into the present, and the community was better for it, despite the highways diverting their traffic away. Despite all the changes and the passage of time, the B&B held its own. A relic covered in vines, rust, and still as inviting to visitors as the day it first opened.

Hands on her hips, Jane was a curvy thing in her tight cut-off jeans and light blue crop top. The outfit made her look like a brown-haired model from a clothing ad for high-end stores, where a simple white shirt cost triple the price of a similar thrift shop find. She took pride in being old fashioned, and she loved the old inn with all her soul. On days like this, she wanted to feel alive or at least blend into the current times.

Her hair had been jumbled into a messy bun and she blew a strand from her face as she lit her pipe. An old habit she kept going, though she hadn't seen anyone come through the B&B smoking a pipe in decades. This had always been her one vice, a gift from her beloved husband in fact, and she couldn't part with it. The aromatic cherry tobacco filled the room quickly as she waved the match.

Glancing up, she scowled at the no smoking sign. *Make me,* she thought with a smirk.

Pipe in her lips, she removed her gardening hat and gloves, happy to assist in keeping the old place alive and well. It had been hers for some time, but at last, it had swapped ownership multiple times. The latest owner and management seemed to enjoy its quaint and quirky qualities, quelling her need to quarrel with anyone about it. They had refurbished the rooms in their original design, though modernizing the amenities to encourage pleasant stays for their guests. She hadn't been asked to help, nor did she work there. They simply allowed her to come and go as she pleased, letting guests know she was the former owner and visited from time to time.

The garden is sorted, so now to the next matter. Another college boy is staying the night. Wonder if I can just get by and avoid them altogether. Annoying shit, that business.

Tired from the heat of the day on her bare tan shoulders, she climbed the steps. They had indeed told guests of her coming and going to the point where the local college now made a game out of staying in a room. The college brats took turns, some coming back on multiple occasions, with one goal in mind; see who could lay with the Lady in Blue. She preferred it that way instead of her true namesake, and she'd keep it that way with the rash of blue balls and broken hearts she'd returned to the campus.

A trail of pipe smoke lingered in the air in her wake. Behind the front desk, the receptionist coughed and hacked, waving it from his face. He stared into the darkness with a deep frown, chasing the smoke up the empty stairs.

"There she goes again. I wish she'd stop smoking; it's killing my sinuses." Snuffling his nose, he settled back into his chair. "Now, where was I in this book? Oh, yeah... the jail scene."

Jane wandered the halls, checking that each door was locked and secured. One was cracked and she pulled it shut, nice and quiet as not to wake the old couple spending the week at the B&B. Satisfied all was in order, she spun to her room, then paused at the door. Her blue lamp was on, the glow coming through the bottom of the door, casting an eerie glow across the hall carpet.

Who the hell is in my room? Anger filled her and she pulled her pipe from her plump lips. *Don't tell me... I'm going to kill that pukwudgie. This is his doing!*

Pushing through the door, she stopped at the bathroom door, glaring at her bed. Not one, but two college kids were having the time of their life in her sheets, on her quilt, in *her room*. Crossing her arms, she watched them with jealous intrigue. The blonde was naked, her pale skin blue under the lamp's light as she rode atop the man. Her body thin, she was petite compared to Jane. There was a level of admiration though, the way her body waved as she straddled her lover, torso snaking provocatively as she grinded against the cock she rode.

Athletic arms reached up, cupping her subtle breasts, making her pink nipples more pronounced. Jane's face grew hot as she followed the overlapping layers of muscles back to their owner's face. He bit his bottom lip, his lustful eyes making Jane completely jealous. They both moaned, arching against each other. Sweat painted their bodies, showing how long they'd been at it, neither paying heed to Jane's presence in the room. His caramel skin a sexy contrast against the milk of her slender body. Long black locks of hair stuck to his face, his expression tense and focused.

He muttered between groans, crooning in Spanish. It was enough to even make Jane wish she'd been in the girl's place but she shook her head. After all, she had been waging war against the hazing ritual they had rudely made her part of. Until they stopped, she refused to give into their game. Last thing she wanted was her B&B becoming the Blue Lady's Whorehouse. She snorted, thinking about how her belated husband would roll over in his grave if she let their dream home become twisted in such a way.

Her eyes fell on the man's lips, thick and plump as they spoke foreign words of lust and love. *Lips like that, he's gotta be a good kisser.*

A phone buzzed on the bathroom vanity, scattering Jane's thoughts. Curious, she picked it up, safely assuming the pink glittery case belonged to the blonde harlot shrieking in pleasure. She unlocked the phone and read the text. If they were going to invade her space, she would do the same, in the only means she had: *their phones.*

[Mark: Hey Babe. Where u at?]

Oh? Another man is looking for her. She's a busy one.
From the room, she heard the girl mutter, "Phillipe! Oh, oh, harder baby. Deeper... y-yes..."

Another wave of Spanish and moaning came from her partner. Jane rolled her eyes.

She dove into the string of texts between this Karen and Phillipe. There, she found sexting and fanned herself. She didn't need to watch them anymore. *Jackpot!* She had found a trove of dick pics and sultry pics exchanged between the two.

The size of that man's cock! Another shriek came from the room and Jane's face flushed. *I'd be singing like a banshee if that was for dessert! MERCY ME! Where'd she fit all that!*

Another buzz and a new text disrupted Jane's viewing.

[Mark: I stopped by your place to bring you soup but your roommate said you were spending the weekend with your new boyfriend.]

Ouch. If he's her man, then she bailed on his ass this weekend for caliente caramel, sweetheart. Twisting her lips, her curiosity peaked. *What have you been sending, Mark? Looks like her last reply was this morning saying she had the flu and stay away. Ha! I want to catch the flu if that's what we're calling Mister Spanish Lover!*

[Mark: And apparently, that's not me.]

Oh, it's definitely not you this weekend, sweetheart. Maybe she'll cash you in next weekend? Jane snickered to herself, despite the creaking of her bed under the fucking couple annoying her. *In fact, who are these other pictures she has of... how does Mark stack up against Mr. Caliente Caramel?*

[Mark: Did you forget to break up with me or something?]

Jane ignored the text, flipping through the photo gallery. Her stomach knotted and she blinked, marveling over the dark-haired brute. Everything about him was *her type* and she cursed the girl for giving something like that up. She peeked back into the bedroom, baffled that they still had stamina, his hands gripping her hips, pushing himself deeper into her as she gasped with each thrust.

The phone started ringing and she hit ignore. *Poor guy. She's a little too busy to talk.*

Another text buzzed through and Jane cringed, watching as the couple started to peak. The man repeating over and over, *my lovely.* With a howl and deep arch, Karen's ecstasy hit, bracing against his muscular thighs as she took in his throbbing cock, both coming hard.

[Mark: Karen!! Call me ASAP!!!!!!]

Fuck this. Jane snapped a photo with Karen's phone. *Sent. Let's see if this answers your question Mark. Shouldn't be long before...*

[Mark: WHAT THE FUCK!!!!!!!!!!!!!! FUCK YOU!!!!! YOU CHEATING BITCH!!!!]

A smile crested Jane's face. *No one fucks in my room besides me.*

2

The Flu My Ass

Mark Wilder scowled at his cell phone, taking another swig of his beer. The broad-shouldered college sophomore was more irritated than relaxed as his two friends narrowed their eyes at him across the table. He ran a hand through his thick black hair, stewing in anger while his leg jittered on the bar stool. His girlfriend of almost two years, Karen, was supposed to be sick with the flu. Instead, she had other plans...

Come on. At least show me some respect. A vein pulsed in his temple, a revelation rising in his mind. *Unless, all those times she'd visited sick relatives were bullshit too... Son-of-a-bitch! She's been sleeping around on me for our entire relationship!*

"You okay, Mark? You look royally pissed." Timmy took a slow drag of his beer before leaning in. "Look, if this wasn't a good weekend for me to visit from Jersey, I could've easily grabbed a work shift. Dylan's a nice boss like that."

Mark sighed, shaking his head. "I just caught my girl cheating on me. This fucking sucks ass... dammit!"

"Ouch," Axle chimed in, arching a brow. "That sucks. You've been together for a while, right?"

Mark lowered his brow and glared back. "Thanks. I'm fully aware of that fact. And I can't help but wonder if she's been sleeping around this whole fucking time. She said she had the flu. How many other times has she faked being sick?"

"I wanna catch the flu." Axle flinched as Mark shot him an angry glare.

"Let's change topics!" Timmy flagged down a waitress. "Two buckets, one full of Bud Light and the other... you got Shiner Bock?"

"Yes, we do, though that bucket has an upcharge." She smiled, shifting so her breasts bounced and called all their eyes to them. "You okay with that? I'll go grab it."

"Perfect. It's on my tab." Timmy turned back, rubbing his jawline.

Mark punched the keys on his cell phone aggressively, his face a shade of red, his emotions already past the stages of grief. He was pissed. *If she didn't want to be with me, why didn't she bother breaking up with me? And give me the chance to screw all the girls like a normal single guy.*

He sucked on his inner cheek as he hit send.

[Mark: Did you forget to break up with me or something?]

Tossing the phone upside down on the table, he drained the last of his beer, then crushed the can into the bucket. The others sat; eyes wide as they glanced at one another. Their faces told him exactly what they thought, and how he felt, *it's going to be a long night.*

"SO!" Timmy slapped the table, drawing everyone's attention to him. "Is the fraternity still doing that thing?"

"What thing?" Mark drawled.

The waitress slid two buckets onto the table and spirited away the other without a word or glance.

Mark grabbed a Shiner Bock, cracking it open. "You mean that stupid B&B thing?"

"Yeah, the hazing ritual I started!" Timmy's eyes sparkled.

"Well, it outgrew the fraternity," announced Axel, rubbing his shaved head. "Now all the local colleges compete to reserve a room. Granted, the Blue Lady has been leaving behind a trail of blue balls since you left."

"Oh shit." Timmy took a drink, looking off as if guilty for something. "It wasn't supposed to be a multi-university tradition. Shit. Oh man, she must have it out for me..."

"I don't believe in poltergeists, and why the hell would anyone from the 1800s want to fuck some college dork? Especially now that we have those horny stallions from AbraXus Tasker College mixed in?" Mark was bitter, his eye glaring at the phone. "I refuse to participate. Where did you get the ridiculous idea for this anyhow, Tim?"

"You can say my former college at Bridgewater Trinity *inspired* me." He laughed, finishing his own beer, eyes shooting off sideways as if hiding behind a half-truth. "So, has anyone hooked up with her?"

"No, but she has been known to leave countless blue balls and dry, unenthusiastic handjobs in her wake." Axel chuckled. "Though, I don't know if I believe those stories either."

"Ghost stories," corrected Mark, rolling his eyes. "You can't convince me that some ghost woman is waiting in a small-town B&B, ready to get laid."

"Technically, only the first part is true. I was the one who declared the last part. She didn't ask for a wave of college boys to come to her rescue. In fact, why did I pick..." Timmy's eyes looked up, recalling a memory. "Oh yeah. Satch made it into a game back home; who could hook up with the most... never mind. Just know, I can't keep up with that guy, and I thought the impossible would give me an ace up the sleeve."

"Satch sounds like a man-whore." Mark chuckled. "I think it's just an excuse to go on a mini-vacation, hook up with a local girl, then call it a day."

"Last weekend, Levi swore he saw a ghost. Said in the middle of the night, someone felt him up and by morning, he was blue balling so hard he went home." Axel grabbed a Bud Light and held it a moment. "Now I know why they call them 'blue' after I took him to the doctor's on Monday. It was rough stuff."

"Stop it. That annoying asshole probably got kicked in the gonads for being too bold." Timmy watched as Mark slid the phone closer, hesitating to flip the screen up. "So, Mark, did you ever go?"

"Hell no." Glaring at the phone, he took a slow sip of his beer.

"What about you, Axel?" Tim shifted. "You ever go?"

"Actually..." He rubbed the back of his neck, embarrassment building on his face. "I get it next, for an entire week in fact. Like Mark said, I thought it sounded like a chance to relax, have fun, and satisfy my curiosity."

"Ha." Mark grabbed up the phone, unwilling to cave in front of his friends. "Well, I gotta piss."

Mark bypassed the bathroom and slipped out the back door. Half the dive bar's patrons bar pissed on the back fence while waving to passing Amtrak trains. He relieved himself, confident no one could hear what conversation that may unfold. He dialed Karen's cell number. He zipped himself up, it rang once, and he was sent to voicemail.

Anger boiled up from his core. She knew he had caught her and now she had the gall to ignore him. *You'll have to come back home eventually, Karen!* Marching back into the bar, he punched in his next text to her.

[Mark: Karen!! Call me ASAP!!!!!!]

Hitting send, he sat there and finished his beer.

"Then who has the B&B reserved this weekend?" Tim disregarded the angry state of his friend and pressed on with the conversation.

Axel shrugged. "Some assclown from AbraXus has it. Bill? Phil? The kicker on the football team, that guy."

"Aren't they horny horses or some shit." Tim's commentary sent them into another round of chuckling.

"And what's with those colors?" At this rate, Mark was feeling depressed, but he clung to the conversation. "Pink, purple, or is that more magenta and fuchsia?"

Tim choked on his beer. "What kind of color is fuchsia?" he asked. "Is that more pink or more pur–"

A text buzzed on Mark's phone, halting the conversation as all eyes fell to the backlit screen. Mark glanced down, his face paling before shifting to maroon, veins pulsing. He lifted it up, showing the entire table the provocative image of Karen atop a caramel skinned athlete. Both faces very visible and full of pleasure. A blue light cast across them and everything about the room screamed *small-town B&B.*

You, fucking bitch. After a moment of huffing, Mark managed to get the words out. "This guy? Isn't that the kicker and your B&B with my girl on top of him?"

"Oh shit." Axel and Timmy gripped their beers.

"I can't..." Depression weighed him down and Mark covered his face in defeat.

"Look, Mark. Fuck her," declared Timmy, scooting his barstool closer. "There are way better chicks out there. Sometimes, they can walk into your life when you least expect them. Literally."

"What do you know about love?" Mark leaned on the table. "Maybe I should convince her to stay with me? Maybe I did something wrong?"

"No, don't you dare go down that road." Axel downed the last of his beer. "You're a good guy, Mark. She's a shitty person. It has nothing to do with you."

There was a pause, then Mark muttered, "Will I find love again?" *Depression stage initiated.*

"Nope, don't do that either." Timmy made him sit upright, pulling his hand from his puckered and pitiful expression. "Look, we never thought Dylan Johnson was the type to settle down. Then Abby walked in and changed that. You just haven't found the right girl."

"I want to see it." Mark gulped down his beer, then grabbed another from the bucket. "That stupid B&B. What was so special about it that she'd rather be there with him and not me?"

"Fine." Axel pulled out his cell phone, making several swipes on the screen. "There's my confirmation for next week. If it makes you feel better, you'll see she's shit and that there's nothing special about that place besides an old ghost story."

Timmy cringed, then after a minute, he smirked at the picture still glowing on the table. "If you're lucky, maybe you'll hook up with a local and get a chance to take a picture of your own. Then, send that shit to her as revenge. There's no way Karen will be happy if you break things up with her first."

Mark grabbed his phone. Karen was calling and he ignored it. A text flashed.

[Karen: I can explain!!! PICK UP!]

"Yeah. I like that idea."

[Mark: FUCK YOU. We're done.]

3

Speak to the Manager

T he sun poured down, brighter than ever. Pausing from weed pulling, Jane stood and stretched her back. The quaint little garden had been laid in bricks and pavers, a collage of missing brickwork. A small bench in the shade sat before a row of hibiscus and above that was a porch overlooking the site. A small white picket fence matched by evergreens with spurts of Japanese boxwood. For color, Mexican petunias, Wichita blue juniper, and red-tipped photinia filled in the larger sections, while spurts of perennials, in the form of a variety of lilies, occasionally filled in the gaps.

Star jasmine grew to cover the side yard mess near the building. Often, they bloomed at night, filling the air with its sweet scent. For attracting butterflies, there were rosebushes, vining plants, and an assortment of sage to maintain the appetites of hungry little caterpillars. It had taken years to get the garden to look this way, and she wasn't letting the weeds ruin them after the last gardener quit.

What a brat. To blame me as the reason to quit, when I was just trying to point out his mistake when he plucked my lilies surrounding the willow.

Glancing at her pocket watch, it was nearing check-out time. Like a staged event, the bickering disrupted the peaceful morning and brought a smile to Jane's face. By now, the boyfriend would have called. Even more wonderous, there'd be a picture of her and her caliente lover magically sent via her own text.

Jane bit her lip, getting aroused thinking about the man's lean and gorgeous body, but her ex-lover Mark, now he's one she wanted to see sans clothes. *That's more of my kind of fun in the sheets. What on earth would've possessed you to give him up? Greed? Lust? Is he bad in bed? I mean, you didn't even send sultry pictures to your actual boyfriend. That's a problem, girlie.*

Karen marched out of the little B&B and paced the main sidewalk between the porch and gate. "Mark, I swear! It won't happen again!"

Close behind her was her lover, Phillipe. "Look, I paid for the room, but we need to go. I got practice later today."

"Shut up, Phillipe," she hissed, covering the receiver.

Phillipe threw up his hands, then marched pass her. "Look, I had a great time but unless you get in the car, you'll have to find another way home. I didn't sign up for this drama. You said you two broke it off, and everyone *knows*—you don't *fuck* with Mark Wilder. He was one of the best defensive guards before he quit."

"Dammit, Phillipe!" Her shout came through the phone, Mark's own voice blasting from the device and she doubled back. "No, baby. He's not here. I ditched him for you." Her voice softened. "I don't know who sent you that picture, but it wasn't me. We've been together six months... er... right, two years..." She cringed at her mistake. "No, I was thinking... no... Mark, please..."

There was a long pause, Phillipe stopped at the gate, watching Karen unravel. Her face beamed red, her hair a wreck from each time she'd tugged on it. Her pacing accelerated. Jane watched with amusement as her lips widened, only to be cut off from her ex-lover's words.

Karen had *fucked up*. On more than one level.

How the hell do you not know how long you've been with a man? Jane gnawed on her pipe, lighting it with a snort. *How many men has she had on the side, to muddle that number to hell? A significant difference between six months and two years.*

"It wasn't me," she pleaded, her voice trembling. "No, I mean, I'm sick, don't you remember? I have the flu." She paused, fanning herself and forcing herself to hyperventilate as if she were crying. "A-are you calling me a *liar*? How could you say that, Mark?"

Wow. She's laying it on thick. And yet not a single tear shed. Jane blew smoke from her pursed lips, making rings that circled Karen's face like a picture frame. *You're a vile one, a regular Jezebel worthy of bad karma, madame. I don't even feel guilty for what I did. Sounds like I did him a huge favor!*

Karen's face twisted. "Okay, so it was me. I didn't realize you could see my tramp stamp. How the hell could... oh." She took another breath, then resumed her pacing. "Look, if you were around more, then... well... I know I cancelled the last six times, but I had better things to do! I have a life too!"

She bit her lip and pulled the phone back. Mark roared, "FUCKING HALF OF ABRAXUS TASKER COLLEGE APPARENTLY!"

Jane raised her brow, crossing her arms, still grinning over the majesty of this conversation. *Oh, he's no fool, now that she's been caught. She's flailing now. Bad.*

"What? But... no, you can't end our relationship!" Another fist full of hair, scowling as she hissed over the phone. "You can't break up with me! I break up–" She glared at her phone in shock. "He... he... he hung up on me!"

"Look, let's just go so I can take you home and you can clear this up." Phillipe rubbed the back of his neck.

"No." She spun on her heels, facing the B&B entrance. "I want to speak with a manager! Someone working the late shift must've taken this picture. Who else would've had a key to our room?" She marched forward, determination written on her face. "In fact, I'll get your money back."

"Oh, this ought to be good." Jane brushed the dirt off her knees and butt, then sashayed towards the porch where she could hear Karen's formal complaint. "That man will not refund that room after the mess they left in it. Hell, I don't think anyone has weaseled a refund from him. He's quick witted and the shit he knows about folks at a glance is unnerving."

"I demand a refund!" Karen had her volume on max, shifting into full attack mode. "Someone took an inappropriate photo of us! In our room! Last night!"

"Excuse me?" The manager lowered the book he'd been reading and lifted an eyebrow. "And what does that have to do with refunding you the room you slept in and made a mess in?"

Karen's face flushed once again. "I demand to know who works the night shift, who would've had access to our room."

"No one." His eyes returned to his book, his demeanor unmoved by her tantrum as he flipped to the next page. "If you hadn't noticed, we're a small family owned and operated establishment. We can't afford additional staff besides myself and the maid who cleans in the morning after guests such as yourself."

She pointed to her phone. "Someone took a photo of us."

"May I see?" He peeked over the top of the book, and she gasped. "N-no!"

"Well, how can I verify if you're telling the truth?" He marveled, a wicked glint in his eyes.

"Haven't you heard, *the customer is always right?*" hissed Karen.

"Yes, and it's a bit dated. As I recall, that term was coined during the Wild West days when customers were more honest and loyal." Clearing his throat, he said, "Produce proof or I can't dispute your claim."

"I'm not showing you a picture of... of..." Her face turned a deeper shade of red.

"Who else stayed in that room besides you? Did you ask them if they took the picture?" Another arching eyebrow silenced Karen, deflating some of her ego.

Jane puffed on her pipe of cherry tobacco, watching as Karen marched out and towards Phillipe. She snickered. The girl was a force to be reckoned with when mad. Though, her circumstance was of her own creation. Taking a puff of the pipe, she watched as the next round of shouting began. Karen was out for blood, and it didn't matter who was injured in the process.

"Did you do this?" She held up her phone to her Spanish lover. "Did you take this?"

"Take what?" Phillipe unlatched the gate, baffled. "Let's go already. Now, you're embarrassing me, and I can't be late for practice."

"Did you take this picture of us fucking, then sent it to Mark?" she declared.

"No. How could I when I was stuck under you, while you cowgirl styled my dick with your pussy." He laughed, shaking his head. "Come on. Let's go."

She was rendered speechless as she followed Phillipe out to the main sidewalk, then descended the path. Jane stood, watching as they went.

Karen paused in her steps, taking a double look.

Again, her face flushed, and she stormed to the fence. Inhaling deep, she shouted with all her might. "YOU! YOU THERE IN BLUE!"

Phillipe looked to where she shouted, confused. "Who in the hell are you screaming at?"

"The gardener," she hissed. But when she turned back, Jane had disappeared. "The... woman. In blue."

"Real funny." He continued walking, shaking his head. "It's just a ghost story."

"Are you calling me a liar?" she asked as she chased after him. "This is the third *fucking* time I've been accused of lying today! This is bullshit!"

Jane took a few more puffs of her pipe. She had sat on the garden bench, fully aware the hedgerow and old willow blocked her from of view. They were long gone, the birds continued to sing and the butterflies fluttered above the garden.

The manager appeared on the front porch and yawned, then he choked on her pipe smoke. "Dammit, Jane. That can't be good for people." It was a statement more than a threat. "Not like anyone can stop you."

Jane smiled to herself, dumping the last of her pipe tobacco. "Fine, you win. I'll cut it out for the rest of the day. You earned enough of my respect after the way you handled that unruly woman."

"Man, she *was* a bitch." He scratched his jaw, then lowered his gaze to the garden. "Man, you'd think I hired a professional gardener. I suppose I should say thank you."

"You're welcome." She stood, walking around the willow tree, admiring her handiwork. "But you still need to hire a gardener. I'm getting too old for this."

"Yeah, I'll make a couple calls. I wonder if old man Ted still runs his landscaping business."

"Oh man, is that what he ended up doing? Landscaping." She grinned and squatted to pluck a weed from between the pavers. "And to think he nearly crashed his car through this very garden as a kid. Life spins us in funny ways."

Looking up, the manager had disappeared inside, making Jane's chest ached. She hated the way it snuck up on her, that drowning sensation of being alone and depressed. Ever since her husband left this world, she couldn't bear to see everything that stood for him and their relationship go to ruin. This was the home they had shared before he passed. She couldn't let it rot away so easily, even if she no longer owned it.

Besides, I'm too ornery to die just yet...

4

The Gardener

Mark stood before the B&B with mixed emotions. Much to his disappointment, there wasn't much to the place. He could confirm they didn't hook up in a romantic setting. Old vegetation covered the building, while paint peeled off the two-story building that should've fallen down decades ago. Adjusting the duffel bag strap on his shoulder, he pushed through the tiny gate.

Halfway down the front walkway, he paused, covering his face. *What the hell am I doing here? Why the fuck would I stay in a room where my ex-girlfriend cheated on me?*

Inhaling deep, he held it. Then he buried the turbulent emotions rolling in his chest deep once more. Looking back to the building, he realized he hadn't seen any signage. Circling back to the gate, he checked it and came up blank. Craning his neck , he spotted someone in the garden. Curious to know if he had found the right place or some old man's house, he cleared his throat, announcing himself.

The girl, bent over pulling weeds from the base of an old willow tree, didn't flinch. His eyes wandered across her body, everything about her was *his type.* The baby blue jean cut-offs with brass rivets fit her ass tightly, leaving little to the imagination for what lay in between. Her skin peeked out of the top before escaping into her light blue crop top.

At this angle, he had a glance at her soft blue lacy bra, and his breath hitched. *Holy shit, she's gorgeous.*

She shuffled over and continued pulling weeds surrounding a batch of lilies. Her hands were in leather gloves, her arms muscular, and sweat rolled down the side of her cheek. Far as he could tell, she had been at this all morning. A hat obscured the top half of her face, nothing but high cheekbone and pale pink lips making him aroused.

What am I doing? Just standing here like a creepy stalker with a hard-on? Say something!

"Excuse me." His eyes darted away, sliding his duffle bag to block the bulge inside his jeans. "Is this the Story Bed & Breakfast?"

Again, she kept working and Mark wondered if he had mumbled his words. Squatting down, he made himself semi-eyelevel with her, tapping her arm to make her aware of his presence.

She froze. Slowly, she turned to face where his fingers met her arm, before tracing the appendage until their eyes met. Pimples rolled across her tan skin, and he held his breath like he had disturbed the surface of a glassy lake.

Wide eyed, her blue eyes seemed to glow in the light. "Are you..." She squinted, reading his face. "Are you touching me?"

"Sorry, I didn't mean to startle you." He blinked, unsure of how to gauge her reaction. "Wait, shit, are you deaf?"

"What? No!" She laughed, shaking her head. "I'm not. Not many people show up here wanting to chat with the gardener, is all. They kind of don't notice me most of the time, if not *all* the time. I'm sorry, what are you asking me?"

"Well, you were the first person I saw." She motioned for him to stand, and he did so, hugging the duffle bag to his front as his eyes dipped to her flushed cleavage. "Is this, uh, is this the Story B&B?"

"Yes, it is. It's been here for as long as the town, in fact." They walked side-by-side, then stopped when they reached the main entrance. "The manager should be in there, reading his book. I don't think they have any other guests here besides an old couple in town visiting for a family reunion."

Mark took in the admiration on her face. "You love this place. Why?"

Her face flushed and she locked eyes with him. "Well, my... well, it was in the family name for some time."

Shit! She was an owner! And I'm eating her alive like eye candy!

Mark's face turned red. "I'm sorry! I'm Mark, Mark Wilder and you are?"

"Jane..." He held out a hand and she smirked, pulling her own from the gardening gloves and gripped it tight. "Just Jane."

"Little old fashioned."

She paled. "What's old fashioned?"

"Your name, Jane. I like it." Mark looked to the entrance, then back at Jane. "Do you stay here or live in the area?"

"Yeah... you can say I live here at the B&B." Her eyes scanned him from head to toe, lingering on his lips once more. "Are you checking in or applying for the gardening job?"

He blinked. "Checking in. And no offense, it seems like you have this under control? Or are you retiring?"

"Retiring..." She tilted her head, arching her eyebrows. "I'm just stepping in to maintain the B&B's most important feature. I can't have the place full of weeds and falling apart."

Mark gave her another scan, licking his lips and running his hand through his hair. "I don't normally do this, but..." *What the hell did I have to lose?* "Would you like to join me upstairs in the shower?"

Jane opened her mouth and paused.

Mark held his breath, unsure if he'd been too bold or offended her.

He watched as she covered her mouth, gazing at her unfinished work. Again, his eyes flowed over to her sharp jawline, her slender neck, and the way her collarbone returned his stare back to her freckled chest. A hint of the lacy blue bra dared to peek out of her crop top. At last, she swiveled her face back to him, her expression obscured by her hand as she looked him up and down.

Unable to take the growing embarrassment, Mark turned and started up the steps. "I'm sorry, forget it. That was—"

"Which room?" Her voice made him stop, and he twisted to face her, but all he could see was her back. "I'm long overdue for some fun of that kind."

Mark shook his head, taking a moment to absorb her answer. "Uh, my friend booked the... um, the..." He dug into his pockets, pulling out a folded paper and unraveled it. "Blue room?"

"Really?" At last, she shot a glance over her shoulder, her eyes glowing bright in the sunlight. "I'll be up in a moment, just gotta put away some things."

"R-right!" He couldn't contain the smile on his face. "Let me check in and... see you upstairs, Jane."

He rushed through the front door and the manager put his book down. "Checking in? Mister Axel... oh. No. Mark Wilder. Aren't you a lucky man today?"

"Yes, sir, that's me." Mark pulled his wallet out, but the manager pulled a key fob and key from the hook and slid it to him. "Upstairs on the left. The blue door. It's all been paid for."

"Um, don't you need my ID or something." The manager had returned to his book, waving Mark on as he lost himself to the novel. "I guess not..."

Mark snatched the key, then raced upstairs. On the second landing, he spotted the room with the plaque immediately, and as promised, bearing a blue door. Reaching for the knob, it creaked open and he paused, confused. *Did the maid forget to lock it or is it a faulty knob?* Pushing into the room, he closed the door, pushing it tight and checking the lock.

"It's not broken." Jane's voice jolted him, and there she stood in the room, her hat and gloves gone. "I just beat you here, is all."

"I see that." Mark flipped the lock, biting his bottom lip in anticipation. "Just going to dump the duffle at the foot of the bed and..."

He let it slide off his shoulder, rolling the stiff muscle as he turned to face her. The silence between them lingered, awkward and enthralling. Her brown hair clung to her sweat-soaked face, and he reached out to brush it from her brow. She cupped his hand, the gauging look meeting his eyes as if she somehow knew him, recognized him from somewhere.

Mark leaned in, his lips hovering so close to hers the heat of them teased of what could happen next. *Am I being too bold? Is she afraid... of this sudden desire to just be lustful for a moment in my life?*

Jane's fingers balled his shirt in them, and she yanked him forward, their lips connecting. She deepened the kiss and whatever hesitation had haunted him dissolved. He moaned into her mouth, enjoying the way their tongues tangled with one another. Her body was hot against his as he pulled her into him. She seemed hungry to have his passion, never slowing the voracity of her kissing as he weaseled his hand under the back of her crop top.

With a fluid motion, he had unlatched the back of her bra, and she broke the kiss with a laugh.

"You're good." She buried her face into his chest. "I have to admit, it's been a while."

"That's okay." He snorted. "To be honest, I'm on the rebound after catching my ex cheating on me."

Her fingers snaked down his chest, rolling over his abdomen and began unbuckling his pants. "Then let me help you forget all about her." She had pulled away from him some, now unbuckling her own jeans as if to make the playing field fair. "I have to confess; this isn't something I normally do. Hooking up for the fun of it."

"Really? And here I thought you were only saying yes to the shower," he teased, pulling his shirt off in a rush. "To be honest, I didn't think you'd say yes." All he desired was to feel her touching his skin, the thought made him harder with each passing moment.

"I didn't think I'd say yes either." She laughed, removing her top and bra, letting them fall to the floor. "You okay with a hot shower?" Her hips swung left and right, her jean shorts rolling off her hips.

Blue lacy thongs... that's not proper gardening undergarments. Mark smirked. *But I'm not complaining!*

5

Hot Shower

He may look like my husband, but that body and cock are on a whole new level.

Jane's heart raced as she led Mark to the bathroom, jeans left on the threshold and her thongs sliding past her knees. He rushed to the doorway, struggling to kick off his own jeans as they tangled at his feet. They both laughed, the excitement and lust building between them taking them into an unexpected ride.

She reached in, turning on the shower. Steam started to fill the span, goosebumps waving over her skin.

He doesn't have to know how long it's been since you let someone touch you. She swallowed back the nervous tension building at her core as he freed his last foot. *He doesn't know the last man you were intimate with was your belated husband.* Mark locked eyes with her, and he smiled, making her heart flutter. *They look so much alike, but...*

Her breath caught as he closed the gap between them. Lips pressing against hers and again she deepened it. She wanted to feel the heat of his body against hers, anywhere and everywhere all at once. The loneliness that had haunted her, kept her in such a restless state, slowly started to fade to the throes of passion.

They stumbled into the walk-in shower, the hot water pelting them. Her back pressed against the cold tiles and she pulled his body against hers.

His erection slid between her thighs, making her loins throb with want. Rivulets of hot water flowed down their bodies, the rush of it streaming down his back, to where her hands clung to him. *I want to feel alive again.* She rubbed her tongue against his, diving into his mouth and he throbbed between her thighs once more. His hands belonged to someone used to hard labor, the callouses adding to the visceral sensation travelling down the sides of her torso before squeezing her ass cheeks. Another throb of his cock, his hips tilting slowly to rub it against her pussy, making her wet.

Their kiss broke and they stared at one another, marveling over their instant connection. She couldn't slow her beating heart or the way her breath quickened with excitement. He began kissing her neck, and she leaned all her weight against the wall, arching and stretching so he could have full access to her body. Mark's hands slid across her hips, up her abdomen until they groped a breast in each palm.

She moaned, this time tilting her hip to slide her pussy across the top of his dick. He moaned into her neck, sucking and licking, building a hickie that she'd gladly wear. *To be touched like this... with no barriers, no restrictions, and...*

Her hands flowed across the muscular torso, diving between them where she could rub and grip his cock. Again, he moaned and throbbed against her. *I've never wanted sex with someone so desperately. This might be my only chance.*

She stroked him with one hand, and he hardened in her palm. Biting her lip, she dove her other hand inside her pussy. Her fingers slick, she guided his erection into her pussy. Both of them moaned as he pressed deep inside her.

Dropping a hand from a breast, it gripped her thigh and lifted it to his hip. The angle made her gasp as he thrusted, slow and steady, in and out. He abandoned his play at her neck, eyes locked on her face. She kept one hand between where they connected, enjoying how the base of his cock slid between her fingers, the shaft long and hard, slippery from her pussy.

As he gathered speed, she arched further, her other hand braced on his shoulder and he tightened his grip on her thigh.

"Don't stop," she breathed. "I don't have ovaries... please, don't stop."

Another throb escaped his dick and she moaned. "Did you just give me the greenlight to cum inside you?" He pushed deeper inside her and froze, taking in her face. "Are you sure? No chance of... you know..." His eyes dropped to her belly.

She laughed. "I said don't stop, Mark." She grinded against him, tightening around the hard cock inside her, and he grunted. "I need ovaries for that to happen."

He smirked. "But I wanted this to last a little longer. You feel so good, and... and..."

She abandoned her grip on his cock, pulling him to her so she could whisper into his ear. "Don't stop. I'm almost there, please..."

He rocked in and out, and she arched again, her head pressing hard against the tiled wall. The hot water did nothing to cool the heat building between them as their arousal began to peak. He kissed her neck, leaving a trail across her collarbone and she shuddered. Lips wrapped around a nipple, hot as his teeth pinched it and she tightened. Mark thrusted faster, fucking her harder as he latched onto her breast, aggressive and hungry.

"Yes... a little... more..." Her eyes shut tight, her body buzzing with the rising orgasm.

Adjusting his grip on her thigh, he lifted it higher and she felt them connect deeper. Another thrust against her, hard and eager, and her orgasm peaked. A scream of pleasure escaped her lips.

Fingernails biting into his skin sent him moaning as her pussy tightened in waves on his rock-hard cock. He slowed, moaning into her breasts as he too came. At last, he pressed his pelvis hard against her, throbbing inside her as they rode out their orgasms as one.

Releasing her nipple, he panted and leaned on the shower wall. "Holy shit."

"You're good." Her whole body vibrated, a mixture of wanting and ecstasy. "Or I just went too long without."

He laughed, shaking his head. "Honestly, that's the best I've had... and I don't know if it's the fact we just hooked up out of left field."

Jane laughed, pressing a short and fleeting kiss him to his lips. "I wouldn't mind doing that again."

Mark arched a brow. "Really?"

He slid himself out, enjoying the hourglass figure against the hodge-podge of tiles in all shades of blue. A shudder shook her, the lack of his body heat making her skin pimple and nipples erect. Jane watched how his eyes took her body in and they followed her hands. She fondled her breasts before sliding down her torso and dove between her thighs. Diving her fingers between her folds she pulled his cum over her clit, the sensation riveting as she started to pleasure herself.

"That's no fair." He watched, his cock losing its hardness. "I have a good five minutes before I get hard again."

"Oh?" She grinned, gripping her breast with the other hand as she dipped her fingers once more between her swollen pussy. "Only five minutes?"

He ran a hand through his hair and shrugged. "I timed it."

Rolling her eyes, she focused on keeping the buzz of her orgasm rolling. Wanting to play with herself more, she pulled her cum-covered fingers back to her clit, circling the swollen jewel. With his eyes on her, she moaned enjoying the provocativeness of what she allowed herself to do in his presence. Everything about this was more erotic than she had ever been willing to do or attempt to do in her past. She began rocking her hips, lingering on the way he had felt inside her, the way his body against hers had felt. Her eyes closed and her body tensed. She was nearing a second orgasm, and she dipped her finger in and out, frustrated that she couldn't bring back the pleasure he had bestowed her.

"Let me help with that." His voice gruffed into her ear, breath hot against her neck.

Again, the string of kisses at her neck made her shiver with anticipation. Lips burnt a trail down her body, only pausing to tease a nipple before licking and sucking down her stomach. She abandoned her play, wanting to only feel him and the way he touched her. He kept going, lower than any man had been on her until her breath caught. Shouldering one of her legs, the heat of his mouth wrapped around her clit and she shrieked, body folding onto him.

How long I've waited just to feel another person's touch, but this isn't what I had in mind! She bit her lip, snuffing the thoughts out so she could enjoy every intimate moment.

One strong arm road back up her body, unfolding her and placing her flat against the tiles once more. Her eyes wide, fingers tangling in his hair, her mouth opened but was at a loss for words. Like he'd done to her nipple, the tip of his tongue circled her clit and she gasped. It was electrifying, shooting through her body, and building on her orgasm in a way she didn't know possible. She fought with herself, unsure to pull him away or hold him into her.

Do I dare say I feel alive again? What is it about this man that makes him different from all the others who have come here in search of a night with the Blue Lady?

He moaned into her pussy and she rocked into him. She didn't want him to stop. He kissed her there as deeply as he had done with her lips and her heart pounded with excitement. Shifting, she opened her thighs a little wider, wanting more. He responded to the motion, breaking his suckling from her clit made her squeak.

Hot and silky, he ran his tongue across her throbbing opening, teasing that he may dip his tongue inside. She inhaled deep and swift, holding it there as her knees began to shake.

What on earth did he just do to my body! Can I even stay standing at this rate?

6

Hungry Lover

Mark stole a glance at Jane's face and smirked.

She's never had someone go down on her!

The idea he would be the first excited him, though he hated the refractory period, even if he had been blessed with a five-minute wait unlike some of his colleagues. Still, seeing her please herself with his cum had made him hot and bothered. He wanted to keep playing with her, pleasuring her for his own lustful desires. Teasing the opening of her pussy, dripping wet with his playful suckling, her legs shook.

Good girl... opening those legs for Daddy.

He pushed his tongue between the folds, licking inside her pussy like a hot apple pie. She moaned, rocking her hips in a way that let him taste her further, deeper. Her fingers gripped his hair and she began losing herself to the sensation of his hungry eating. The moaning and gasps grew, her hips rocking faster against his face. Tensing as the roughness of his five o'clock shadow prickled into her sensitive flesh. Holding onto her leg against his shoulder, he sucked and slurped, moaning into her pussy. Again, her legs shook.

He reached down, rubbing his cock. *Just a little longer... I'm slowly getting hard again.*

Rolling his tongue up, he returned to her clit. Wrapping his lips on her hard-swollen bean and sucked long and hard. She folded over him, his arm gone and unable to keep her stretched against the wall. His cock throbbed in his palm. He didn't want her to cum, not until he could bend her over and be back inside her to enjoying the tight pulsing of how hard she came like before. He wanted that one more time. He wanted to feel her orgasm on his dick.

This might be the only time I hook up with her.

He flicked his tongue on the jewel and she shrieked, legs wobbling to the point she slid down on the wall. Every muscle in her body locked and shook. He had her teetering and he slowed his playful eating to allow her to waver off the edge. That he would save for when he pounded her to his delight.

I'm going to savor everything I can from this moment. I want to enjoy every second of this as long as she's willing to keep going. As long as she can keep up with me...

She braced herself on the shower walls, releasing his hair. The water pouring over them turned cold as her searching hand knocked into the knob. The chilling streams added to the visceral sensations rattling them. He throbbed in his palm.

That's it, just a little harder...

He abandoned her clit and began kissing up her body to the other breast and sampled the nipple, hard against the tip of his tongue. His hand slid between her thighs and he thrust two fingers inside. She leaned into him, unable to fold over with his body against hers. They both shivered under the icy water, neither of them willing to break away from the heat of their passion to right the mistake. He thrust in and out of her, enjoying how she tightened on his fingers. With his other hand, he stroked himself, his erection almost to its peak once more. Catching her nipple in his teeth, her pussy tightened. The sensation of it finally making him rock hard. At last, he released her breast.

"Turn around," he huffed, goosebumps making him shudder.

She tilted her head, confused. "Why?"

Mark searched her eyes a moment before smirking. "Forgive me for asking but..." He licked his lips before leaning into her ear. "Is it wrong to assume you've only done missionary style?"

Her hands balled against his chest and her body stiffened in defense at the comment. She didn't say a word. Sensing her rising anger and embarrassment, he began suckling on her ear. A shiver shook her. Sliding his fingers out of her, he gripped her hips and spun her into position, rubbing his hard cock between her thighs. Her body heated under him in response, excited at the thought he was ready again. She reached down and he gripped her wrists.

"It's my turn to play with you," he demanded.

Holding her wrists above her head, he held them tight against the tiles. Watching between them, he rubbed the tip of his cock against her hot pussy. Shuffling, she spread her legs a little wider and tilting her hip. He pressed hard and slipped inside. Again, she tightened around him, inhaling swiftly as he pressed his length all the way inside. At first, he rocked in and out, slow and agonizing. Her legs trembled, body still riding on the pleasure of their foreplay. With each thrust, his cock grew harder and slicker.

Look at you, being naughty and trying something new.

Jane panted, pinned between his body and the tiles. As he gained momentum, she moaned, pushing her ass against him to allow him to full access. His body buzzed, his own orgasm already threatening to end his fun earlier than expected for his second time. Releasing her wrists, his hands rode down her arms and to the front of her torso. He groped a breast in one hand while the other hand continued to snake downward. Like she had done before, he mimicked her motion feeling where his cock slid in and out of her. He moaned as she tensed around his throbbing dick.

Shit, I'm going to cum too fast.

Changing tactics, he pulled her hips away from the wall. The cold water blasting over him, knocking back the rising orgasm. She moaned at the new angle, rocking herself on his dick. His hands retreated to her hips and he watched his length pull out of her before slowly entering her. Each time he swore her body gushed and rattled with delight, gasps coming from her. At last she looked over her shoulder with a pitiful expression.

"Please..." she begged.

He locked eyes with her, watching the pleasure on her face as he pushed slow and teasingly back inside her wanton heat. "Please?"

"Faster." She braced herself on the wall. "I want you to go faster."

His cock throbbed inside her and she tightened in response. "Faster or harder?"

Her brow knitted. "I don't know what either of those mean."

A laugh escaped him. "You're amazing."

"Don't laugh." Her face flushed. "I just, I didn't think I'd like this so much and you're not fucking me fast enough."

"Hard enough," he corrected with a smirk. "Faster means you want me to cum sooner. Harder means you want me to thrust more aggressively."

Puffing out her cheeks, she looked back to the wall. "Fuck me harder."

"Then stand up straighter, I don't need you breaking your nose against the tiles." Mark chuckled, liking their exchange. "We can't do it here at this angle."

"I'll be fine, fuck me hard just like this," she inhaled deep, holding it to wait for the onslaught of whatever she thought she enacted.

"Jane, if you like this angle, then we should move to the bed." He shut off the water and pulled away from her to grab a towel.

I can use this to back off my orgasm some and gain back some lost ground.

"Don't leave. I wasn't done." She stood in alarm. "I don't understand how the bed will help. I'm enjoying it just fine in the shower."

His eyebrows lifted high at the tantrum she started to throw. "Glad you approve, but..." He bit his lip a moment as his eyes trailed down to her knees. "But I don't think your knees will be able to hold you up much longer. You got pretty wobbly there."

Looking to her legs, she looked betrayed. "Well, if you insist and promise to go... harder."

Mark snorted. "The whole B&B might hear us, but how can I say no."

Jane paled. "Can they hear us?" She rushed pass him, covering her face. "Oh... is it like that one couple? Where... Aunt May called the manager? I don't think I can live with myself."

Mark spun her, shoving her forward until she stumbled into the bed. "Let them hear us."

"M-mark!" Before she could stand up straight, his cock slid inside her. "Ooh!"

Her fists balled the blanket in them, and his fingers dug tight into her hips. He wasted no time, her breasts swaying as her grinded hard and fast against her. The bed squeaked as they rocked against it. Her ass slapped against his thighs, her body growing hot under his reckless thrusting. She could only gasp, growing tighter with each inhale. Moaning, he was starting to peak unable to resist how her heat wrapped around his rock-hard cock. A screech escaped her, a gush of hot fluid rushing between them.

Oh, we came hard... I guess it's my turn to make a mess.

He held onto her, trying his best not to lose his momentum. At last, he couldn't hold back as he too peaked. Pressing hard against her, he groaned as he came. Her back arched and she grinded into him, fingers gliding to touch where they connected. A shiver rattled through his spine.

Something about how she wants to feel where I slide inside her just makes this so much sweeter.

Releasing her hips, he glided under her, groping her breasts, and pulling her to stand and lean into him. She touched and played with herself, all while he still lingered inside her pussy. He kissed her neck and shoulders, massaging her breasts. The cherry tobacco smell wafted from her hair. He inhaled deep, holding the scent as she rocked her hips riding out her orgasm. As her breath caught and began to whimper, he bit her shoulder and pinched her nipples. Her pussy grew tight, and he had found her preference: *Jane liked it rough.*

Did she just cum again? How many times was that for her?

"Feel better?" He cooed as the tension in her body melted away.

"I haven't felt anything in a while…" Swallowing, she caught her breath. "Now what?"

Hugging onto her, he inhaled the tangy scent once more. "How about you spend the whole weekend here in this room with me? No obligations, just you and me enjoying each other like this until my time's up." Nuzzling her neck, he kissed it.

"I can't say I'm not curious to see what else you can do with this." Her finger rubbed where they were still connected, his hardness fading.

He laughed, pulling away, then fell on his back atop the bed. "Forgive me, Jane. I think I need a nap." Managing to grab her wrist, he tugged her onto the bed beside him. "How about we rest up and start this again when we wake up?"

His eyelids felt heavy, drained, worse than what he normally felt after two sessions.

Was it the drive that drained me? Maybe all the stress with Karen and being able to just, let it all go just now.

He could feel her fingers pacing to and fro along his forearm, the muscles twitching and a smile coming to his face.

I don't think I've ever been with a girl who prefers it rough. Fuck, Karen. I think I'm in love with Jane.

7

Something for Later

Mark had fallen asleep fast and she covered him up before bolting through the door. She felt like a runaway bride, the way she hesitated at the top of the stairs to steal one last look at the closed door. Shaking herself from the longing and haunting sensations of his hot hands all over her body, she let herself break away. Once more, Jane puffed her cheeks out and rushed down the steps. For a moment, she thought the manager saw her rush out the front door. The way he had stiffened and peeked over the book, looking where she had just flown down the steps as if he heard the tapping of her feet.

There's no way he saw me too! What the hell is happening to me? Who is this Mark Wilder, really?

Stumbling to a stop on the porch, she sidled to her spot on the top step and sat. Eyes wide with racing thoughts, she searched her pockets for the pipe and tobacco tin. It didn't take her long to pack the pipe and strike a match on the wood post to bring the smoking behemoth to life. A long pull brought her nerves to a calm, her panic slowing to a dull roar as she held it in for a minute and released it.

Did that really happen?

The smoke curled from her lips like a bad omen and her blue eyes glowed. Looking at the willow tree, she could see where she stopped pulling the weeds and her chest ached. For the last few weeks, she had just kept the garden going, until someone more skilled and permanent could be hired. Sure, she had made a few people do double-takes during the day as of late, but none of it had been ill-intended. Not like you'd expect from a poltergeist.

"I didn't even know he was talking to me." Mumbling to herself, she didn't bother to pull the pipe from her lips. "No one talks to the gardener, and no one openly approaches apparitions of the Blue Lady either."

Rubbing her forehead, she thought back to last weekend. Upstairs was the man Karen had abandoned and he somehow landed himself in her room and bed. Worse, how could she say no to...

"Son of a bitch." She gnawed on the pipe as her frustration rose. "What the hell was I thinking following that kid upstairs. But shit, who could say no? I've been... the last time I could... I mean, it was my husband and I, dating back... no one could say no to an offer like that. It seemed like a miracle and..."

Goosebumps rolled over her skin. After a few more puffs of her pipe, she pulled one more item from her pocket: *Mark's cell phone.* A mischievous grin crossed her face. Part of her was disappointed as she searched the most private areas of his phone. Unlike his beloved Karen's gallery, he had no dick pics and apparently, she never bothered to share any pussy shots with him, not even a decent nipple or cleavage shot.

Raw deal. The heat rose in her face over this idea. *What a nasty whore. Lock in that man and not provide him with eye candy like her boy toys. She did him dirty. Someone needs to make it up to that man. Two years of dry spell...*

Pursing her lips to hold the pipe, she let it hover over own cleavage. Her upper arms squeezed her girls together, pushing them up and her blue lacy bra slid out of the low-cut crop top. A couple of clicks and she took a look around. The B&B was quiet and the town all around lifeless for a Saturday evening. Goaded by the thought she could fill the gap Karen left in Mark's gallery, she sashayed to the side yard where the shade of large bushes and unkempt lilies might offer great photo mates.

If she won't give it to him, I will!

Right on cue, a text buzzed through, dumping Jane from camera mode.

"Speak of the devil."

[Karen: Mark, let's meet up. I want to talk. Please, let me make this up to you.]

Jane pulled the pipe from her lips. Smoke billowing out and slamming against the screen. Dumping her pipe out, she smirked as her fingers tapped away with authority.

[Mark: The Blue Lady Room. Midnight.]

She watched as the text status shifted from delivered to read. Karen began to type more, but Jane was faster, blocking the number. She chuckled, satisfied with the plan she had cooked up. Her eyes took in the overgrown cubby of foliage all around.

"If I can't see out, no one should be able to see in." Flipping back to the camera, she thought back to Karen's naughty pictures. "Fuck her. I can do better. Someone's about to have the rarest footage of the B&B's very own Jane Story in the nude."

With a snap of her fingers, her clothes shifted into a vintage white petticoat and corset. She shook her hair out of the bun and snapped a downward shot, catching her smirk and cleavage in the sultry shot. After a few clicks, she pulled the phone to her to evaluate her handiwork. Her heart fluttered, the idea of what she would be leaving behind for him thrilling and arousing. Inhaling deep, she reached back and began unlacing her corset.

Something tells me he's going to really appreciate these.

An ache swelled in her chest and she swallowed it down. Flicking her fingers, the phone floated in the air, hovering around snapping shots. On occasion she would look to the phone, giving him a look, one she knew he'd understand the weight of after what they had done moments before. Jane paced herself, shedding the corset and the petticoat. The phone captured her at all different angles until she found herself in the nude among the fading sunlight.

Now, what do I take pictures of?

Blinking, she pondered and shook her head.

Am I really going that far?

Staring at the phone, a flash of his smile and hungry eyes on her body made her body buzz with want.

Yeah, I'm fucking going all in.

She found herself sitting on the grass, goosebumps rolling across her skin like ripples on a lake. Gathering her courage, she aimed to relax, focus on close and erotic shots of her body. Peaks of hard nipples and self-groping, her own hand sliding down her torso, and her sucking on her own fingers. The thought he would see these, see her so raw and vulnerable, and would even pleasure himself looking at them made her arousal grow. Her pussy throbbed with want and she caved to the final round of photos she aimed to leave him.

He just makes me want to touch myself more...

Her thighs parted and she began to roll her finger over her swollen jewel. The other hand groped her breast, fingers pinching her nipple in an attempt to mimic how he had groped them. Pictures snapped, catching every play and the moment her finger dove between her pink folds. A moan escaped her, biting her lip to muffle his name. Her entire body shook with the rising orgasm, the lingering thoughts, and thrills of how his cock thrusted in and out.

Fuck, I want him back inside me one more time...

Body arching, she inhaled sharp as the stimulation peaked. The arousal and ecstasy slamming into her. More clicks of the camera caught as her juices gushed from her, fingers pulling out of the way to show him all that she offered, all that he had taken enjoyment of and how much she wanted him all over again. Panting from the orgasm, she flipped through the phone. Some photos she deleted, *we can't have blurred or half-assed shots like she had.* She intentionally cherry-picked the ones she wanted, the stolen glances, the sultry moment of her body reacting to thoughts of him. Those where she hoped she could get a literal rise out of him and his cock.

"Dammit." Her smile faltered and she frowned. "How in the hell can I explain to him that I'm nothing more than a ghost?"

Closing her eyes, she anguished over the idea. Thoughts mangled; honesty obscured by passion. The leaves rustled and she snapped her eyes open, relieved to see it was nothing more than the breeze.

Whatever reaction I had with him is fading, I didn't feel the breeze in the same level. In fact, after he touched me, I could feel again. The heat of the sun, the tickle of a strand of hair on my face, and the sliding of sweat on my skin. Sure, I can physically manipulate things and sweat under the sun, but there's another layer I've been missing since I died all those centuries ago.

The phone buzzed again, and she pulled it up.

[Timmy: Hey, how's it going?]

Twisting her lips, she sat up and snapped once more. Like that, she was back to her crop top now paired with cutoff shorts. Prying into his phone, she found a picture of the friend and furrowed her brow. Zooming in she blinked, and rage filled her. Without further ado, she called this Timmy to have a word with him and the chaos he had thrown in her direction.

"Hey, Mark!" Timmy answered immediately. "How's it going?"

"You!" Jane fussed over the phone. "You're that pukwudgie that started this mess!"

Silence fell over the phone.

"You better not hang up or I will find a way to come haunt your ass over this bullshit!" She stood and began pacing, throwing an arm out. "You came here, found me, and after that I've been dealing with a flood of college boys invoking my name for sex like I'm some loose floozy handing out sex in handbaskets! Are you kidding me? Do I look like I'm running a paranormal whorehouse, you little creep!"

"I... I can explain..."

"Then explain it to me." She crossed her arms, fuming.

"It's about Mark." He hesitated.

"Yes?" her heart fluttered, the conversation steering in a different way then she had expected. "What about Mark?" *Was this never about me?*

"You see, I don't think he knows." Clearing his throat, he lowered his voice. "He keeps hooking up with all these girls, but he's draining them. Not on purpose, I don't think he knows he's doing it and well, they don't last long in bed with him and... I just thought. If I found someone for him... like you?"

Jane's brow folded and covered her mouth as she tried to grasp what he was trying to say. *Fucking pukwudgies, always beating around the bush and meddling. Anything to cause a bit of chaos...*

"I heard about you haunting the inn. It's not often an entity stays in an active place that long, so I thought if I could just entice him to go there, that maybe if you two meet and well..."

"Well what?" She shook her head, still grasping for what Timmy was implying. "Exactly what does Mark not know about himself that your mischief causing kind would take stock in?"

"Ask him about his dad." The comment was blunt. "You're from the Victorian days, you remember the superstitions about the co-walker? Wraith doppelgangers?"

Jane swallowed, her mind reaching for a time she had let go of ages ago. "The shadow guardians who fulfill dying wishes. The male banshee stories. When you see your doppelganger, death is coming for you. That story?"

"I think he's part wraith." Jane inhaled as Timmy pitched his suspicions. "Wait, if you have his phone, what happened? Is he okay?"

"What makes you an expert on spirits and the undead?" she demanded, blood rushing.

"I majored in Celestial and Spirit Anatomy."

"Gross," Jane muttered.

"Bear with me... and a PhD in Undead and Necromancy."

"I thought you were a casino bellhop?" she countered, questioning the trickster creature on the phone.

"Yeah, because a Jersey Devil works there."

She rubbed her forehead. "Of course, and you needed an in to get close and cause mischief."

"Maybe," he cooed. "My magic knows no boundaries."

"Yeah, I've noticed." Swallowing, she double backed to the initial fact. "He doesn't know?"

"Pretty sure of it." There was a long pause, a huff, then he added, "He doesn't know your dead. That you're a ghost."

"I noticed."

"So, what makes him different? Can he touch you? Turn you on?"

Jane's face flushed. "You, little creep."

With that she hung up the phone, coming out of the bushes to watch Mark leave the inn. She waited until he crossed the street and headed for the convenience store. Returning to her spot on the steps, she sat there feeling sick to her stomach. Lifting her pipe, she abandoned it. Shaking her head, she marched back to the bushes, looking through the gallery of photos wondering if she should just wipe them out.

Shit, not even smoking will bring my nerves to a calm. How could he not know?

8

Cherry Tobacco

Mark sat up in bed, shuddering awake from his slumber. The sunlight had started to change hues outside, and he reached over to find Jane gone. His chest ached seeing her clothes had disappeared from the floor as well. Holding his head, he fell straight back and groaned. It had been amazing, but for the first time he had run out of energy first. Usually the girl bailed, or practically suffered a narcolepsy level nap session by the time he could get off twice.

Dammit, what a bad time for a nap. And to think, to hook up with a girl so willing to try new shit and inexperienced and enjoying herself. Wonder if she'll come back...

Cherry tobacco lingered in his nostrils, he could still smell her on him and in the room, even in the sheets. His cock hardened and he grunted. Pulling the covers off, he stomped back into the bathroom and sighed.

Just shake this off in the shower, maybe it's the cherry tobacco getting me all aroused again.

A shiver shook his shoulders. He wanted to taste her one more time, feel her fingers reach between them... another grunt escaped him. The lustful want building in him goaded him to turn the shower on once more. Drowning his head in the water, his skin crawled. Biting his lip, his hand slid down, gripping his hardened shaft. He stroked, slow at first as his eyes squeezed shut. He could feel the haunting heat of her body.

The way her eyes glowed and face flushed. And when she dipped her fingers to play with herself with my...

Stroking faster and firmer, he released with a moan. His heart pounded as he watched his cum slide down the drain. He searched the air a moment, chasing the fleeting thoughts that tried to bring calm to the growing desire boiling at his core. Jane couldn't be far.

Small town, gardener of the local B&B... Maybe she ran to the little convenience store across the street?

Armed with that thought, he turned off the shower and began toweling off in a rush. He had to find her, just spend another moment with her. Whether this was long term or just for the weekend, it was worth the chase. Sniffing a shirt, he frowned and searched for a different one. He had been so lost in bitter thoughts about Karen he hadn't bothered to check if everything he shoved in the duffle bag had been clean. Pulling one leg, then the other through a pair of cargo shorts, he almost didn't circle back to slide on his flipflops.

Aiming for the exit, he paused and turned to the manager reading his book. "Hey, where's the gardener."

"Gone," he drawled.

"No, I meant the lady in blue."

He peeked over his book and arched an eyebrow. "Funny. That's a cute one. Though I was thinking the same thing."

"Same thing?" Mark could feel a chill snaking up his back, his gut twisting.

"How long has this place been without a gardener?" Mark's mouth ran dry as he dared to ask the question.

"A few months." Sitting the book down, he stifled a yawn before revealing more information. "But its painfully obvious someone has been keeping the garden in shape. I swear, it hasn't been me or the maid. They say the previous owner hasn't left this place since it opened in the late 1880s."

"The lady in blue..." Mark looked at the man, deadpanned. "Jane."

"Yeah, see you know the history. Jane Story is known to leave behind the smell of..."

"Cherry Tobacco."

"There. You got all the information you need." He grabbed up the book and cracked it open. "I keep smelling it today, she's rather active. If you're lucky, you might see her again." He laughed.

"I think I did more than that," muttered Mark, paling as he covered his mouth.

"What was that?" he broke from the book again.

"Never mind."

Mark wandered out of the B&B, lost in thought as he walked to the convenience store. Without making eye contact or a single sound, he pulled a 24-pack of beer from the wall cooler and marched to the counter. His eyes fell out of focus, his mind choking on disbelief as he tried to digest what or who he had been smitten with.

Could it just be a local hot chick playing the part? I mean, I had sex with her. Didn't I? Am I even awake?

"Hey, I said it's $27.99." The cashier chewed on her bubblegum, popping a bubble. "And I need your ID still."

"R-right." Blinking, he handed her his license and credit card. "Does a girl by the name of Jane live in town?"

"No." Then she smirked. "Except for the ghost in the B&B. Why?"

He shook his head, the information only securing his fears.

"Is this everything?" she asked as she smacked her chewing gum, mouth opened.

Someone should let her know how unattractive that is. He glanced at the wall of tobacco products and he tilted his head, "You got any cherry flavored cigarillos?"

She folded her brow at him. "Like what my Aunt Kathy smokes?" Reaching under the counter, she produced a box of cherry flavored mini cigars. "These?"

Clearing his throat, Mark could feel the heat in his cheeks, "Yeah, those."

She giggled as she rung them up. "You smoke these?"

He narrowed his eyes. "What if I do."

Shrugging, she grinned. "Just seems odd. Unmanly."

"Well, when you grow up and stop chewing gum like a five year old, call me up."

There was silence. She closed her mouth, leaned over and spit her gum in the trash can. "You want my number? I'm ready, big boy."

"Next time, sweetheart." He winked at her, loving her acute response to his snarky comment.

"Come see me when you're back in town, the name's Sam." With that, she slid his license and card back to him.

"Depends if I settle for Jane first," and Mark stomped off with his bagged purchase.

If I can figure out if she's a ghost or a person or... it can't be.

His heart beat hard against his chest, the idea that Jane was a phantom. Other questions crept forward, and he gripped the bag tighter as he crossed the empty street.

Could there be something different about me to make... now I'm just thinking like a b-rated movie. Might as well be the plotline to a bad paranormal themed porno. All it needs is a pizza delivery boy.

Shoulders shuddering, the streetlamps began to flicker to life, exposing how barren of life the town was for a Saturday night. Still, he couldn't shake the doubts and wonderings. His gut twisted every time he circled back to words like *ghost, phantom, or dead.*

Did I have a mental break? Maybe she gave me a false name? No, that's not it.

He paused at the gate, swallowing as something deep inside shook his core.

The door never closed and opened. Not once. There's only one set of stairs up and she wouldn't have made it pass me. It's a tight fit in that foyer. And if that's the case then...

Bushes beside the B&B shook and out came Jane. His heart skipped a beat and again he swallowed. She froze, their eyes meeting. Every fiber in his body wanted her, wanted to drag her back through those bushes and...

Dammit, I must know who she is before I proceed further!

Pushing through the gate, he headed for the front porch steps of the B&B. He broke their stare, choosing to ignore her. Sitting down, he riffled through the bag, ripping the cardboard open and pulling a bottle out. Twisting the cap off, he chucked it to the ground and began guzzling. Jane walked up, reaching down to retrieve it with an annoyed expression.

"I'd appreciate it if you wouldn't throw your trash everywhere." His expression made her blink and she frowned. "C-can I sit with you?"

Shit, she knows something's up.

He slid over, unsure if he should speak. Reaching into the cardboard, he pulled out a beer. Holding it to her, he felt like someone might see him and think he was trying to drink with his imaginary friend. Relief washed over him when she took it from him and popped the cap. She chucked both caps into his bag and he guzzled down the rest of his beer. Without so much as glancing at her, heart racing, he popped the top on another.

"From the way you're acting, I suppose you've figured out who I am." She took a sip, her eyes demanding he look at her and he refused. "Or is the thought more of a what am I?"

"How..." He lost his words. *I can't just say, 'How is it possible to fuck a ghost' can I?*

"When you touched my arm, that was my first thought, *how*." Tilting her head, she took another sip and continued. "Then you offered to have sex and all I could think was how long it had been since the last time I felt the warmth of another human being. Sure, I can feel the heat of the sun and the cold of snow, but what good is that if I'm... well, you can imagine having so many pass through me like I'm made of air, and here you come like it was nothing."

His chest stung. "So you're really her, the Lady in Blue."

"Y-yeah."

He downed his beer, then opened another. *Fuck me. I'm in over my head.*

"I'm sorry, you were just looking for some fun and..." her voice faltered, she finished her beer and reached over him for a second.

Her breast slid over his thighs and he became hard. Cursing under his breath, she paused. There was something electric about thinking of her, but feeling her against him brought out a side of him he didn't even know existed. The chemistry in their touch was off the charts and he knew she could feel it, beyond just the dick poking into her tits. There was this hunger for companionship and lust that resonated between them. She pulled away with her beer and smiled to herself.

"Look, Mark. If you want to fool around, I'm game. You're the only man I can do that with anyhow." The beer hissed as it opened, and the cap landed in the cardboard. "You are welcome to hit me up anytime. Plus, your girlfriend is a piece of shit."

"You? You took the picture of Karen?" She sighed, satisfied to finally have his eyes meet hers. "Of course, you did."

"I just found it annoying. Seems like she was sleeping around on you... a lot."

"It always happens that way…" He shifted forward, leaning on his knees, a weak attempt to hide the tent in his shorts. "Every girlfriend I've had has either left me or cheated on me. I swear it's the sex, but…"

"It is," Jane intercepted. "That and well, the other thing…"

He narrowed his eyes. "What other thing? What about the sex? What the hell am I doing wrong?"

What did I miss? Is there something wrong with me? This whole time was it really something wrong with me?

9

Bring Me to Life

Jane faltered from taking a sip of her beer, nearly spewing it. Mark's pitiful expression told her volumes of heartbreak and guilt, as if he had failed his previous loves in the bedroom department. After what little she had in her previous life, he had been leagues better than her belated husband and far outclassed the racy gossip she had heard. In fact, she had been rotten, playing with herself watching the living have intercourse for some sort of release. Regardless, his face said he had convinced himself he was the failure in the sheets, not them.

Poor guy!

Just the flashback of the way he had made love to her hours ago made her shift. A flush of arousal hit her, and she prayed the heat in her face didn't make her cheeks red. The sky was a deep lavender, the moths tinging off the porch light from above. In the yellow lighting, Mark seemed worn down.

What on earth went wrong? she wondered.

She scowled and remembered what the pukwudgie had said, *he doesn't know.* Finishing her beer, she inhaled a deep breath.

Ask him about his dad.

Jane's lips twisted, hesitant to follow a trickster's advice, but they don't befriend and not eat a human often. She had only run into a few of them in passing, marveled the insight and mischief they caused the B&B, a resident, or even the whole damn town. Regardless, some part of her felt keeping something like this secret from someone was right-down wrong.

I just wanted to feel alive in his arms one more time, but I can't shake the feeling this is important. Why can I feel him as if we are on the same physical plane.

"Tell me about your dad," she demanded.

His eyes widened. "Why?"

"Let's just say a little gremlin said I'd know the answer if I asked."

"Why would you want to know?" His face tensed, his eyes darkening. "What answer are you looking for?"

"Why this is possible..." She ran her hand over his bicep and down his arm but jerked back before clasping her fingers into his. "So, tell me something unusual about your parents."

He started to open a pack of cigarillos.

"That bad?"

"He died before I was born." Pulling one free, he flustered. "Dammit, I didn't get any matches or a lighter."

"Here." She flicked a match against the porch and handed it to him. "What's that? It smells a little sweeter than what I've been putting in my pipe. Is that a cigarette? Cigar?"

"Something in between. It's called a cigarillo and they come in a lot of flavors. Try one," he handed her the pack and billowed smoke out. "So, Mom tells this story about my dad. Everyone reassured me it was just a story, but Mom swears it happened and I can't say she's ever been one for ghost stories."

"Ghost story?" She pulled his cigarillo from his lips and used it to light her own before placing it back. "Go on."

"They say he died in the plane crash, but my mom swears by her Bible he came home at the time the black box says the crash happened." He took another drag, the scent of the smoke like the cherry tobacco from her pipe. Strangely, it calmed him. "He didn't say a word. Wouldn't answer her when she asked why he abandoned his flight so suddenly. He just kissed her, made passionate love to her until he uttered her name at last. When she woke up, he was gone, so gone, she said he didn't even leave the usual indentation of his body in the sheets and pillow. Like his spirit laid with her one last time before passing from this world, to do what they had been trying to do in three years of marriage. She swears that's when she got pregnant but... anyway, it's just a... or I thought it... then if... if... never mind."

Jane leaned on her knees, holding her head in disbelief. "It was a wraith."

"W-what did you say?" He leaned into her view and nudged her knee. "It's just a ghost story, you should be used to those by now."

"You're half wraith," she said, collecting herself.

Mark choked on his beer. "Um, what?" he repeated, to breathe. "I'm a what?"

"Wraith. Look, there's old stories about the Co-walker, the doppelganger showing itself when your life is to end and fulfilling one last wish." She downed a beer, then motioned for another.

He paled. "My mom, that night, it wasn't dad but... a doppelganger."

Swallowing the beer, she sputtered, "Right. A type of wraith or banshee. You're not completely human, and you're not completely corporeal because of it."

"I'm not drunk enough for this shit." Mark started to drink faster, his heart racing.

"Look, wraith's often feed off of human life or energy. The more powerful, the more likely they can take on a new corporeal form when the adjacent spirit dies, or it sucks them dry. Let me ask this, do all your sex partners pass out during or after sexual contact?"

He snorted his beer out and dropped his cigarillo down the steps.

"That's part of it, but with me..." She looked away, face flushing as she took a long drag off her cigarillo. "You can't suck me dry, and I am more likely to do that to you if I'm not paying attention."

He stood, stomping the cigarillo out and glared at her. "Then why do you have a physical form near me?"

Blowing out a long stream of smoke, she shrugged. "Maybe it's because you're not dead? You provide a link between the dead and living?"

"Wouldn't this happen sooner to me?" Despair filled his face.

"Like a ghost would tell you what they are."

He leaned over her, nose to nose. "Were you planning to tell me?"

Jane's heart raced. She had thought to tell him, maybe at the end of the fun weekend. Her eyes fell to his lips lingering so close. Sweet cherry smoke filled the air, his hard cock pressing against her knee through his shorts, making her wet for him. Caving to the arousal, she pressed her lips against his. He deepened the kiss, the force of it making her abandon and snuff out her cigarillo on the porch beside them.

I wanted to have you think of me as alive a little longer in fear I couldn't have another moment like this.

The bitter taste of cheap beer and cherry tobacco filled her senses. She wanted more of it, more of him. His tongue dipped into her mouth and she suckled it, making it stay. Her knees parted as she laid back onto the porch, moaning as the tent in his pants rubbed against the crotch of her shorts. Wrapping her arms around him, she pulled him closer. The heat of his hand slid under her crop top and she responded with lashing her tongue into his mouth where he captured it, sucking on it.

His fingers weaseled under the cup of her bra, squeezing her breast tight. Her heart fluttered as she felt him throb where their hips pressed tight. Breaking away, he sucked and nipped on her neck and she arched into him. The heat of his body made her own warm, the rush of life filling her like nothing had ever done before. His breath hot against her skin made her own pimple and she reached down to grope his ass.

He moaned into her neck. "I want to take you over and over again."

A wave of arousal made her shudder. "And I will let you have your way with me over and over again."

His tongue ran up her neck until his lips captured her earlobe. Another wave of goosebumps rolled over her and his cock throbbed. Fingers pinched her nipple and she ached to have his hardened length back inside her. The provocative want for his skin against her own made her whole being buzz with desire. Her hand slipped under his shorts, and grinned to feel he had gone commando to come looking for her. Again, she squeezed his ass cheek and his dick throbbed against her pussy.

Damn these clothes!

"Fuck me right here," she purred in lust.

He nuzzled her ear. "What if they see us?"

"No one comes around on Saturday." She slipped her other hand into the back of his shorts, grinding into his cock and earning a grunt from him. "I bet you can cum twice before we're caught."

Mark giggled and she tensed against his stubble chin. "They might just see me with a hard-on humping the porch."

"Shit." The color drained from her face and she pulled her hands out. "I'm sorry I didn't think about the fact–"

"Mr. Wilder." The manager's voice made Jane's blood run cold, staring at him wide-eyed where they froze in their embrace. "Not that it's my business what you and this young lady intend to do, but please take it to the privacy of your room upstairs. Small towns frown upon such public displays of affection."

Did he… did he imply he can see me! What the hell is happening?

10

Taking It Slow

"**Y**-yes sir." Mark shot a glance in her direction and they scrambled to their feet. "I meant to tell you; Jane will be staying the night. Not sure if that's an extra charge or..."

"Of course not." Tapping the book on his leg, looking at her, confused. "Jane?" The man was tall, his goatee only made his mouth sterner and the glasses obscured his expression completely from where Mark stood. "Is that really your name, girl in blue?"

"Y-Yes." She looked to Mark, then to the manager, both wondering if the manager could even hear her.

His brow folded and he scratched his jaw in thought.

"I'm local?" Jane cringed, not confident in her focus. "That's right, Mr. Buckley, I just wanted to surprise my boyfriend this weekend." Shuffling over, she hooked an arm with Mark's and picked up the bag of beer. "He's been gone to college and said he was returning home so we rented the Blue Lady room."

"R-right." Now the manager squinted his eyes at them in suspicion. "And that's why the room was registered under his friend's name?"

"About that..." Mark mentally grasped for everything, anything to patch the story they crafted. "I didn't want her to catch on to me coming for a surprise visit."

"Right!" Jane nodded, following his lead. "And well, he didn't know I've been gone. Dealing with..." She inhaled sharply.

Shit, she hit a dead end. Come on, come on, think!

"Taking care of family property." Mark shrugged.

"Yes! That's right."

The manager chuckled. "Just get upstairs with this before old Aunt May across the street calls me or the sheriff." He shook his head, "You don't have to explain shit to me, just don't trash the room like last weekend's couple."

Mark flinched, but Jane pinched him in the ribs. "Ouch. Why'd you do that for?"

"You heard the man. Upstairs. Now. Before anyone *sees*," she hissed, tugging him into the room.

The door shut behind her and she leaned against it. Mark held his head, and they both stared at one another in shock. He managed to motion to her and couldn't find the words. She lipped *I know!* Blue eyes wide and chest rising and falling with her quickened breath. Mark looked to the ceiling, still holding his head in disbelief.

Is that what I can do? Make ghost flesh for a fleeting moment?

A rush of heat pressed hard against him. Jane had buried herself into his chest. Arms wrapping him tight, fists balling his shirt as she clung to him. Blinking, registering what was happening, he wrapped his own arms around her. She was crying, sobbing into him. He rested a cheek on the top of her head, sighing as he let her carry on.

And to be dead, haunting your home for this long. What does this mean if I leave her? Does she go back to that life? Back to an afterlife of barely existing.

His chest burned, swallowing the fear rattling him at his core. "Will you be okay?" He spoke in a soft voice soft as he held her tight.

Catching her breath, she at last answered, "I'll deal, I've gone this long but..."

"But?" She released him at last and he wiped a tear.

Holding his hand there, her eyes glowed and took his breath away. "Would it be too wrong to ask that you visit again? To let me feel alive for a night or day?"

"That's a hard thing to promise." It broke him to say it, but they both needed to assess the situation. "So, I could see you and hear you. There's so much to digest. It's amazing, he could hear and see you."

She laughed. "I swear he's been doing that the whole time. That man comes out to the porch and talks to me all the time."

Mark snorted. "From what I hear, you've made a lot of folks very aware you were here long before I made this happen."

"How are you doing it?" She sniffled and he shrugged.

"Honestly? I have no idea."

"I suppose you should ask Tim." She puffed out her cheeks.

"Tim? My friend Tim?" His mind spiraled. "Why would he know anything?"

"He's a pukwudgie with a Ph.D." Mark's face must have revealed his mind was spinning circles to nowhere. "Oh no, you didn't know? You really don't know anything at all." Puffing out her cheeks once more, she flustered, "Dammit. He's just causing havoc, that little twerp."

Mark smirked, seeing that flare of anger and annoyance she had given him that first moment he had touched her. He kissed her, hands gliding back under her shirt. This time his hand drifted to her back and unlatched the bra, again, with speed and accuracy. She inhaled, a shiver making her shake against him. Breaking away, he lifted her shirt and bra off, eager to see her naked before him, hungry to touch and taste her. A grin grew on her face and she reached down and began to unbutton his shorts. Tugging off his own shirt, he moaned as the heat of her fingers wrapped around his cock.

Which way do I want to take her first? She's been dead, she can feel for the first time in ages... I can take it slow, make sure I keep myself teetering on the edge.

Tilting his hip, he pressed his cock into her palm, and she tightened her grip, stroking firmer. Tracing her cheek with his fingers, he looked at her with endearment. They flowed over the pronounced collarbone and between her subtle breasts. Her skin pimpled, pink nipples erect as he travelled down the center of her torso. A sharp inhale escaped her lips, the stroking fingers on his dick halting.

To think, this gorgeous woman is dead, watching life come and go for centuries. I get her all to myself, mine, and mine alone. Someone to enjoy endless...

His fingers stopped at the waistband and he frowned. "These are in the way."

"Then remove them," she challenged.

Biting his bottom lip, he was slow with the way he unbuttoned her shorts. "So, tell me, how does a late 1800's ghost end up in a pair of Daisy Dukes?"

She abandoned her play and buried her face in his bare chest. "I learned really fast that I could materialize my favorite items, so I thought maybe I could mimic things I saw."

"And you chose this?" He unzipped her shorts, slow as he felt each notch unhook.

"If you don't like it, then take it off me."

His eyes locked with hers as she looked up. "Can't a guy enjoy a hot chick undressing for just a minute or two?"

She laughed and it made his heart flutter. Her hands slipped over his hip, shoving his own pants down and they fell to the floor. Arching his eyebrows high, the zipper finally couldn't travel any farther. The room grew dark, casting deep shadows over their bodies as the last of her own clothes joined his at their feet. Kissing her, he groped her ass, walking her backwards until her knees locked on the bed. She fell back and his hands raced up her thighs, parting them as he kneeled on the floor.

I want to make her scream like a banshee... everyone will know her voice by the time I finish with her tonight. Jane Story will be heard by the entire town by the time I'm done with her.

Running his tongue across her pussy and ending with a flick to her clit. She moaned, legs shaking as she fought to close them around him. Again, he licked the length of her opening, tasting her until he wrapped his lips around the swollen jewel. Suckling, he slipped a finger inside her wet heat, and she arched, knees raising until her legs rested on either shoulder. Mark moaned and felt her tighten around his finger. A second digit joined, and he stroked her slow.

The jittering in her legs told him that at last, with a twist of his wrist, he had found a sweet spot for his fingers to rub. Sucking more aggressive on her clit, locking it in his lips, he flicked it with the tip of his tongue. She squealed, her pussy squeezing on his fingers. He stroked hard and fast, focusing on the spot that had made her body jolt. A visceral scream exploded from her. Back arching, heels digging into his backside as her thighs threatened to clamp shut around him.

That's the scream I was looking for. Good girl. Keep howling. Let them hear you!

Leaning back, he shook her legs off, elbows pushing her thighs apart once more. He rubbed her clit with his fingers, still stroking her hard and heavy. Another wail and a gush of hot fluid rushed from her pussy. A fountain of ecstasy escaped her and he at last looked up to her sparkling blue eyes. They were wide with surprise, cheeks red as her hands rushed down to pull him from his fun.

"First time coming that hard?" He slowed his thrusting fingers until he pulled them from her throbbing pussy.

"Y-yes," she panted.

"Let's see how many more times I can get you there again."

Before she could refuse, his tongue slide over her swollen pussy and she inhaled sharp. Fingers clenched the hair on his head, but he paid no heed to them. She tasted so sweet, the way her body flinched and shook, shooting waves of stimulating sensations through her whole being. His cock throbbed with want, but he pushed the aching aside, focusing on the task before him.

I want her to beg me to stop or ask me for more...

11

Put on Your Blue Light

Jane's body buzzed in new ways. The hot silk of Mark's tongue slipped between her folds and she sat up, threatening to fold atop him. She had never gushed during an orgasm and now he lapped it up like a man desperate to satisfy his thirst. Moaning, her fingers tangled in his hair. Arms wrapped around her hips, his hands pulling her pussy into his hungry jowls. She lost herself to the erotic pulses. Her hips rocked and his tongue dove deeper, wiggling inside her. Her breath caught as he slipped in and out before sucking on her clit once more.

To think this man just made me orgasm with his mouth! MERCY ME!

Teeth teased the swollen flesh, bringing on a new level of pleasure. Now she tried to remove him from her thighs. He became more voracious, a hand dropping over her hip and across her inner thigh. Lips wrapped tight, sucking hard on her jewel. Two fingers slid into her dripping folds and rubbed her slow and with purpose once more. They changed location repeatedly until her body betrayed her all over again, flinching the moment he rolled his stroking fingers over a sweet spot. Teeth nibbled at her clit and he rubbed and thrusted in and out. She wailed.

He's going to eat me alive and I want him to devour everything in his path!

Arching back into the bed, she had given up pulling him from her. The orgasm unfolding both inside her pulsing pussy and captivated clit made her muscles tense and legs rattle. Another hot gush escaped her, and he pulled his fingers from her. Rocking back on his heels, she felt his eyes taking in his handiwork, proud and triumphant. An enthralling shiver rolled through her. Never had she orgasmed so deeply, so wholly.

He's fucking me, body and soul like I've never felt when even alive!

Mark didn't stay there long, tasting and kissing his way up the center of her body. She ached for him to latch onto her nipple, but he denied her. Nuzzling at her neck, the tip of his cock rubbing against her opening. Her pussy throbbed and ached to have him inside her. Flashes of the shower making her impatient. Reaching down for his cock, he stopped her. Strong hands gripping her wrists, flinging her back onto the bed, arms pinned under his hands.

"I didn't give you permission to touch that," his voice grumbled, and chills rattled her.

"Oh?" She grinned, excitement building through her as her heart raced. "Since when did I need permission? I didn't need it a moment ago?"

"I'm not done playing with you."

She swallowed, her mouth running dry as his body towered over her. The hardened length of his cock rubbing against her pussy, her thighs hot with the heat of his torso. Her eyes lingered on his lips, marveling over how they had pleased her and how badly she wanted to taste herself on his tongue.

Was I that delicious to you?

"Kiss me," she whispered.

He pressed his lips against hers and the tip of his cock gliding inside her. She moaned, tilting her hips, wanting more of his dick inside. Deepening his kiss, his body weighed heavy against hers. Nipples hard against the hard planes of his torso, she arched into him. His grip on her wrists tightened. She lashed her tongue into his mouth, chasing him. His cock thrusted slow inside her and she moaned with want.

Pulling away, he searched her face. "So, in your time was missionary the only known position?"

She arched an eyebrow. "It's all mine gave me, not everyone was a–" She squeaked, a quick thrust coming from him made her tighten on the throbbing dick inside her.

"Was a what?" Mark smirked, aiming to make her suffer.

"You're being mean." She tightened around his throbbing cock.

"Now, you're being mean." He completely pulled out, leaning into her ear, his voice low, "Did anyone ever make you feel this good?"

Slow and agonizing, the rock-hard cock slid in until their hips pressed tight against one another. He throbbed inside her and she squeezed her pussy around him. Eyes locked, he began rocking against her, grinding in and out. She mimicked the motion, deepening the sensation, frustrated to have her hands pressed firm on the mattress.

"You really like feeling where I enter your pussy, don't you?" His smirk sent her heart fluttering.

"What if I do?" Her arms wiggled and she couldn't break free. "Please...let me feel you."

"I can't," he pressed hard against her, throbbing inside her wet heat.

"Why not?" She continued to rock against him, verging on another orgasm.

"It'll make me want to cum before I'm done playing." Another playful jump of his cock. "It's hard enough with as tight as you get."

"Like this?" She squeezed her pussy around his dick, grinding slow.

His head fell in defeat. "But I want you to cum for me in missionary."

"Why?" She laughed.

His eyes met hers. "So I can prove I'm better at it."

She looked at him, baffled and astonished for a moment in the darkness of the room. Inhaling deep, she held his words there in her mind, weighing her own emotions.

He means that. He's thought about my situation and intends to give me everything he has to offer.

Hooking her feet together behind him brought his hip tight against hers. He leaned in, the heat of his body against hers, wrists aching under the stress of him atop her. Arching her body, her nipples slid over his muscled chest and both of them shuddered, enthralled with the sensation.

"Then fuck me harder," she demanded.

"You really want it rough, don't you?" He released her wrists, his hands trailing down her arms and over her breasts and torso as he stood tall. "Shouldn't we make a safe word?"

"Why?" Her hands groped her own breasts, licking her lips. "I'm dead, remember?"

"I don't think you understand." He grinded against her, his cock hard inside her throbbing heat as he leaned down to her ear. "You might beg me to stop. This won't be gentle like before."

"Prove it," she hissed back.

"The safe word is," he suckled her ear before rumbling, "cherry."

She laughed. "Fine. Cherry if I can't take anymore, huh?"

"That's right," again the sliding of hands crossed the length of her body making her shudder and tighten her pussy. "I got into a lot of BDSM in hopes I could keep my partners awake, but as you know, that wasn't the issue so, I'm looking forward to breaking you in."

"You make it sound like a conquest." He took a step back, studying her body laying across the bed. "What's wrong?"

"Absolutely nothing." He flicked his finger, signaling she turn around. "I want to take you from behind, you seemed to enjoy that earlier. We'll start there, instead."

"Start there?" Scooting to the edge of the bed, she stood and kissed him.

He deepened it, parting her lips with his own, moaning as the heat of her hands glided over his ribs, flowing down the divot of his spine to grope his ass. His hardened length throbbed between their bodies. Her tongue licked the length of his own and he lashed out. Wrapping and twisting, tasting one another and the subtle hint of cherry tobacco still lingering in one another's mouth. Jane arched into him, her breasts pressing into him making his hunger to fuck her tantalizing as he shuddered. Breaking the kiss, he gripped her shoulders and twisted her in position.

Leaning back into him, she reached down and held his cock against her opening. Heart racing, anxious to see what he had in mind for her next. With new aggression, Mark's arms wrapped around her, an arm angling up to grasp her throat. She stiffened and he knew he had her attention. Her pulse quickened, breath catching. The rock-hard heat of his forearm made it clear he wouldn't allow her to go anywhere. His other hand groped her breast, twisting her nipple hard. She tried to whimper but the slight tightening of his hand on her throat silenced her.

"Good girl." The provocative sound of his voice only matched the way he fondled her breast.

How exciting to feel him get rough... I want more, more of this dominating...

She slowed her breathing, submitting to him and the new-found roughness. Letting go, he moved forward with reassured confidence. Shoving her down onto the bed, he pulled her arms behind her. With a single grip, he bound them behind the small of her back. A slap against an ass cheek made her flinch, his handprint leaving a blossom of red as it surfaced on her skin. Again and again, switching ass cheeks every so often, he smacked her until she no longer flinched and whimpered. The heat of the rushing blood made her sense of touch heighten.

My body nervous, unsure when his touch will be rough and soft. I can't stand it...

His cock teased the opening of her pussy. Her wetness growing with each step of gaining dominance over her. So much so, her thighs had become wet, making the grinding, and rubbing between her legs add to her ache for him to enter her. Mark adjusted his grip on her bound arms pressing down on her as his other hand gripped the nape of her neck. Pulsing his grasp from tight to loose, her breath quickening and he shuddered with excitement.

"Please... fuck me..." she whimpered.

I have never wanted a cock inside me so desperately in all my years on this earth!

12

Call Me Daddy

Mark didn't even react as the blue lamp flickered to life. The blue ambience only added to the mood, the curves of her body mesmerizing in the color. His cock throbbed against her hot, wet pussy. He wanted to take her, but that was the hardest part of playing the dominate one. Deep down he cursed himself for not bringing any of the toys, a satchel filled with vibrators, cuffs, nipple clamps, and more. It had been abandoned under his bed, haunting him, and now he had found someone to play with him.

I wonder if I can make her scream cherry without them?

Licking his lip, he pressed his weight into her, teasing her with the idea he might enter her at any moment. She whimpered in hushed tones, pleading for him to fuck her. Releasing the back of her neck, he towered over her. Spanking her over and over again, her grinding against his cock telling him how desperately she wanted him inside her. The blue light caught a trickle of her juice run down her leg. She had only gotten wetter with each move he made.

She's very into this. I don't think I've ever seen a girl get this wet at this stage of the dominance.

"Mark, fuck me, please." She tried the push back into him and he held her in place by her arms. "Please, I can't take it anymore–"

His arm scooped under her, making her arch as his powerful forearm slide between her breasts. Fingers wrapped around her throat and muffled her words. A shudder rattled her, and he could tell she was excited. He didn't make it impossible for her to talk, no he still wanted to hear her scream after all and wanted to satisfaction to hear her utter *cherry*. He nuzzled into her neck and shoulder, sucking hard and nibbling at her like some predator. She tasted sweet and salty on his tongue. As he played and teased her, he waited for the calm to hit her breathing and pulse. The high and lows of adrenaline were his favorite to toy with.

"Beg me some more," his voice rumbled, and his cock throbbed. "Punish me."

He smirked; *she's catching on.*

"Please, punish me," she breathed. "Show me how bad I've been."

"Wasn't your spanking enough?" He caught her earlobe between his teeth, then whispered, "I loved your dessert." His cock rubbed across her opening. "Beg Daddy for more. Tell me what you want me to do with this."

"Fill me up until I burst, please, Daddy." The weight of desire in her voice proved more than he could resist.

Tilting his hips, the tip of his cock entered her pussy. Her body was on fire, he had worked her up to a breaking point. Arching her body, one hand locking her arms behind her while the other still held her throat. Pushing deep inside her, he took his time as she tensed and relaxed, like her pussy gobbling up his dick. She was soaking wet, whimpering as he rode through her. At last he couldn't push himself any deeper, biting at her neck like he threatened to devour her on every level her body could provide him. She tried to speak, and he threatened to tighten his fingers.

In the window, he caught their reflection. They looked like phantoms with the way the blue light hit them. Two creatures feeling corporeal for the first time in their ghostly presence. One invisible, the other denied the ecstasy of connecting with the living in the way he ensnared her. Her eyes glowed, and he blinked for a moment. Even his own shared the eerie glow of something more.

Half wraith… feeding on the living… but with her… I feel… complete.

Rocking his hips, thrusting his cock in and out of her swollen folds she moaned. He loved how wet she grew with each stroke. She tightened, soaking the front of his thighs with her juices. His balls ached with the need for release, but he fought it back. There was still much work to do but the temptation to let himself cum inside her once more never left the back of his mind. Thoughts crept back to the shower and he grunted, tightening his hold on her.

I can't stand it; I can't hold back. I want to take her. After this, I should be able to hold out longer… I'm going to have to cave.

Releasing her throat, he let her bend over, face against the bed. Now he gripped her arms with both hands like fleshy guard rails. Pressing deep inside her, he waited, gauging her body a moment. Goosebumps rippled across her skin, shimmering in the blue light of the lamp. Biting his bottom lip, he prepared himself for the next move. Pushing his weight on her arms and hips, he began thrusting hard and fast, like a racehorse fresh out of the gate. He couldn't hold the rapid succession thrusting for long, but she had been more than primed to orgasm.

A scream erupted from her. He didn't slow, pounding her as her pussy tightened. The smacking of their bodies filling his ears and driving him forward. His grip tightened, his cock hardening as he teetered on the edge of his own orgasm. Exhaling, he moaned as he released inside her, pushed hard against her to fill her in her deepest depths. Her shrieking shifted to heavy panting, sweat painting both their bodies from the rapid grinding he had given her.

Releasing her arms, he grabbed her ass cheeks, spreading her so he could watch his dick slide, in and out of her swollen pussy. At last, the tip came free and he smirked, watching his cum drizzle out of her. He rubbed his cock's tip in the sticky liquid and shoved it back into her heat with force. She yelped, tightening. He wasn't nowhere as hard before, but he loved the state he had broken her into. Every touch he gave her would set her back to near peak. Her pussy throbbed and he pulled out, more cum sliding from between her folds before using his cock to force it back into her. Another shriek and her body gushed.

He met her eyes in the window's reflection and smiled. "Well?"

"I thought..." She hummed as he grinded slow against her.

"You thought?"

Inhaling deep, she tried to speak again, "You were going to rip me apart with your dick, or I'd catch fire from the speed you pounded it into me."

"Maybe I was trying to start a fire." His eyes fell to her ass, watching as his cock slid out and this time, he let his cum escape, dripping down between her thighs.

"Like what you see?" She grinned when he met her reflection again.

"I like everything about you, Jane." His hand slid down over her pussy, making them slick from their juices as he rode between her folds until he found the hard nub of flesh. "I suppose I should let you choose what we do next?"

"I want to..." She tensed, fighting back a whimper of pleasure as he rubbed the tender flesh. "I want to sit on top."

"On top? Cowgirl position?" He arched a brow and stepped back. "If that's what you want."

She rolled over, standing to her feet with a bashful expression. "B-but I've never done it. I just... watched."

Mark laughed. "We're breaking a lot of firsts for you today, aren't we?"

"Well, fucking me from behind is a new favorite. What's that position called? Do they all have such ironic names?"

"That one's called Doggy style." He laughed at her grimace. "I like it because I can reach all the fun places so..." His eyes glided over her, making her hyper aware he meant breasts and clit. "So you want to have to do something new?"

Her hands glided over his torso, eyes hungry as she gripped his cock and made him moan. "I want to ride on this, please Daddy."

"Oh, how can I say no to that?" He kissed her, then bit her bottom lip before releasing it. "If I let you on top..." He spun them so he could back into the bed. "You have to do every position I want, without a fuss. You promise to be a good girl, for Daddy?"

"T-there's more than one on top position for me to do?" Her eyes widened.

"Oh yeah..." He broke away, laying on the bed stroking himself to stay hard. "Let Daddy teach you. Bad girls should do their homework after all."

"Is this..." Jane straddled his legs, her breathing quickened as her eyes fell to his dick. "Is this also part of my punishment?"

"Oh yeah..." He motioned for her to crawl closer. "That's a good girl, let's get you on the saddle."

"Aren't you tired?" She was close enough to the tip of his cock that it rubbed against her lower belly, precum making her skin slick.

"Not if you're gonna take over." He grabbed her thighs and slid her into place. "Now, be a good girl and guide Daddy's cock inside."

The goosebumps rolling over her made him excited. She had wanted to do this, was starving for a chance to try all the new things only he could offer her. Her body trembled, her hands reaching down between them as she rose to hover over his cock. The expression of helplessness made him throb in her hand and she scowled.

"What next?" she hissed.

"Sit on it." He tilted his hips, his cock slick as it slid in her hand and pressed against her pussy.

"Just sit on it? That's it?"

"No, but that's the first step." Gliding his hands up her body, he squeezed her breasts, massaging them. "Be a good girl and sit for Daddy."

Humming, she guided him into her opening and eased down until she sat on top of him. His cock flinched inside her and she gasped. She looked down at him, smirking.

Oh, she's already into this!

13

Cowgirl Jane

Jane's heart pounded, sitting on him, legs straddled on either side of his torso, his cock inside her as she glared down at him. The pose was provocative and new. His hungry hands gripped her breasts, twisting her nipples. Inside her pussy she could feel his cock throb. She tightened and loosened, fascinated to the new array of pleasurable sensations that invaded her body. Shifting forward some, he slid inside a little more and she inhaled sharply.

"Rock your hips for me."

A shudder rattled her. His voice had become deep and demanding. Everything about it added to the eroticism unfolding between them. She wanted to learn more until she knew how to make him orgasm as easily as he made hers peak. Rocking her hips, she could feel how her body moved his cock inside her, rubbing in several places. She mimicked the way she had seen other girls had done. Her entire torso snaking so she could move his cock in ways to please herself.

It's like fucking myself, but I'm using his cock. Does... does he feel this?

Reaching down, she braced herself on his torso, shifting into a more favorable position as she rocked her hips. Now she had her thighs lifting and dropping her along the length of his cock, wanting to feel him, mimic what he had done and more. She began moaning, enjoying how the way he felt inside her and all under her control. The heat of his hands released her breasts and gripped her hips, rocking in rhythm with her movements.

"Good Girl... ride Daddy until you cum."

"Y-yes..." She picked up speed, enjoying how they grinded against one another like a sexual dance. "This feels... this feels..."

"Tell me. Tell me how much you like Daddy's cock inside you." He slid a hand off her hip, a thumb pushing between them and to rub her clit.

Jane jerked upright, leaning back until she braced herself on his thighs.

"I'm sorry, did I ruin your fun?" He smirked.

"N-no." She started to rock again. *This angle is completely different but just as... as...*

Thoughts derailed, the arousal and pleasure consumed every part of her. He continued playing with her clit, the new angle exposing another level of indulgence to her. With each motion, she was coming closer to another orgasm. Her pussy tightened and he pulled away his thumb, making her falter. Looking down at him he laughed at the way she pouted.

"No fair!" Then she paused.

"You can reach, why do I have to do all the work." He had a glint in his eyes, playful as he placed his arms behind his head. "I wanna see the bad girl orgasm from my cock."

Her expression turned serious. With one arm still bracing against his thigh, she slid her hand between them. Her fingers were soaked, making her breath catch at the idea she had been gushing so heavily during everything. At first, she rocked, fingers rubbing where his shaft slid in and out. At last, her fingers trailed up and began circling her clit. Instantly, her legs began to shake, everything already tender. Her gaze met his, both of them serious and intense as she rocked harder. The rising orgasm made her tighten, his cock hardened and throbbed in response.

At last, the orgasm peaked, making her fall forward as she moaned. Before she could finish riding out the peak, his arms wrapped around her. Pressed tightly into him, he pounded her with the burst of speed from before. She wailed, back arching and arms hard as stone locking her there. Straddled over him, hard cock fucking her fast, she gushed once more. He slowed and let go and she collapsed against him, panting.

"Good girl," he whispered, licking her ear. "Now sit on Daddy's face and eat my cock."

She pulled herself into a sitting position, his cock still hard inside her. "And how can I do both simultaneously?"

He flicked his finger, motioning she turn around. "Turn it around, love. Keep your knees above my shoulder so I can eat you while you suck my cock."

Inhaling deep, her face seemed red even in the blue light. "Is this a favorite of yours?"

Mark twisted his lips and answered, "To be honest, every man on this earth is merciless the moment their dick reaches a girl's mouth."

"Is that so?" She braced against his torso, standing to reveal the wetness between her thigh and legs. "Mercy me. My dam's broke."

He chuckled. "Hurry up. It's cold."

She shushed him, hesitant to kneel above his face. "Are you sure about this?"

"Sit down already."

He gripped her ass cheeks, shoving her down onto him. The ferocity of his lips and tongue against her sensitive pussy had her folding over him, lips lingering close to his hard cock. She gripped him stroking and at last wrapped her lips around the tip. He tilted his hip, sliding his shaft a little deeper and she realized she needed to mimic the movements he needed to cum. She began sucking and wiggling her tongue, both of them rocking themselves into each other, wanting more. She managed to have the tip hit the back of her throat and he rewarded her with his tongue inside her, wiggling as they both moaned with the pleasure of it all. Jane enjoyed the tit-for-tat game it became, learning fast what he liked, experimenting with ways to use her tongue, lips, and hands could make him moan into her pussy.

The door opened and Karen stumbled in. Jane deep throated, sucking hard as she fondled his balls. His moaning escalated as she kept the hard suckling going riding her lips up and down his hardened shaft. Cum squirted hot and thick into her mouth, eyes still locked with Karen's. Satisfied he emptied it all into her, she sat up, rocking her hips on his face.

Opening her mouth, cum rolling on her tongue broke the cheating harlot. Swallowing, Jane was starting orgasm again, his tongue inside her flickering and thrusting. Karen snapped a photo and Jane grinned wildly at the idea.

And one more photo for his collection.

"I swallowed it all, Daddy." She couldn't stop moaning, he continued play verging into the unbearable with Karen watching.

Karen's cheeks puffed out. At last, she turned and left as Jane shouted her next words.

"Please, punish me. Eat me, teach me, make me to cum for you, Daddy, please!"

Mark's hands slid up her torso and groped her breasts. She came hard, again lunging forward. She tried to crawl away, but again strong arms kept her locked into place. Screaming, visceral and wild, she could take it. He wasn't stopping. Lips suckling her clit, everything on fire with overwhelming pleasure. Teeth teased the swollen flesh and–

"CHERRY!"

She inhaled sharp, shocked she had screamed it. He had paused and released her clit. Arms released her and she crawled away some and looked over her shoulder. Mark smiled, propping himself up by his elbows, his face, neck and chest soaked.

Clearing his throat, he tilted his head. "Did you just shout, cherry?"

She twisted around and covered her face.

"Well, I am pretty sure I heard the safe word."

Dropping her hands, she confessed, "I said... cherry."

He collapsed back, covering his face.

"Wh-what's wrong?" She climbed up to him. "You won. You knew I would cave."

This time, he lowered his hands. "For a moment there, during that blowjob, I thought I might have to call it. You had me, I was done for and I put you there."

They started to laugh. After a long silent moment, they took a shower, both sore and exhausted. It didn't take long before they spooned in the covers, falling asleep in the heat of one another's naked bodies.

"Please, tell me this wasn't a dream." He sounded sad.

She sighed. "No, this was no dream," she said. "Just come back to me. Just one more time later in this short life you have."

"Promise..."

And then, he dozed off.

14

Mark's Long Lost Girlfriend

Mark woke to the sound of knocking.

"Mr. Wilder, check out time is in an hour."

"Y-yes sir. Showering and checking out," he shouted.

"Very well," and he could hear his steps fade.

Groaning, his body ached from the night long excursion of sex. Part of him felt relieved, as if a knot in his core had been untangled. Perhaps it had been the ability to let go completely on a sexual level for the first time. Sure, he had tried going to an orgy once, thinking he was *broken*. At the end of that experience and picking up some new tricks, he realized he rather be monogamous. The idea to master someone's body, know all their secrets and learn new ways to exploit them got him hot and bothered.

He rolled over and frowned. "Dammit, she's gone again without a trace."

Mark stumbled his way to the shower. Hot water beating on his sore muscles were a warm welcome, his skin still felt sticky and salty from a night of ecstasy, despite the shower they took. He looked down at his flaccid cock and laughed.

I don't think it'll want to see any action for a while...

Drowning his face in the stream of water, flashes of the night rattled through him. At one point, he swore he saw Karen.

In the window, like she walked in on us and took a picture? Couldn't have been... Granted I was a little busy eating pussy to really care after cumming so hard.

Shaking off the thought, he focused on scrubbing faster.

Shit, where's my phone?

He tilted his head, lathering up every inch of skin for good measure.

Man, I can't tell if I'm sticky from sweat, cum, or...her.

Another brazen grin curved his lips as he began rinsing the soap off.

Oh, shit, I didn't think about recording any of last night...

His face grew red at the thought as he cut the water off. "Would she even let me? I mean, it would be for me later and not to post on some site to proclaim *I fucked the Blue Lady.*"

Dressing, he scrambled around gathering what little he had brought along. Still no phone. In fact, a lot of the mess they had created was gone as if it all had been an apparition. Even the sheet lacked the large wet stain of when he made her gush not once, but twice before pounding her so mercilessly. Checking in the drawers, under the bed and nightstand, he still couldn't find his phone.

"Maybe she cleaned up to hide the mess?" Scratching his chin, he headed downstairs. "But where the hell is my phone?"

Leaving out the door, he gave the room one last look. *Wonder if I come back if she'll show up again.*

Making his way to the front counter, he slid the key to the manager. "Here you go with just a few minutes to spare."

The man lowered his book and sized him up. "And your lady friend?"

His face flushed. "She left before me."

"You two must've had quite a night." The manager closed his book and smirked. "The *whole* night it seems."

"Sorry for the noise?" Mark didn't know what to say.

"Didn't bother me." He chuckled. "But your girl screamed so good and loud that old Aunt May across the street left plenty of voicemails about it. She's got a set of lungs or you're that good."

Mark shrugged. "It's been a while since either of us have hooked up. What can I say?"

"And the town now knows that much." He picked the book up.

"Uh, have you seen a cell phone?" Mark changed topics, already unnerved about the volume in which they had reached. *Careful what I wish for, I suppose. The town indeed heard Jane Story last night.*

"This one?" It was like a magic trick as he pulled the cell phone from thin air. "Found it on the front porch after I shooed you two upstairs."

"Oh, that makes sense." It wouldn't turn on. "Damn, dead battery. Look, do I owe you any more for the stay?"

The manager wouldn't meet his gaze. "None, Mr. Wilder. Do return though, and maybe a little sooner and not later if this is the result of an extended time away."

"R-right." Mark started for the door but paused. "What book are you reading?"

"Bound by Fire," he drawled. "Plucked it from a guest and it's rather good. I suppose I should return it so she can finish writing it."

Mark made a confused expression. "Typically, they write it, then it becomes a book."

"I'm very aware of the fact, Mr. Wilder." He cleared his throat and lowered his voice. "And typically, my guests don't fuck and date the undead."

"Wait, what?" Mark rushed the counter, unsure of the rasping whisper.

"Good day, Mr. Wilder. Give Jane my regards." He spun the chair away, giving Mark the cold shoulder.

Sighing, Mark pushed out to the front porch and paused. A breeze blew pass him and he could smell a hint of cherry tobacco, more along the lines of the cigarillos. He smiled. Even if he couldn't see her, the idea he could leave her with something new to enjoy made him happy. Marching down the walkway, he paused at the gate and took a look back. It seemed odd now, looking where he had seen her gardening on that first day. He hadn't even noticed anything abnormal about her. Part of him ached to see her one more time, say goodbye.

Maybe her time was up? Or could it be she can only show herself during certain times?

Slumping his shoulders, he made his way to his car. Sliding into the driver seat, he tossed the duffle bag into the back and started the engine, cranking the air conditioning to high. Plugging in his phone, he started it. In an instant the cell phone came to life with missed texts and voicemails, and most of them were from Karen. Rolling his eyes, he pulled up the chain of texts and paled.

"What the fuck is this?"

There on the screen was a picture of Jane sitting on his face, his cock standing erect, from Karen simply stating:

[Karen: I get it. You wanted to get caught like I did. Thanks. I don't need this bullshit. Enjoy your new whore of a girlfriend, asshole!]

Not a bad shot, her titties are in full focus and that look on her face, ooh!

He felt himself get a little hard and scrolled up to see the text someone had sent her. Covering his mouth, he grinned. Karen had been set up and he now knew he *had seen* her in the middle of their fun. Saving the photo of Jane, he flipped to the gallery and his eyes widened.

"Well look at that!" He shifted in his driver seat, heart racing. "Jane was a busy girl. When did she sneak off with my phone to do…" Face red, he thumbed through the collection of racy and seductive photos. "Oh, these are going to keep me busy for a while."

Another text pinged through.

[Timmy: You okay? Figured you'd be heading home by now. Please tell me you're okay?]

[Mark: Yeah. Just got to my car. Phone died.]

[Timmy: Did you have fun? Hook up with someone?]

Mark covered his face pondering whether to say something. At last, he sent a less racy and more seductive photo of Jane. He couldn't hold back showing off someone so beautiful and amazing.

[Mark: The gardener. *Picture*]

[Timmy: Uh… we need to talk about your new girlfriend, buddy.]

[Mark: Well, not exactly girlfriend… I hooked up, not exactly a girl I can take home to mom, even if I wanted to.]

There was a long pause, the writing indicator stopping and starting a few times before at last the text came through.

[Timmy: Did she tell you?]

Mark blinked at the question and it all came flooding back. Jane had said something about Timmy, and how a lot of her own tribulations were his doing. Swallowing, Mark remembered the weird questions he'd received the first night he'd met Tim at a fraternity party. He dialed the number, waiting for him to pick up.

"Hey, Mark?" Timmy's voice gave nothing away.

"Tim. Is this… is this about my Dad?" His throat and chest tightened with anxiety.

"Yeah, look… I'm not very truthful about who or what I am, but you need help or you…" He halted as if afraid to go too far. "We need to talk face to face. What are the chances you are willing to take a drive with me to Bridgewater Trinity College? Oh, and you're gonna have to bring Jane, I may have made a large miscalculation on how this would affect you."

"What the hell is…" Mark swallowed, his hand on the wheel semi-transparent. "FUCK!"

"The Manager gave me a call and said the two of you have… flipped roles. SURPRISE!" Tim waited, the silence haunting. "Now, go get your poltergeist of a girlfriend and head my way. Stay close together, should keep you both corporeal until we can fix the natural order of things or get you something to help you two through this."

Epilogue

Karen stood outside of the B&B, a little past midnight. The whole town seemed barren, almost to the point of a ghost town. Upstairs she could see the blue light coming from the window of her aimed destination. Mark awaited her. A wicked grin crawled across her face. He had taken longer than she expected to make up with her, but this was borderline hot.

Was he jealous and wanted to fuck me here in this cheezy B&B? I knew he'd come around and forgive me. Besides, men don't break it off with me... I break up with them. I'll have fun, but after this he can kiss my ass. About time I go back to finding some fresh meat, someone with more money and can spoil me on occasion. Damn shame that Satch guy at the casino didn't work out last summer. Would have totally broke it off with Mark sooner for a man like that! Man, could he eat a pussy!

A shudder rolled through her, but she pushed down the walkway and up the porch through the entrance. The manager's counter was empty, and she snorted. *Good riddance! That man was an asshole!* Eyeing the stairs, she pulled out her phone and read Mark's text once more.

[Mark: The Blue Lady Room. Midnight.]

Glancing at the clock, it was pushing closer to two in the morning. "Hope I'm not too late."

Besides, I needed him to sweat. Break his heart, revive it, and shatter it later. That's what he gets for breaking up with me over a damn texted picture. So what if I fucked a football player, what does it matter to him whose dick I fuck when I can't stay awake for his!

Gripping her phone tight, she headed to the top floor.

Bringing me back here where I–

Sounds of a couple fucking couple halted her steps.

She paled. *He wouldn't dare! And with who! No way that loser found someone to screw in just under a week's time.*

She rushed to the Blue Lady room door and found it cracked open. Pushing the door open wide, the whole place was lit with the blue light from the lamp on the nightstand. Her eyes fell on a girl choking down a cock. From here she stood, they were locked into the sixty-nine position. The moaning from the man told her he was cumming– *no, Mark. That's how Mark sounds when...* She searched the floor, seeing the familiar duffle bag with his last name *Wilder* embroidered into it.

Rage filled Karen, glancing back to the interlocked couple. Jane locked eyes with her, stroking and sucking him, making his orgasm linger a little longer as she rocked her hips on his face. Pulling her lips off his swollen shaft, she cracks her mouth open to show off the cum rolling on her tongue. Karen's eyes widen, shaking with anger and rendered speechless.

Jane swallowed, sitting up, still grinding into his face. "I swallowed it all, Daddy."

Karen's cheeks puff out, her mind spiraling. *That's what I call him in the bedroom, bitch!*

Inhaling deep, Karen raised her phone to threaten to take a picture, as someone had done to her. Mark moaned under the rocking hips. His hands crawling up Jane's body, one groping her breast and the other gripping her neck. Jane's breath caught, as she started to orgasm. Karen snapped the shot, but they didn't slow. Spinning on her heels, she had seen more than what she bargained for.

"Please, punish me." Jane gave Karen a wicked grin. "Eat me, teach me, make me cum for you, Daddy, please!"

Spiteful tears rolled down her cheeks as she flew down the stairs and out the door. She pulled up the image, the way the girl stared at her seemed ghostly.

Eyes don't glow like that! Could he really be fucking the Lady in Blue? Fuck this!

She sent a text, ending it for good.

[Karen: I get it. You caught me, now I've caught you. I'm out of your life, enjoy your ghost girl asshole! *Picture*]

[Phillipe: Hey. Booty call?]

[Karen: Fuck you!]

[Phillipe: Um. That's the point.]

Karen throws her phone to the ground, smashing it under her heel. "This is bullshit!"

The End

Wanton
WOMAN in WHITE

Honey Cummings

Urban Legend Erotica Collection

Table of Contents

Dedication

To Nita

These are the kind of relationship
goals everyone needs in their life!

XOXO
Honey Cummings

1

The Bachelor

Remi Adama stared at his phone. His nerves tightened, mind spiraling in a mixture of emotions. On one hand, he could laugh at the ridiculous idea he had jumped into; on the other hand, he imagined it couldn't be any worse. After running from a bad relationship—*no, straight up abusive relationship that has evolved into a level five stalker situation—what do I have to lose?*

His phone buzzed, and he waited to see who was calling before answering. The screen lit up: *Show Bailey*. With a relieved sigh, he answered right away.

"Hey there, Bailey," he sounded cheerful, even excited. *Just get on with it.*

"Remi! Thank you for sending the contracts for the show back so fast," the Talent Coordinator said, her voice coolly professional. "In a moment, I will do a three-way call, and you and the mystery bride-to-be will have a moment to get acquainted. Mind you—there are rules involved."

"R-right," he stuttered, his nerves rising high once more. "So, in short, you guys are really marrying me to a stranger like some arranged marriage?"

"That's the gist of it," she chuckled. "We were having a hard time finding enough male contestants. A lot of them backed out after the phone calls, so... now we monitor them. Anyhow, who scouted you again? His information isn't on here."

"Oh, uh..." Remi scrambled through the scattered papers on his computer desk, knocking over a tower of empty pre-made boxes.

"A-are you okay?" Bailey had been startled by the sounds coming over the receiver.

"Y-yeah. It's just boxes for my online business." He found the piece of paper and squinted at his scribbled writing. Even with his glasses on, it seemed cryptic. "Man, my chicken scratch sucks ass... uh, Timmy? Tommy? No—Timmy. That's definitely an 'i' there."

"Huh. Timmy..." He could hear her rifling through paperwork and typing away on her keyboard. "Weird. We didn't have a Timmy listed... but I'll make a note." She finished a whirlwind of typing, paused, then continued. "Okay, now for the rules. You can't say names or locations of where you currently live. Talking about a hometown is okay... but no perverted or sexual commentary, or we'll terminate your contract. We do not payout on the contract until you tie the knot. If you need assistance to make the trip to the filming location in St. Augustine, Florida next week, please let me know."

"Right, right." Remi rubbed his forehead, eyebrows raised. "I need to be there some time on Friday, right? I'll be driving, so I just need the address. Text it to me if you can, Ms. Bailey."

"Absolutely, Remi." There was some tapping, and his phone buzzed. "Did it come through?" she asked.

"Perfect. Yes."

"Now, the three-way call."

Remi waited as he was placed on hold. His leg jittered, and he glared at the boxes scattered across his tiny bedroom. With a grunt, he started to stack them, not noticing he had placed the smaller boxes on the bottom until he put the last box on top. Scoffing, he laughed at himself, leaning down to put his elbows on his knees.

"Remi?" Bailey's voice made him jolt, and he sat up, banging his head on his desk.

"Shit!"

"A-are you okay?"

"Y-yeah." Clearing his throat, he reassured her. "I was picking something off the floor. Sorry about that."

"Hi there," a softer, new voice cut across the receiver. "I guess we're getting married next week?"

"Uh, yeah. That seems to be the case." Remi leaned back in his chair, brow furrowing. "So... what do you do for a living?"

"Is he allowed to ask me that?" She sounded offended.

"He is." Bailey sighed, the sound blowing across the phone.

"Look, I run my own business out of my home," offered Remi, motioning to the towers of boxes filling the tiny apartment bedroom.

"Oh?" the sweet voice seemed intrigued. "And is it successful?"

Remi's muscles tensed as he pushed forward in the conversation. "Well, I guess that depends on your definition of success?"

"Money," she blurted in frustration. "Does it make a lot of money? It must not if you're still running it out of your room."

Remi blinked, shaking the shock off and defended himself. "It pays my bills. I'm not one of those guys who has a billion starter ideas and abandons them before getting them off the ground."

"Well, please understand, I want a man who can support me and the lifestyle I want to live."

Tilting his head, Remi tried again, "And what do you do for a living?"

"I'm unemployed. I intend to be a wife and nothing more or less." She sounded entitled. "As your beloved wife, I promise to always be at my best. Salon hair and nails and dressed in the finest clothes and shoes. I am your trophy after all."

Eyes wide, Remi stuttered, "Wait, what?"

Shit. What kind of person am I about to be stuck with?

"We'll end the phone call here." Cutting in, Bailey dumped the bride-to-be off the phone. "You will get to meet her in person when you get to St. Augustine." She gave a nervous laugh.

"I see why the others bailed."

"Please! Look, I'll double the money." She dropped the bribe like a ton of bricks. "Remi, no one else is getting that offer from the show. You cannot disclose this deal with anyone. Marry her, and we'll pay you double."

Remi rubbed his forehead, "That's a lot of cash. I can buy a house and a car... and pay for an assistant." He looked around the room. "If she doesn't spend it first. I thought the money went to a joint venture?"

"We'll put half in a private account for only you," Bailey promised.

Silence fell. Remi covered his mouth, absorbing the offer. *They are desperate to marry this girl off, but why?*

"I've gotta ask," he inhaled deeply, "why not dissolve her contract if she's been so difficult rather than offer me double?"

Bailey groaned. "Okay, you can't say anything. Turns out she's the main investor's step-daughter, and he's shipping her out. She's been a mooch, and he's tired of her and figured the drama she would stir would make for great TV for the show."

"There it is." Remi smirked.

I can take advantage of this. The contract says we have to stay hitched for 180-days. I can milk it until then and annul the marriage. Yeah... yeah. I think I can do this. Why not? Treat myself since I can't seem to find a decent fucking woman.

"Triple it," he countered. "Double in the private account, so she stays out of it."

There was a long silence. "Let me put you on hold."

Remi shuffled the papers around on his desk. The coffee-stained copy of the contract revealed itself and he glanced through the pages for the price. At last he found it: *$300,000.00 USD*. Triple that, and he would almost have a million dollars. Granted, the crazy bride-to-be would be getting a third of that, but still...

Over half a million dollars. Now that should get me off the ground for good. Warehouse or no, just a bigger place should do it.

Bailey cleared her throat. "Mr. Adama?"

"Yeah?"

"We have a deal. Check your inbox for the revised contract, and this time, we're going to veri-sign digitally. There will be no getting out of this unless–" She choked, almost letting the name slip. "Unless the bride decides otherwise."

"Fine with me." Remi smiled ear to ear.

"The lawyer is revising it... so give it an hour or two to make it back your way." Bailey typed away on her keyboard. "Pleasure doing business with you, Mr. Adama. Look forward to seeing you in St. Augustine next week."

"Same–" Remi glared at the phone. "Huh, she hung up on me."

With a huff, he turned his attention back to his computer. Wiggling the mouse revealed a paused YouTube video, and he minimized that. Behind lay his prize: a porn site displayed tiles of all kinds of combinations and scenes. Clicking on one, he jumped the video ahead to where the girl dropped the last stitch of lingerie. Settling into his computer desk, it squeaked, and he took a pump of lotion. Slapping a hand towel like a ball net across his thighs, he leaned back, waiting for what would come next.

Another night, and another porn to keep me satisfied. No baggage, no bitching... the perfect jerk-bait girlfriend a man could ask for.

He watched, growing hard as the woman took a thick cock between her lips, gagging and drooling. Her enthusiasm to suck and choke on the baseball bat-sized dick only made him think of how easily she could take in his own cock. Closing his eyes, he focused on the moaning, slurping, and pop of lips. The heat and stiffness built as his thoughts dug deeper. He imagined her tongue wiggling under his shaft. Tightening his grip, he stroked faster, firmer. The gagging sounds shifting his imagination, and he could picture shoving himself deep into her mouth, holding her there as the tip...

With a groan, he released. Leaning forward, he folded the hand towel over and finished cleaning himself off. His phone buzzed and he reached for it, still in a haze. Riding out his euphoria, he didn't glance at the name on the screen before he answered.

"Remi!" Monica's voice sobered him quickly, and he sat up stiffly, wiping himself. "When are you going to give me my fucking cat back!"

"Are you kidding me?" Remi marveled. "You took him to the shelter a week before we broke up because he liked me more than you!"

Dammit, fell for it... shit.

"Oh! So you are going to talk to me, huh?" She seemed pleased to get a rise out of him.

"Look. I'm moving to Florida. We're done." He hung up.

Shit. Will this mystery bride be any better? Let's hope so...

2

The Woman in White

The wind still held the heat of the day as it blew through Jenifer Rosalind's hair. Even late September in St. Augustine, Florida, proved no different from a summer's day elsewhere in the world. Over the horizon, the sky faded from neon pink and orange to peach and lavender. She watched it from the same bridge over and over again.

She looked down to the creek, the current flowing fast beneath the bridge, but the water level was lower than it had been in previous seasons. Though the brackish water was on par with saltwater, the quality didn't keep the bullfrogs and catfish from swimming through the waterway, occasionally disturbing the calm surface. The cicadas screamed until at last they caved to the symphony of crickets and southern toads as the last sliver of sunlight faded.

The light pollution from the college area didn't completely wipe out the stars from where she stood alone. The breeze was already cooling down. Without the heat from the sun, the humid air quickly chilled at night, cutting right through her white wedding dress. Her skin, still damp from the day's heat, pebbled immediately, and she shuddered, cursing the lacy halter top and the thin fabric of the skirt's layers pressed hard against her legs. On the dark horizon, lightning chased itself through the incoming clouds. The moon and stars were swallowed, the spiderweb of white and orange streaks making bitterness rise in her gut.

Frowning, she looked down the bridge first one way, then the other, but she hadn't seen a car on it in months. Settling into the nook of railing, she smirked. Since it seemed she would be alone, and bored out of her mind, what better way could she pass the time other than...? She bit her lip, inching the skirts up and over her knees.

"Dammit, I'm so pale I fucking glow," she muttered, awestruck as ever at the sight of her skin.

Shaking her head, she regained her aim. Fingers slid between her thighs, and she leaned back into the icy metal that braced her. Raising a foot, she balanced her leg to gain greater access to the pink jewel she desired. Her skirts flapped in the wind, and in the distance, a whippoorwill sang loudly between the rumbles of thunder. With the incoming thunderstorm, the temperature fell even more rapidly, a good ten or more degrees as the humidity left her skin sticky.

Goosebumps rolled across her skin, nipples hard as her fingers glided over her opening. She was slick with her wanton desire, the loneliness and thoughts of being taken. A bride abandoned on this very bridge during a hurricane ages ago, all she wanted was to rid herself of the past, to move on, and to be taken by a man worthy of her body.

So tired of doing this...

She inhaled, fingers dipping between her folds, thrusting and rubbing. Her leg jittered, and she slid her fingertips out, hot and wet as they began circling her clit. The swollen, hard jewel rose to the occasion. Electricity shot through her in tandem with a lightning strike. Thunder vibrated through the steel so cold and wet through the skirts of her dress. She arched, her orgasm rising. Head drooped back, eyes shut tight, she inhaled sharply.

A little more...

Icy raindrops started to pitter and patter all around. One hit her cheek, prompting her to speed up. Biting her lip, she moaned, trying desperately to draw the orgasm forward. The rain thickened, spattering her exposed legs, arms, and...

Fuck me!

Abandoning her play, she rose to her feet and threw a bird to the sky, "Fuck you too!"

Rain thick and hard fell relentlessly across Jenifer and her world. The creek was no longer visible from the bridge. Nothing but the pouring rain, wind, and thunder filled the air where once nature had played a sweet serenade to her. Crossing her arms, teeth chattering, she stood in the middle of the bridge with nowhere to go and nowhere for shelter... *again.*

Stumbling to the middle of the bridge, she faced south and frowned.

If I could go that direction, it would take me home. Would I even have a place to go back to?

Twisting, she faced north where the road curved up a small hillside.

If I could go that way, it would take me to the old farmhouse. Granted, I was supposed to be married there, but they might take me in. Surely that place is still open to travelers?

Looking down at her feet, she huffed. They were pale and ghostly... a*nd growing brighter?*

She turned and saw headlights coming at her fast. The wheels squealed and skidded across the wet road. Wide eyed, she watched as the man at the wheel struggled to turn. He swerved around her, and she covered her mouth, chasing the brake lights as he hydroplaned to the other end. By some small miracle, he managed not to ping-pong off the railing and at last exited the bridge and high-centered on the curb.

The little blue *(or was it purple?)* Ford Focus teetered as the man stumbled out. He held his head, walking backwards to assess his car in the rain and wind. At last, he spun and shouted something. Jenifer blinked, impressed she could hear him this far with a thunderstorm in full swing. He ran full stride back down the length of the bridge. Gripping her shoulder, he looked her over, his face smooshed as he squinted.

"Are you okay? I didn't hit you, did I?"

"So loud!" Jen lowered her brow, wondering if something had happened to affect her hearing.

"Sorry, I just… dammit, I can't see shit without my glasses." He glanced over her again and looked all around. "You're not hurt? I don't need to get help, do I?"

"I'm fine, but…" Jen pushed him back, the rain and pitch-dark night making it hard to pick apart his features. "Who are you? What are you doing driving down this bridge so late?"

"I'm Remi. Look, Miss…?" He was shouting over the weather.

"Jenifer," she offered.

"Miss Jenifer, I was going to ask you why you were standing here in the rain so late," he retorted. "Here, let's get in the car and out of the rain, so we don't have to shout over the–"

Thunder muted his words, and before she could say anything else, he tugged her along by her hand. As they reached the threshold where the bridge met the paved road, she slipped from his grip. She stared, nervous and unknowing at the line the two made. In the past, she had tried to take a step, to dare to push herself to make the rest of the trip to the old farmhouse, but inevitably, it failed or she'd feel faint.

It's not that I didn't want to get married; it's just the weather got so bad…Then the storm surge sent the creek–

"Come on. It's okay. I don't care if that piece of shit gets wet." Remi scooped her around the waist and thrust her forward.

"W-wait..." she sputtered, looking over her shoulder in confusion. "How did you...?"

"Here." He shoved her into the passenger side and shut the door.

Jenifer watched him with growing interest as Remi slid in the car with water dripping from his goatee. She couldn't help herself. "Who are you again? Are you even from here? *Why* are you out here?"

"Me?" Remi pointed at himself, his brow furrowed. "I'm Remi. And you're... Yennefer?"

"Jenifer. We already exchanged names, Remi." She narrowed her eyes at him, noticing how his gaze didn't seem to focus on her. "Where are you going?" Twisting, she glanced back behind her, trying to look out the window. "What are you even looking at?"

"Uh, good question." He scrambled around the tiny car, bumping into her leg. "S-sorry, just... oh, here it is. My phone's GPS stopped working, and all I remember is Bailey saying to go over a bridge and the farmhouse was just up the way."

"Y-you're going to the farmhouse?" She leaned in closer, enjoying the heat of his body so close to hers. *When was the last time I even felt another person's body heat? Before my accident? Wait, this is my chance to make it to the farmhouse! Just maybe this curse can be broken after all!* "Please take me with you! I'm headed there, too!"

"Is that why you were standing out there?" Shuffling around, he reached below the dashboard and came back up with glasses. "Found them."

"Well, you could say I was stuck on the bridge for having cold feet." Jen laughed nervously.

Remi cleaned the lenses and pulled on his glasses. The lightning flashed, and as they locked eyes, Remi inhaled sharply. Jenifer cringed, the reaction making her fear the worst. His eyes flowed over her, down and up again before at last, he smiled. *Last time a man shot me that look...* She tilted her head, visible confusion building on her face.

"You're a bride?" Remi scoffed. "I can't believe they'd leave you wandering around out here like this. And in a storm!"

"Yes, but I was the one who..." He flipped on the dome light, and she blinked. *My Adonis... I have found you!*

He was handsome. Nothing like her former fiancé, this man looked strong, like he could build a barn solo if he had no other choice in the matter. Her eyes slid over his thick hands, muscular arms, and at last lingered on his plump lips. Reaching out, her fingertips caressed the heat of his arm, and he visibly shuddered. As she crested his shoulder, his other hand cupped hers.

"So warm..." she whispered.

"Wow, you're cold." He twisted to the back of the car, cursing under his breath. "I don't have anything in the back... I might have a jacket in the trunk. I can go get it... hold on."

Lightning lit the car up once more, and her pale face reflected in his glasses for a split-second, gaunt and ghostly. He reached for the car door, stuttering about the jacket in disjointed bits. Jenifer gripped his shirt and pulled him back to her, across the tiny center console. He spun and their lips locked. She deepened the kiss, his lips parting. Willingly, he teased the tip of her tongue before overpowering her. With a jerk, it ended, his hands on her shoulders with a wild expression.

"We're supposed to wait until we get married first!" he exclaimed.

"Wait, what?"

What in the blazes is he going on about?

3

Late Arrival

Remi's heart beat loud and fast. He couldn't tell if his movements or the storm winds outside made the tiny Focus rock on the curb, teeter-tottering here and there. Regardless, he clutched the strange bride before him. His glasses were starting to fog up. He flung them onto the dashboard and kissed her once more.

Who am I to resist? She's so damn gorgeous and...

She crawled across the car, the Focus shifting with a clunk as it tilted hard. An icy hand gripped his wrist and shoved his palm onto her breast. Remi squeezed, and she deepened the kiss, moaning. Her other hand slid down his torso and rubbed the hardening length under his zipper. He broke the kiss off once more.

"Wait-wait-wait-wait," he muttered, the cramp and confined quarters making it clear it would be near impossible to have sex. "There's not enough room to... you know..." He motioned at her dress and the backseat filled with boxes. "I didn't buy the Focus for fucking..." He cringed.

"Oh." Jenifer took in the cramped situation, her dress filling up her side of the car. "Oh! Oh no." She turned her attention back to Remi. "But you're hard already, and," she winced, "it's all my fault."

"Look, when we get to the farmhouse—" Remi looked away, cursing his glasses on the dashboard, her face blurred and unreadable. "We can hook up, but it's gotta be secret."

"R-right, but still, I think there's enough room for at least this." Her fingers were quick, his pants unfastened and her hands gripping his hard-on in a few seconds.

"Dammit!" he cursed, surprised and shocked, but glad he never bothered with underwear.

"What's wrong?" She looked up at him, all doe-eyed, and his heart fluttered.

Shaking in admiration, he mumbled, "Y-your hands are cold."

"But not my mouth," she winked, leaning down.

Remi moaned as his cock slid into the wet heat of her mouth. Her tongue wiggled and rubbed on the underbelly of his shaft, sending chills across his entire being. At last, the tip of his cock hit the back of her throat, and she sucked hard, letting him linger there. Pulling off his dick, she stopped at the cap, tongue circling once, twice, and repeating the slow motion over and over. He moaned each time he connected to the back of her throat, his balls tensing with the urge to cum.

Fingers gently caressed his testicles, and he groaned, becoming rock-hard. He cursed, unable to shift into a more comfortable position. He already had the seat all the way back for driving and... She picked up speed, and he fought the urge to hold her down on his cock. He gripped the steering well, head tilting back, his eyes closing.

His cell phone started ringing.

Alarmed, Jenifer pulled off his dick with a pop. "What is that?"

"M-my phone." He caved and glanced at the screen: *Show Bailey.* "Shit, it's the Coordinator." Reluctantly, he picked it up. "B-bailey."

"Mr. Adama, where are you? It's an hour past midnight, and you were supposed to be here by now." She sounded beyond pissed. "We had an agreement, or do you intend to back out of our deal?"

"Whoa-whoa-whoa-whoa." Now Remi sounded miffed. "I am stuck over by the bridge."

"The bridge?" she echoed.

"Yea, I almost hit a woman on the bridge, but we're both okay. My car's stuck on the cur—"Remi's words faltered as Jenifer began stroking his cock.

She gave sheepish grin as he looked down at her. *Is this a challenge? To see if I can sustain my conversation while she plays with my dick?*

"Stuck where, Mr. Adama?" Bailey's voice made him inhale, trying to fight the building pleasure.

"The curb right after you cross." His voice broke some as a hot tongue licked the length of his shaft from the base to the tip.

"I see. I suppose the storm is rather bad tonight." Bailey babbled about a possible *tropical storm,* but Remi couldn't focus on her words.

Jenifer began kissing and licking his dick in earnest. He relished the way her lips felt hot and soft against his hardened strength, the lashing of her tongue and warm breath washing over him. A moan escaped him, and he dropped the phone. Jenifer snickered, handing it back to him.

"R-Remi? Remi?" Bailey's voice blasted loud over the receiver.

Fumbling with the phone, Remi finally replied, "Y-yes! I-I dropped the phone."

"Are you in pain?" Bailey seemed concerned.

"Wait, what?" Remi furrowed his brow and stifled a moan as Jenifer went down on him.

"Y-you're groaning an awful a lot." She declared.

"Am I?" He gripped the steering wheel, biting his lip as his cock connected with the back of her throat. "Well..." She began thrusting up and down his shaft, and he teetered with the car on the edge of an orgasm. "I can't...." He inhaled swiftly, fighting the urge to cum. "I can't..." He was sweating from his battle of sheer will to hold back. "I..."

"Can't what?" demanded Bailey.

"The car. It's stuck! Send help!"

Lightning flashed as he hung up and threw the phone on the dash next to his glasses. "Fuck, I'm..."

Jenifer pulled all of him into her mouth, sucking hard, tongue rubbing purposefully against his shaft as she deep-throated his cock. White-knuckled grip on the steering wheel, Remi moaned, cumming into her sealed suction of his cock. She pushed down, swallowing, and he groaned again. At last she slid slowly and purposefully off. He panted and relief washed over him, his grip releasing the steering wheel.

"Feel better?" she chuckled.

"That was harder to do than I expected." He laughed. "I was trying to let you know..."

"I know. And no offense, I could tell." She leaned back in her chair and stared out the window as the storm continued. "So, who was that? Your bride?"

"No, no, that was Bailey the Talent Coordinator. Surely you've talked to her too?" Remi tucked himself away, zipping his pants as a flash of headlights appeared. "Shit, we weren't far from the farmhouse after all."

"N-no. It's just behind the sand dune there." Jenifer frowned. "I suppose this is where we part ways."

"Wait, you're giving up just like that?" A SUV came to a stop behind the teetering Focus that clunked when he shifted to look. "Look, I bet that's the production crew coming to get us both."

He couldn't see her face, scrambling for his glasses on the dash. "I get the feeling you're giving me sad eyes. My sight is shit."

"Remi, you should know, I'm really a—" The car horn honked, muting her words.

"I know, I know. A bride for the show. Look, I'm a groom. Granted, we're not each other's bride and groom..." Another honk. "Let me run out there and see if they have space for us both."

Before Jenifer could say much more, Remi rushed out into the thunderous storm. The rain fell in large icy drops, lightning lighting the area up. He got out of the car, which teetered on the chassis and seemingly had no wheels on the ground. Cursing under his breath, he ran to the SUV and cracked the door open. The 90s emo male intern blinked at him, jerking in the driver seat.

"You have room for two of us?" he demanded.

"Y-yeah?" His reply was almost too low to be heard over the pelting rain, squeaking windshield wipers, and rolling thunder.

Remi wasted no time, spinning back to the Focus. He hurried to the passenger side and threw the door open, startling Jenifer. He grabbed her hand and pulled her along through the darkness. She tightened her grip on his grip, looking up at him in wonder. He pushed her into the passenger side of the SUV and spun, turning back.

Shit, my keys! I left the car running like a moron. Remi made his way back to the car, turning off the ignition, and taking the keys with him.

By the time he pulled himself into the SUV, water dripped from his beard, and his clothes and body clung to the vinyl seats. He squeaked into place. Pulling on the seat belt, Jenifer and the intern spun to glare at him in the back. His face flushed.

"Okay, let's go," he said, hoping it would prompt them to stop staring.

"The headlights," announced Jenifer.

"You left the headlights on. The battery will die, won't it?" added the intern.

Remi turned, squinting to see the rocking Focus with its lights on. "Fuck me!"

With a huff, he slung the seatbelt back off and went back out to weather the storm once more. He scrambled to the driver's side, flipping the headlights off and grabbing his ringing cell phone off the dash. Lightning flashed and he winced, the strike so close the thunder shook the ground at his feet and the air in his lungs. Shaking it off, he climbed back into the SUV, panting. He felt drained.

The intern's cell phone rang, and he picked up, "Yeah, I got him and the missing bride. We're heading back now, Ms. Bailey." Hanging back, he looked back at Remi. "Anything else you need?"

"Nah, man." Remi shook his head. "It can all wait until tomorrow when it's not raining."

The SUV started to make its U-turn. "Hate to say it, but there's a tropical storm slowly making its way in. This is just the precursor. Granted, tomorrow you might be able to get things between rain bands. Oh, and I think Ms. Bailey made arrangements for a tow truck to bring the car to the farmhouse."

"Wait, we're going to the farmhouse?" Jenifer panicked.

"Y-yeah?" Remi and the intern replied in confusion.

Jenifer covered her mouth then at last pulled her hands away. "Sorry. I guess you could say wedding jitters, still?" She gave a nervous laugh. "I made it this far so... why not the farmhouse?"

"You're weird." The intern rolled his eyes and pulled in front of the old two-story house that could pass for a vintage hotel.

"I like weird girls. I mean..." Remi covered his face, realizing that he'd left his glasses in the car. *That came out all wrong.*

"And I like men who are willing to wade through a storm without question," she countered, laughing.

4

Farmhouse Folly

Walking into the entrance of the Farmhouse, Jenifer froze. The space was nothing like she remembered. Candleholders were long gone, and the new electricity ran everywhere. Large wires were taped to the wooden floors, black lines running to the clusters of film equipment setup everywhere she looked. The walls had been painted, furniture changed, and entire area far more embellished than when she had visited with her fiancé. Looking down at her bare feet, she marveled at her surroundings.

I made it. From the bridge, I finally made it this far after more than a hundred years.

"Remi!" A middle-aged red-head exploded from a corridor, the woman locking eyes with Jenifer as she stumbled to a stop. "You're not Remi..." She looked Jenifer up and down. "And you're not Karen either."

"I can leave..." Jenifer offered slowly, her chest aching at the idea.

"Wait. She may be a no-show after all." The glimmer in the woman's eyes made Jenifer's eye twitch. *I know a conman, or woman, when I see one.*

"Bailey! Thank for sending someone so fast!" Remi's voice boomed through the old farmhouse, echoing against the walls. Jenifer thought the display of wine glasses clattered.

"Hush! Everyone is asleep," hissed Bailey, holding up a finger. She turned to her cell phone, thumb swiping left and right. "Mystery bride, what's your name? Who was your recruiter?"

"Jenifer and... recruiter?" she tried, stepping backward, but managed to bump into Remi. His heavy hands fell on her shoulders. *Dammit, I'm trapped.*

"Are you not signed up?" Remi paled when she gritted her teeth and mouthed *no.* "It was Timmy, right?" he said confidently.

"T-timmy?" Jenifer and Bailey asked in unison.

"Your recruiter, like me. It was Timmy. I thought that's what you said in the car?" Remi spun Jenifer to face him and lipped, *say yes.*

"Y-yes, Timmy." Jenifer's voice shook.

"Ah, not that guy. I can't find his information... that means you don't have a contract written up either!" Holding her head, Bailey paced back and forth. "The producer is going to kill me! First, the investor's daughter is a no-show, no-call, no-answer... and now I have a non-contracted bride drenched in rain almost run over by one of our grooms! This has workman's comp written all over it!"

Jenifer shuddered once, then twice. She hadn't done that since...
Am I cold? I haven't been cold since the day I...

She leaned into Remi, the heat of his body against hers making her blood rush. *What on earth is happening to me?* She pinched her arm. *Dammit, that hurt. Holy crap...*

"I'm... I am..." Jenifer's teeth were chattering, her words struggling.

"Hey, she's freezing." Remi wrapped his arms around her. "Anywhere she can change close by, maybe a hot shower?"

Covering her mouth, Bailey's eyes searched the air for several minutes as she considered. They waited, and she finally shrugged, shaking her head. "Whatever. Sure. Straight back this way. She can take Karen's room. Bobby, show them where it is." With a glance at Jenifer's wedding dress, she added, "There should be some spare sweats for everyone on the table when you pass."

Bobby, their emo-driver from before, pushed past them, and they followed in silence. The old wooden floors creaked underfoot as they climbed the stairs to the divided hallway. There, as promised, was a table filled with all kinds of amenities. Toothpaste, shampoo, and sweats bearing the show's logo were piled in a glorious mini-buffet of necessities.

Remi stopped, strangely excited about all of it, but Jenifer kept walking with Bobby. He opened a door at the end of the hall and smirked, studying her from head to toe, taking in the shape of her body beneath the semi-transparent gown. Running a hand through his hair, he glanced at Remi, the larger man loading his arms up with goodies and clothes from the table.

"How about you and I ditch this geek and have a little fun before you tie the knot?" He flicked his eyebrows for good measure as he surveyed her again, more slowly this time.

"Uh, no thanks." Jenifer's annoyance made the lights flicker, and she held her breath.

"Look, I got you a tiny shampoo." Remi had caught up to them. He glanced up at the flickering light above their heads. "Man, old houses seem to have the worst electrical problems."

The lights stopped buzzing as his hand hit her shoulder. "Is this the room where we can take a shower?"

"Y-yeah." Bobby the intern paled, looking small in comparison to how Remi towered behind her, adding to her ominous presence. "Otherwise you'd have to use the community bathroom on the other end of the hall. This is the master bedroom–"

"Alright!" Remi pushed past him, pushing Jenifer through the door in front of him. He closed the door in the emo-kid's face and rushed to unload his prize pickings onto the bed. The room was arranged around the large bed, a dresser pressed against the far wall and a desk tucked into a corner beneath the wide window. A small lamp sat on the desk, the dim light bathing the room. There was a wooden door in the wall to her right, probably leading to a private bathroom.

Jenifer smirked, admiring the excitement he carried for the smallest of treats.

He's a groom. I'm a bride. And for one night I'm alive to do—what exactly? Screw this. I know what I've been dying to do...

Biting her lip, she reached behind her and locked the door. By the time she tip-toed into reach, he had separated his items from what he had grabbed for her, and the gesture made her pause. Tilting her head, she looked at the display as he spun around, eyes sparkling and grin wide on his face.

"There! I suppose you should use the shower first," he announced, puffing out his chest in pride. He frowned as he saw the look on her face. "W-wait, what are–"

A devilish smirk crossed her lips as she untied the ribbon that cinched the waist, slipping the wet wedding dress off first one shoulder and then the other. The fabric slid down her body, the train sewn to the waist piling in waves of white, and she stepped out of it, moving closer to him. "Before that, there's something I want to do..."

"Look, we just met and..." Remi stumbled as the dress fell heavily on the ground. His eyes followed it, then scanned hungrily upwards. At last, he breathed, "Dammit, you're gorgeous."

Jenifer reached out to run her hands down his torso, her ghostly fingers bypassing his clothes to glide over his skin. A shudder shook his shoulders, and she pushed her body closer to his, relishing the heat of a living body. A twinkle of her nose, and his pants unfastened and fell to the floor. He jolted in surprise, taking a step back and out of his pants to land awkwardly against the bed. She pushed him into a sitting position. Shaking his head but still smiling, he pulled his shirt off, muttering about his missing glasses.

He flung his wet shirt to the ground with a thud, and Jenifer straddled his lap. Their lips locked, her hand snaking between them until she gripped his hardened shaft. Remi moaned, his tongue deepening their kiss as she began stroking him. His big arms pulled her against him, the heat of his body making her feel alive again. Her wanton desire made her impatient.

I've waited a good century for a wedding night like this and in this very farmhouse no less!

Arching back, she broke their kiss. Eyes locked, she guided his cock inside her pussy. The pleasure on his face thrilled her as she let him slide slowly and purposefully deeper. Hot fingers trailed down the line of her spine before resting on her hips. He pulled her forward, a firm and knowing direction and pushed deeper inside her. A gasp escaped her, the sensation invigorating and satisfying.

She rocked, his hands showing her when to grind forward and arch backward. The lightning from the storm outside lit the room, shadows of their bodies moving together illuminated in quick flashes. Rolling thunder let her moan her pleasure. Her fingers lingered near where he entered her, and she enjoyed feeling him there inside her. Remi licked and suckled at her breast, his own pleasure muffled by her flesh. Her body buzzed with the rising orgasm, her blood running hot as her heart thudded loud.

I feel so... so... alive.

Fingers slick from her pussy, she began circling her swollen clit. "You feel so amazing..." she told him.

She tightened, and Remi released her nipple to moan, "You're so... so..."

He seemed breathless, and she pushed him back into his treasure trove of toiletries. "I want you to watch me ride your cock."

"O-okay." His hands slid across her hips and gripped her thighs.

She wiggled into position, allowing his dick to slide in and out of her as she bounced on top of him. Her breasts moved with the motion, leaning back so her fingers could continue their play. His fingers dug into her thighs, his cock growing stiffer inside her. She slowed, sitting firmly on him until every inch of his dick was inside her. Arching back, she rolled her fingers over her clit harder, firmer. Her pussy tightened hard on his shaft, and it jumped with excitement. Grinding against him, she could feel her orgasm building with each circle.

"So tight..." moaned Remi.

"Oh I wanted this so bad..." she breathed. "A big cock inside me..."

Remi smirked. "You like how that feels, hm?"

"Don't you move!" she demanded, her other hand gripping her breast. "I'm... I'm almost there."

The heat of his hand slid up to her other breast, pinching it. "Let me help."

"Oh, touch me more," she pleaded.

"If you insist," he rocked under her, making his cock rub inside her pussy. "When I'm done, you'll be begging me to stop."

"Please... I want..." Her breath caught, her pussy tight with her orgasm as she lunged forward.

FINALLY! A REAL ORGASM!

5

The Bathroom

Wrapping his arms around her, Remi pulled her body into him and thrust hard and fast. She felt so amazing, so tight and wet. *The way she looks so haunting on top of me like that...*
Seeing her touch herself had been more than enough to make him agonize over coming too soon. Biting his tongue, he fought to hold it back, wanting to make her cum one more time. She shrieked like a banshee, arching in his arms, nipples hard and pressing into his chest.

Her skin was on fire, finally warming up. A gush and another tight lock on his cock signaled she had cum once more in the short window of wanton peak. He pushed her back, lifting her off him onto his thighs, and gripped his cock with a grunt. He looked left and right. Everything was a blur, but he didn't want to dump his load in the only dry clothes they had.

"Shit, I need something to release in!" He groped at things, hating that he couldn't see shit without his glasses.

Hot lips wrapped around the top of his dick and sucked. She shoved his hands away, taking his cock all the way in as he released. This time his breath caught as she made his own orgasm linger longer. Again, she swallowed, and he moaned at the way her tongue danced against the length of his shaft. He rocked in and out of her lips, slowly as the last ejaculation let go. Jenifer pulled her mouth off his cock, and they looked at one another, both grinning broadly.

"Feel better?" she offered.

"Oh yeah," he inhaled, holding a deep breath for a moment before huffing it out. "You seem to have had a good time of it."

"I'm not done," she warned, beginning to kiss her way back up his body.

"Uh, you do know it takes a man a while to recharge, right?" He marveled at how enthralling her lips felt against his torso.

I've done this to a woman plenty of times, but on me... holy hell I've been missing something in my life!

"What if I told you I might know a way to..." She paused and looked at him, eyes glowing in the haze of his blurry vision.

Is that the lighting in here? Or are my eyes really getting this bad?

"...speed things along," she offered, her fingers beginning to stroke his dick once more.

"Look, I've heard great things about Viagra, but I'm not that kind of guy," he confessed.

Jenifer stopped and sat up. "What is Viagra?"

"Uh, the little blue pill that makes you rock-hard for like hours on end?" He couldn't believe she had no idea. "Like on the late-night infomercials?"

"Forgive me. I've literally been stuck in the middle of nowhere while the world grew around me." She crossed her arms, and the dim desk light began to flicker.

"Oh." Remi bit his lip. *Dammit, I ruined the moment. Now what?* "I'm sorry?" he offered.

Her body language softened, arms uncrossing. "It couldn't be helped. And why are you apologizing?"

"I just assumed everyone knew what Viagra was." He shrugged, shifting his body and making some of the toiletries fall off the bed. "Huh. You'd think they would have fallen sooner?"

"Let's fuck some more." Her voice darkened, and he caught her gaze as icy fingers gripped his cock.

Grunting, he pulled her hand away. "First, you need to warm up in the shower. I mean, you're as cold as a dead body, girl."

He pulled himself to his feet and tugged her behind him. "But Remi..."

"But nothing." His authoritative tone silenced her.

Guiding her along, he managed to push her through the bathroom threshold and flip on the light switch, revealing white tiles and golden fixtures. She gasped, spinning slowly to take in the entire room. He chuckled to see her eyes light up. The huge shower space, the deep garden tub, and monster-sized vanity had her eyes wide with wonder. She rushed to each one, afraid to fully touch it but desperate to reaffirm they were indeed real.

"If you want, I can take the shower and you can take the tub?" Remi suggested. Jenifer spun around and scowled at him. "Or I take the tub?" he tried.

"No, *WE* are taking a bath *together*," she announced.

She looks way too excited about this idea. I can't tell her no. I mean... she's swallowed twice for me now!

Jenifer moved as if to leave the room, and he caught her arm. "Whoa, where are you going?"

"To fetch water." She blinked. "To fill the tub?"

"This may be an old house, darling," he winked, strutting over the fixtures, "but it is up to speed on the basic utilities."

Her eyes widened as he turned the knobs and water came spewing out. "They have indoor plumbing!"

"Y-yeah…" He tilted his head in confusion as she rushed over to dip her hands in.

"And it's hot water!" She gasped, laughing as she stepped into the tub. "This must have cost them a fortune!"

"I guess, since the house wasn't built with it?" Remi shrugged her reaction off. *She must have been brought up by…* "Are you Amish by chance?"

"Amish?" She made a face. "Do you think an Amish girl would suck cock like that?"

He laughed, choking on his own spit.

"Oh, you okay?"

He waved her off, sliding into the tub across from her.

As the huge space began to fill with hot water, he scanned the assortment of bath oils and bubbles lined up on a small shelf along the wall. A grin crossed his face. *Lavender bubbles for the win.* He dumped half the bottle under the flowing water without thinking. The reaction was immediate, a white plume of bubbles that had them both in a fit of giggles until soon Remi couldn't see her… or the bathroom any more. He had poured too much, the volatile concoction far more potent than the dime-store brands he had encountered in the past. The bubbles towered up like some elephant toothpaste chemistry experiment and toppled onto the tiled floor. He swam in them, hands reaching for Jenifer and nearly smacked her in the face.

"Shit! I poured too much!" He paled, but she only laughed harder, kissing him firmly on the lips for a quick second.

"I think this is wonderful!" Her hands cupped his face, her smile making his heart flutter.

"Y-you do?" he blinked. *If I could just read her expression a little more clearly…did I leave my glasses in the car or on the bridge?*

Another kiss planted on his lips, and Jenifer's tongue dipped into his mouth. They licked at one another, the water sloshing as he blindly groped for the knob to shut off the faucet. Her thighs hugged his hips, and he slipped backward until the garden tub caught his back. Slick with bubbles, his hand explored the curves of her body, squeezing and groping, chasing how her body dipped and bloomed. She broke the kiss, giggling again as she wiped bubbles from her face.

Catching a nipple in his lips, he pulled her to him, water slapping against the tub from the motion. She yelped, and he sucked more hungrily. Her fingers pulled him into her breast, goading him on. His teeth teased the hardened nipple, and she gasped. He was getting hard again, and Jenifer reacted. Her hips slid her pussy against the hardened shaft, making waves in the massive tub for two. Both moaned as she shifted, and he slipped inside her. The water added to the heat of the moment, while the bubbles made them blind to one another. Hands gliding across slick planes of flesh without direction, groping and pulling one another closer.

He released her nipple and moved over to the other breast. She tightened on his cock, and he shuddered in delight. Widening his mouth, he took in more of her breast. He rocked his hips, matching her rhythm so he could push deeper inside her. Water slapped across the tub's edge, spilling as it splashed against the tile.

"Faster," she breathed. "I want you to fuck me faster. I'm almost... I'm almost there."

Releasing her breast, he couldn't see her through the bubbles. "I can't at this angle."

"Then change angles!" She gently cleared bubbles, searching for the tub edge. "What if I lean over?"

Remi shuffled onto his knees, the water slapping the tub walls from his rush. "That might just work..."

His hands gripped her hips, lining her up. Straightening himself, he came too short with the way she had bent over the edge. Blowing bubbles from his mouth, he wiped more away, but still managed to smack her ass. She yelped, and when no rebuttal came, he smirked and repeated the action a few more times. Rubbing her ass cheeks with a red blush forming, he dipped his fingers between her thighs.

When his finger rolled over her clit, her thighs tensed. He pressed on, rolling and rubbing the opening of her wet pussy. The water and bubbles added to the surreal moment. *I shouldn't be doing this... but dammit, I might be stuck with a real Karen for the rest of my life instead of...*

He dipped his fingers into her pussy, thrusting hard and fast. Jenifer was on her tippy-toes, squealing with delight. His arm ached, and at last, he broke away and returned his grip to her hip.

"Bend your knees," he told her. He wanted back inside her, his cock throbbing with want. "I can't reach. You're too high."

"Oops." She began bending her knees when—*pop!* "FUCK ME!"

"I'm trying!" Remi's heart raced. *Shit, she's pissed!*

6

She's Back

Pain rolled through her, destroying the arousal. Her knee locked up, no different than it had done in her living state. It all came back in a blinding flash, thunder rolling outside to match the peak of her frustration. She turned, palmed Remi's chest, but his eagerness to rise to his feet and grip her made it clear that he misunderstood her words in the throes of passion.

"My knee... I can't..." she choked back the tears. At last, she saw recognition cross his face. "I forgot how much this hurts..."

Without a word, he scooped her up. She curled into him, hissing with each bounce of his step. He slid in the bubbles, but at least she still had the ability to move objects and righted him with a twinkle of her nose. All she wanted was to let him cradle her in this moment of pain.

She had fallen off the horse, slamming her knee on the only godforsaken rock in the whole damn field. After that point, it never healed right, and worse, she couldn't always bend it. Her toes numbed as another shot of pain made her press harder against his chest.

"I got you. It's going to be okay," he cooed, his voice soft and affectionate, making her heart swell.

I've never had a man talk to me like this before...

He set her on the bed gently, walked back to the bathroom and returned, handing her a fuzzy towel. "Here. I'll go grab some ice..." He rushed to put on the sweats with the obnoxious pink logo reading *Love at First Married.* He spied the open bathroom door. "Crap. Let me close this... the bubbles are dying down but..." He shut the door and the room fell dark with only the dim desk light. "Let me go get ice... I'll be right back. I promise."

With that, he left her alone in the room. She blinked, staring at her swelling knee awestruck. Trying to shift on top of the assortment of toiletries, she winced. The pain brought her back to the day she had fallen off the bridge, swept away with the storm surge. Lightning flashed outside, the wind slapping rain across the window as if agreeing with her.

This is usually the moment I fade away and wake up back on the bridge—or relive the moment.

A chill sent her body into a shudder, and she wrapped the towel tighter around her body. That night, it had stormed like this, but first thing in the morning, she was to marry Beau D. Phallis, the farmer's eldest son. As if by some twist of fate, a storm had blown in fast and hard. It always stormed hard during August, so no one thought anything of it. Her mother hemmed her dress up a little higher so the puddles wouldn't ruin the lace edging. She even pinned the train up for good measure, tucking it behind her.

"Momma, we can reschedule." Jenifer frowned in the mirror at herself before catching the disgruntled glare on her mother's face. "There's no telling when this storm will end."

"True, Babydoll, but I'm not cancelling this wedding. We've already made the food. People are already pouring into Phallis Farm, and they came to see two people get married—today." She finished connecting the train up so it wouldn't drag on the ground. "We'll cut this thread loose once you get into the house over there."

"But Momma," her voice lowered, "what if it's a sign?"

"A sign?" her mother scoffed. "To have the wedding inside? Absolutely! Remember how Rebecca fainted two summers ago at her uncle's funeral? August is a terrible time to wear a dress this elaborate."

"Did you just compare my wedding dress to funeral attire?" She spun with disbelief. "This is all a sign. It has to be."

"For what, Jenny?" Her mother snorted, hands on hips now.

"That... that..." Jenifer's chest tightened, and she couldn't hold her tongue. "We're not meant to marry one another."

"Whoa, did I ever walk in at the wrong time," Michael, her older brother, choked on the cupcake he had snuck from the kitchen.

"Michael van Winkle!" Before either of them could react, her mother had closed the gap and started shooing her brother out of the room. "You are not to ruin this day for your sister! Go get the wagon!"

"Well, Momma, I came to bring you over first. There's no room left thanks to Aunt Cathy being as big as Jimmy's prized sow." Jenifer and Michael chuckled hysterically, earning heated glares powerful enough to silence them.

"Boy, you better apologize to my sister in the buggy." Her mother paused, turning to Jenifer and looking to the window where lightning flashed. "There should be room for Jenny."

"Big Jo is too spooked over the thunder. We don't need a runaway horse and buggy with a bride in it. So only little Penny seems willing to pull it. Just one horse and..."

"Aunt Cathy is too much weight for the old mare," she confessed, flatly. "Fine." She locked eyes with Jenifer. "You want to go alone or I can stay and ride with?"

"Go, Momma." Jenifer managed a soft smile. "Get settled in and enjoy the indoor wedding you cooked so much food for."

"That's my girl. No wedding day jitters, now." She turned to Michael, shoving him out the door. "Now you get going!"

"See you on the other side of the bridge, Sissy!" Michael shouted from the stairs, making her giggle.

The mansion seemed quiet in that moment, more than any other time she had been left there alone. Thunder rolled, rain unyielding, and the gusts of wind made the glass panes rattle. A strike lit the room with blinding light, making her flinch. The floorboards underfoot vibrated with the powerful boom and she inhaled swiftly. It was enough to make her hide away from the windows as she ventured out into the hall and down the spiraling staircase. She sat in the receiving room, staring at the old Polish-made grandfather clock that had made it across the Atlantic and survived the Revolutionary War.

At least the old thing still keeps time. Heavens help us if it ever breaks down.

Time ticked by and she stood, pacing. Her brother should have been back by now.

It's been almost an hour.

Pausing, she turned to the front door and threw it open. Despite being midday, an orange hue covered the world outside. It looked like hell on earth with broken branches scattered about and the white picket fence on the ground in places. The rain stung her face and arms, but she stepped out. Pushing against the gusts of wind, she stumbled into the muddy road, looking toward the farm where she could see the bridge. There were no signs of anyone coming.

Nothing will stop me. Momma spent three days in that kitchen to make this happen. Hell or highwater, my wedding will happen.

She gripped her skirt, hiking it high, and began her march. The mud proved too much for her shoes, and she abandoned them. A gust of wind slammed her, and she stumbled to the side, barely catching the bridge railing. Glancing up, she could see all the way across the bridge. Her brother was there, calming old Penny, who snorted. The buggy sat tilted, a wheel sunken into the mud. Their childhood friends Rory and Claude were trying to pull the buggy out.

Jenifer shouted, but no one seemed to hear her. The river beneath the bridge was choppy and foaming as the salt in the brackish water frothed in the wind. Determined to push on, Jenifer stepped farther onto the bridge. She was already soaked to the bone with her teeth chattering. The farmhouse was just around the bend. Looking at her bare muddy feet, she willed them to move forward. Wind gusts made her skirt flail, and she struggled to stay upright.

Should I turn around…? No. I've made this walk a billion times. I can do this. It's just a thunderstorm…

Each step was arduous as the wind grew stronger. The rain slammed into her, stinging her face like bees, and at last she made eye contact with Michael. Penny reared up, he fell back into the mud, and the others rushed to his side. Jenifer persevered, pushing forward as the old mare ran off around the bend. She was halfway across… The boys could help her from there.

A strange sound met her hears, a cracking and rumbling. This wasn't thunder. This wasn't the wind. The bridge shook, and she looked to the men. They looked down the river, and she saw the whites of their eyes as they began screaming.

RUN! RUN NOW!

She took two strides and slipped, her knee popping. Collapsing to the bridge, she turned. A wall of muddy and debris-laden water came crashing down on her, and the bridge gave way. The water knocked the breath from her. Inhaling brought stinging pain as the saltwater filled her lungs. She tried kicking, but as she twisted and bumped into the unknown, there was no telling up from down. Her knee burned, and the light faded…

More water pressed down on her…

Darkness gripped her.

I can't remember if the snapping sounds came from me or the wooden bridge but... it was so cold. So horribly cold.

7
Show Must Go On

Morning rehearsal buzzed all around Remi as he scratched his chin. Swallowing, he glared at the rack of tuxedos, mind reeling. When he had managed to get an ice pack and brought Bailey to the room, Jenifer had already fallen asleep. She mumbled, tossing and turning from whatever nightmare plagued her. Bailey shooed him out of the master bedroom to his tiny, shared room where he finally fell asleep on the twin bed.

In the morning, he woke to find his roommate Bob pacing the small space. "Wedding day jitters?" chuckled Remi, walking down the hall to the rack of plastic garment bags containing their tuxedos.

Bob paused at his side. "You can say that. Aren't you nervous? I mean, we have no idea who or what we're stuck with…"

"The contract doesn't make us stay with them for life if it doesn't work out." Shrugging, Remi checked the tags on the bags until he found his name. "I hope this fits okay. Unlike my prom tux."

"Man, yeah, you should try this diet I'm on. You gotta cut all the potatoes out." Bob nodded, locating his own bag. "Trust me, I'm a certified therapist. I know what I'm talking about."

Remi furrowed his brow. "And what do a therapist and nutrition have in common?"

"Oh this sounds like a great joke! I don't know. You tell me." Tucking the bag over his arm, Bob rubbed his hands together, leaning in for the punchline.

Remi's eyes widened. *I feel bad for his bride to be.* "Well look at the time!" His booming voice made Bob leap back a little. "We better get ready for dress rehearsal, Bob!"

"Y-yeah."

Remi scanned the hallway, searching for Jenifer. What they had done—or at least started—last night had been amazing. Unfortunately, she wasn't the bride he had spoken to on the phone. She wouldn't be the one he would be married to. No, instead...

Dammit, I just had to make that deal involving the producer's daughter.

He covered his mouth as he dressed, angry at the blind jump after money. His phone buzzed and the name flashed: *UNKNOWN CALLER.* Sending it to voicemail was followed by two more calls without messages. At last, he silenced his phone. A text popped up from a private number.

[PRIVATE NUMBER: Are you fucking kidding me! You'd rather marry on live television with a stranger than me!]

SHIT. It's that crazy bitch Monica.

He worked fast, not reading anything else as he blocked the number.

I hope the filming location hasn't been leaked. This could be bad.

"Mr. Adama. This way. We will be reviewing some of the scripted parts and what to expect." It was the emo-kid from before.

"Thanks." He shoved the phone in his pocket, following the intern to the prep area downstairs.

He walked into a room to see that all the chairs were taken. Bob rushed in behind him, and with that, the door shut. Bailey paced in front of the grooms, most sitting, but a few standing at the back like Remi and Bob. Each one locked eyes with her, and she scribbled something on her clipboard. She circled back to the other end of the room, asking a name to confirm she had indeed memorized each groom. As she did so, more writing was recorded, and the men shot looks to one another, their nervousness building. At last, she returned to the front of the room like a coach and inhaled deeply.

"Listen up! We will be taking each of you one at a time to resolve..." they followed her glance to a scruffy, greasy-haired man who shrank in his chair, "...appearance issues. We are going to be on national television, and if we're lucky, picked up globally or at least on Netflix or Hulu. We are taking you first come, first serve. Get comfortable." She turned to her clipboard. "Okay, Stan, you're first. Follow me this way, and we'll get to work. After that, we will allow you a recorded, blind, in-person session with your future wives."

Stan puffed out his chest, a suave clean-cut man in glasses who sashayed out the door, winking at Remi and Bob like he beat them somehow. "Early to rise, they say."

Remi rolled his eyes, muttering under his breath, "Ass kisser."

Bob chuckled. "Right?"

An hour came and went, the chairs opening up. Remi was glad to sit, but annoyed. He had pulled his phone out a few times, but Monica was still attempting to blow it up. The battery was fading fast, and he scoffed. Placing it in his pocket, his mind wandered until at last it settled back on what happened last night. He had nearly killed a woman, possibly twice when her knee buckled in the tub. A smile came to his lips. She had been so fascinating. Never had he met someone so innocent and naughty in one package and he grunted.

Oh, how I wish I could just get one more chance with her before...

"Hey man." Bob slid over to him and tapped his arm, leaning in to whisper, "So you, uh, you watch adult movies?"

Remi's face wrinkled in confusion. "Do you mean porn?"

"Y-yeah... adult movies," he repeated. "Do you, you know, watch them for... uh..."

"Jerking off?" Remi tilted his head, Bob signaling for him to lower his voice. *Wrong conversation to have with someone as loud as me... but where the hell is he going with this?*

"Right, for *release*." Bob's word choice made Remi snort. "I do. Do you?"

Remi squinted his eyes at the man. "Doesn't everyone?"

"Well," Bob glanced around the room, leaning in and lowering his voice further, "I like them, but I don't watch them if they have a man in them."

Remi narrowed his eyes in confusion. "Um, don't most of them have a man in them?"

Bob scowled, face disgusted. "It's not... well, I mean, looking at another man's dick outside of medical reasons seems... it makes me uncomfortable. I'm just afraid..."

Are you out of your mind? Just pretend that's you pounding that big black beautiful babe from behind! With a smirk, Remi nudged him. "I get it, man. You're afraid you might see a huge cock and decide you like looking at one after all."

Bob paled, tripping on his words. "T-that's n-not what I m-meant?!"

"Man, when I watch them, I just think, *yup! That's me! The baseball bat with veins!* And sit back and enjoy the show." Remi's laughter filled the room, making everyone turn.

Bob's face reddened, embarrassment and anger building. "That's not what I meant." He managed to say, voice stern.

Oh, we're angry.

"Look man, I just don't understand the big fear. You ever been in a locker room growing up?" Remi marveled.

"I was home schooled," declared Bob.

That explains everything...

"Bob, you're next." Bailey's voice cut in, and Remi watched her shoo him out the door. A few moments later, she ushered the two final grooms out, but instead of following them, she turned and slammed the door closed, locking it behind her. "Remi."

He stood in alarm. "What's wrong?"

Again, the pacing started as she rubbed her forehead. "She's not here."

"Who?" He was confused.

"Karen." When he gave her a baffled expression, she started again. "Your bride—the producer's step-daughter Karen. She's supposed to be here by now but..."

"Am I not getting married then?" Remi felt a small wave of relief, though he did his best to hide it.

"Well, about that..." Glancing at her clipboard, she flipped a page up and sighed. "We do have a replacement: the girl you met last night." She shot a look his way, and he smirked. She returned the look. "I thought you might like to hear that good news."

"But the contract?" Remi lowered his voice. "I take it this means I'm back to the original rate."

"You still get double." She sat down and crossed her legs. "You get triple if she shows in time."

Remi puffed out his cheeks. *There's the catch. I get the full amount if I marry Karen last minute...*

"But seeing as no one has heard from her, you might have dodged a bullet, Mr. Adama." She folded her hands on top of the clipboard.

"She can't be that bad..." Shoving his hands in his pockets, his hair stood on end as he gripped his cell phone. *Was I about to marry someone like Monica? I would rather forfeit the fucking money.*

"Never mind that." She changed subject. "Jenifer van Winkle seems to be rather excited about it. So sign here." Bailey presented the marriage certificate written out and signed to be with Jenifer van Winkle.

"Really?" He spun away to hide the excitement on his face. *Maybe my luck is changing for once!* "How's her knee doing?"

"On-site med said to keep it in the brace and try not to bend it. Gave her some pain killers and trying to keep her off her feet until we need her for filming." Bailey stood, tapping him on the shoulder. He turned back, gripping the pen and signing. "Now, let's get you ready for your bride, Mr. Adama."

"R-right." He thought for a moment and curiosity go the better of him. "How many have pulled out of this in the last twenty-four hours?"

"There's only three couples left." She choked on her words, pausing near the door.

"But we had like twelve grooms?" Remi looked back to the room, counting the men he recalled.

"Their brides backed out during the recorded conversation."

"What in the fuck did they say?"

She puffed out her cheeks, unlocking the door. "I can't disclose that private information to you."

Remi's eyebrows lifted as he watched her leave.

Did they miss out on the fact we are going to be on television, and it was a recorded conversation?

8

Last Call

Staring at herself in the mirror, Jenifer didn't know how to feel. They had given her something for the pain in her knee, and it had knocked the ache down, but still she had her leg propped up with ice for swelling. Behind her, the hair dresser was having a hell of a time with the veil they'd chosen for her. She couldn't deny the fact it matched her dress well. Looking to the skirt, she saw that the muddy stains and even the tear had been expertly mended. A tailor had brought the dress back to her, gushing over the vintage quality and refusing to allow anyone to put her in a different dress.

Her heart fluttered. It looked like the day she wore it, and she could almost hear her mother fussing at her all over again. A make-up artist and hair stylist competed for room as they finished preparing her for this *special day*. The excitement of the other brides added to her own, but she paled as thunder rolled and a shutter slapped against the house. Somewhere beyond them, a talking box spoke of the incoming hurricane.

It's happening all over again.

Anxiety crushed her. Her smile faded.

But this time I made it, made it to the farmhouse.

One of the interns came in, drenched even under his poncho. "I lost the damn umbrella. What category are we up to?"

Category? Do they mean the storm has categories? Is it that serious like back when I…

"Just announced it hit category three," sighed another hair dresser, crossing her arms. "They said they were getting gusts up to 112 mile per hour in the Bahamas. Shocked it's not pushing into cat-4."

"Well, ladies." Jenifer jolted as the hair dresser tugging on her hair and veil spoke, "at least this place has a gorgeous dining hall. Those chandeliers are to die for."

"Oh, so true!" agreed a bride, nodding. "I saw it before the setup. Can't wait to see how they dolled it up!"

Jenifer's eyes bounced to each person as she spoke, but her thoughts muted their words. A chill ran through her, the thunder and wind outside rattling the window panes. She inhaled sharply and held it.

I'm alive again, but will the storm sweep me away? Just like last time?

Thunder hit close, the chandeliers rattling, and the other brides yelped. It made her heart race, and she bolted from the chair, ignoring the cries of the stylist. Running past the televisions and dumbstruck staff, she flew up the stairs. She panicked, turning in a circle before running away in long strides, bare feet thudding against the wooden floor.

Bailey flattened herself against the wall to get out of the way of the dashing bride, paling as if a phantom came at her. A shriek filled the hall as Bailey attempted to climb the walls. Remi turned, face curious, just as Jenifer slammed into him.

"Remi!" She realized who the wall of flesh was that had stopped her. "Remi…" Relief filled her, tears welling up as she clenched his tuxedo.

His great big arms wrapped around her. "Let's go someplace private. It seems you scared the shit out of Bailey! She's gasping for air and sunk to her knees in the hall. Come on." He took her hand. "This way."

Jenifer wouldn't let go of his hand, the heat of his body calming her as her shoulders shuddered. He pulled her into a dark room, slamming the door and locking it. At last she pulled away, trying to remove her makeup smudges from his black tuxedo. Gripping her wrists, he tugged her back, then lifted her face with a finger beneath her chin, demanding she look at him. He smiled, and her heart fluttered. A huff escaped him at last as he searched her face.

"Dammit, I wish I had my glasses."

She furrowed her brow. "Where are they?"

He shrugged. "Either on the bridge or in the car. Not sure."

"Oh no, and the storm..." A lightning strike hit close, and she buried herself in him again.

"It seems this has you a little freaked out." He rubbed her back. "Oh, I know what will get your mind off this." His hands gripped her waist and guided her to a desk in the corner.

"I don't think journaling about this will help." Jenifer frowned as the back of her thighs bumped into the dress, the edge softened by the bundled train of the dress.

"That's not what I had in mind," he chuckled, lifting her up to sit her on the desktop.

"I don't understand?" She tilted her head in confusion.

"Oh, you will."

He knelt on the floor before her, making her heart race.

Is... is he proposing?

The heat of his hands slid up her shins, gentle as he caressed her knees, skipping over the brace. She stiffened, gripping the edge of the desk. He pushed her legs apart, squeezing the inside of her thighs with his large hands. Remi paused, thumbing the garter belt.

Wait, that's for...

He moved his hands higher until they found her pussy, rubbing between her folds. She gasped. His finger followed the silken crevasse to the pink pearl. She tried to close her legs in reflex but caught on his broad shoulders. She frowned, hating not being able to see him. Her skirt hid him away, making her rely solely on the sensations and heat of his hands on her body. Slowly, purposefully soft, he circled her clit. Breathing steady, she made herself relax. Closing her eyes, she focused on the pleasure he gave her. The fear that had sent her bolting washed away.

I love how he touches me... Don't stop! Don't ever stop, Remi.

The heat of his breath blew across her pussy, and she throbbed with wanton want. His other hand glided in, rubbing the opening, growing slick with each stroke. At last, he slid a finger inside her wet heat, and she moaned. His stroking added to the pleasure of circling her clit. She spread her legs, wanting to give him more room to play with her. He pressed harder and faster against her swollen jewel. Her legs shook in response, and he began thrusting his fingers quicker, hard and calculated with his circling.

She panted, arching and fighting the urge to close her legs. The rise of an orgasm brought a smile to her face, her eyes closed tight. If the lightning still threatened to strike her down, she had forgotten and paid it no heed. His finger pulled away from her clit, and his tongue took its place. She squealed, biting her lip to hold it in for fear they would be discovered. His fingers abandoned her, leaving her aching until his tongue ran the length of her opening. She moaned. A shiver of pleasure rattled through her entire being. Lips wrapped around her clit, the jolt of her body electrifying. He pulled her to the edge of the desk, leaving her teetering with her legs on his shoulders somewhere beneath the white satin skirt.

Another moan left her trembling lips, his teeth teasing her pearl-sized treasure. Sucking hard and long only made the shaking in her legs increase, the verge of orgasm haunting her. Wanton desire made her pussy ache to have him inside her again. Memories of how good his swollen shaft felt stroking the slick, sensitive...

"Fuck me," she breathed.

He didn't stop his play.

"Please, I want your cock inside me," she begged.

Releasing her jewel, he barked through the skirt. "Not yet. We can't."

"Wait, what?" She released the desk only to grab it again. "R-Remi!"

His fingers slid inside her, and she moaned as he stroked slowly. Dripping wet, she tightened on his fingers, her orgasm nearing its peak. The suckling returned to her clit, shifting so his tongue circled it as his finger had done before. She lurched forward. He switched to two fingers, rubbing in more places, speeding up with each passing second. All at once, she peaked, a wail coming from her as she came hard. She could feel how she squeezed around his fingers and gushed with the wake of her orgasm. He slowed his play, making her ride out the oh-so-sensitive vibrations shooting through her. When Remi climbed out from under her skirt, she had slumped back on the desk, panting. He chuckled as their eyes met.

"We have to save the other for the honeymoon tonight." He shrugged.

"No fair." She swallowed, catching the tightness in his pants. "Are you going to be able to live with that?"

Another shrug. "Something tells me this will be worth the wait when I don't have to keep my tux on."

She laughed. "Thank you for making me... feel better."

The shutter began banging against the side of the building. Jenifer flew off the desk and back into Remi's arms. He hugged her tight, and for the first time, Jenifer felt alive again. It was as if all that time being dead had been just a distant dream, and she had found her soulmate, the one who could anchor her back into the world.

Did I find my second chance? Is this the man I've been waiting for all this time?

9

Groom's Bride

Remi was relieved they had escaped into the master bedroom with the fancy bathroom. He washed his face and hands while Jenifer rested on the bed, feeling faint. He lingered until she fell asleep before heading for the door. The storm outside seemed to be taking a physical toll on her. Granted, with a hurricane fueling the weather, they were in for hours of thunder, wind, rain, and potential tornado warnings with flood advisories to boot. Bailey waited outside the room for him, still pale and shaking.

"Are you okay?" Remi rushed to her. "You look like you saw..."

"G-g-g-g-ghost." He almost didn't hear the stuttering whisper.

"Oh! Is this place haunted?" He looked around, excited. "I've never seen a ghost before."

"The bride," she pointed to the door to the room where Jenifer slept. "She's a ghost!"

"That's rather rude." Remi made a face. "I mean, she is rather pale, but..."

Bailey scoffed, pushing past him. "Are you blind?"

"I lost my glasses, so yes, I am blind."

Bailey swung the door open, but Jenifer was gone. "Look—vanished."

"Oh, well maybe she's in the bathroom?" Remi started in that direction when water hit him; the window was open. "Oh no, did she... run away?"

"She's. A. Ghost." Bailey held her arms out, eyes wild.

"I don't know what you saw, but maybe you need some sleep." Remi couldn't see any signs of Jenifer outside and closed the window. "What should we do?"

Bailey shivered. "She disappeared, Remi."

"Yeah, out the window. I thought she was asleep in the bed." He reassured himself, scratching his jaw.

"Look, she didn't even leave an impression in the bed, Remi!" Bailey waved her hand out as if to provide evidence.

"Uh, maybe she fixed it before she left," countered Remi. "Look, there's a hurricane unfolding out there. It can't be safe. I'm going after her."

He started for the door, but Bailey grabbed his arm. "She's a fucking ghost. If you leave the premises, your contract is void."

Remi pulled his arm free. "Leaving someone in that storm is a risk I'm not okay with. If you're asking me to choose my money or her life, I choose her life."

Before she could say anything else, he rushed down the hall to the stairs. He pulled the bow tie loose and tossed it to the ground. Flying down the steps, his every footstep thundered through the house. The audio guy carrying the boom mic went to yell at him, and he tossed his jacket in his face. Cameras all turned as he dashed out the doorway, and there was his Focus.

He dipped his hand in his pocket, relief filling him. By some strange fate, he had kept his keys close. Hopping into the car, he spied his glasses and put them on, the world snapping into focus. He didn't care that he was soaked from short jog. All that mattered was that he could *save her*. The little car sputtered to life and he followed the road back toward the bridge where they had met.

The little Focus fought to stay on the road as each gust of wind slammed into it. Cursing under his breath, Remi fought to look all around. The road started to make the turn, and there before the bridge, a woman in white stood. Jenifer turned as if she had been trapped there for some time, trying to decide if she dared cross the bridge. Water splashed up as the little river had doubled in volume. Muddy and white-capped water rose, foaming up and flecking into the wind, and the bridge swayed in the wind.

Her wedding dress whipped around, and Jenifer stumbled as a gust rocked the little car. He flashed the high beams at her, and she frowned. At last, he crept the car closer, and she waited. Sucking on his cheek, he understood at last.

"She's going to make me chase her." He put the Focus in park, inhaling a deep breath. "Okay, my little Runaway Bride. Here I come."

Shoving the door open, he walked slowly, expecting her to take off at any moment. He stopped a few feet away, towering over her in the flashes of lightning. She reached for him, then her fingers retreated. The look on her face, reddened from sobbing, told him something had rattled her. His heart skipped a beat.

"Did I do something wrong?" He feared the answer.

"No, no, you didn't, Remi." She shook her head, not breaking their intense stare.

"Why'd you run?" He looked stern, trying to mask the emotions boiling inside him. *Why'd you run away from me? From us? Didn't you feel we had something special? Something that just felt... like destiny?*

"I didn't." She looked back to the bridge. "But I woke up and found myself back here and..."

"Sleepwalking?" He looked at the bridge, waves managing to rise and break across the road.

"Not exactly." Again, she reached for him, pausing just shy of gripping his drenched shirt.

He grabbed her hand, her fingers icy in his own. "Then what? Why run away from what we could be? I know it's intimidating getting married on a television show but..."

She laughed. "I love you."

He smiled. "I love you, too."

"No one has ever made me laugh and look forward to the tiniest of moments together as I have with you, but Remi... I'm..."

Lightning hit the Focus, the sound making Remi scoop Jenifer into his arms and start running. She screamed, fingers digging into him as the car burst into flames. A smell of ozone filled the air, making him tighten his hold. They were halfway across the bridge when the road shook beneath them. Jenifer buried her face in his chest, shaking with fear.

"It's happening again," she kept muttering into him.

A tree, swept up by the river, banged against the bridge, unable to flow under or over. Another tree rode on the storm surge wave. Swallowing, Remi held onto Jenifer tight. His car was fucked and popping and now, the bridge was about to be destroyed.

"Hang on! I refuse to die here before we have a chance to even properly get to know one another!" he shouted.

My bad luck seems to be pulling out the stops. Now if my dumb luck can just kick in for this one moment...

The water was starting to flow over the road, making his footing uneasy. He started sliding as they reached the last few strides. The bridge creaked and popped. Another thud, and he was hydroplaning on his feet.

Is this even possible? Fuck me!

He hit the mud along the side of the river, and his balance gave way. Down they both went, sliding across the ground. They scrambled to their feet, faces and clothes covered. The bridge buckled, the storm surge chasing them down the road as it overflowed the river.

Remi thanked his luck for the uphill run for the first time in his life. Reaching beside him, he locked hands with Jenifer, and they managed to turn the bend, leaving the water behind. She tugged his hand, and he followed her up a steep driveway. The gates to the mansion had been left open as they slowed down and panted.

Leaning against the brick wall, Remi paused to slow his racing heart. The covered porch gave them very little protection from the rain riding on the nonstop winds of the hurricane. Jenifer searched the bricks. He narrowed his eyes at her, realizing he had cracked one of the lenses in his glasses.

"Shit, that was close!" He had finally caught his breath.

She paused, glancing over at him. "Thank you for that." A brick came loose, and she reached in to produce a key.

Remi stared at her. "Well, that was a lucky guess."

"No, not a guess. Granted, this isn't the type of key I expected. It seems the current owner has been keeping the old tradition alive." She handed the key over.

"Should we knock first?" Remi stared at the key in his palm.

Jenifer pointed at a sign on the window reading:

Will be gone until Thanksgiving. Please do not leave packages at door.–TW

"Huh." Remi tilted his head and pushed the key into the lock. "It's an emergency, and we can't stay out here in a hurricane. We can ask for forgiveness later or just cover our tracks."

"R-Right." Jen gripped the back of his shirt.

The locks turned with ease and opened. With a scrape, the door opened wide, and they walked slowly through the foyer. Water tapped on the floor as it dripped off them and onto the wooden floor, waxed and kept to a historical level. Walking into the receiving room, Remi spun, marveling at the space. The Victorian furniture, the grandfather clock and its swinging pendulum, even the lamps were kept mimicking a forgotten time.

Jenifer began to cry. She stood before a massive family portrait, covering her mouth. He approached her to see what the matter was when he locked eyes with one of the girls in the painting.

It's her. That's Jenifer in that painting.

His eyes searched the frame and painting until at last he saw what he looked for: *Van Winkle Family, 1840.*

"That's you." He spoke the words at last. "But how is that even possible?"

"Remi." She turned to face him, demanding his eyes. "I've been trying to tell you this since the bridge. I'm a ghost. I've been dead a long time. On a day much like this, storm and all, the bridge broke and swept me away on my way to get married at the farmhouse."

He paled. *What do we do from here?*

10

Bride's Groom

She waited for the words that would follow, but none came. They stood in silence under her parent's painted gazes. Here she was, home again, but with a different groom than she left to go marry. Her heart raced, and her fingers ached in the cold. She could see Remi's lips turning blue, and he shivered. Panic drove her as she grabbed his arm and tugged him along.

"You're freezing."

Opening a door down the hall behind the stairs, she flustered. The bathroom had been demoed out and, from the look of it, sat that way for some time. A note on the wall said: *Use upstairs bathroom.* She spun Remi around and shoved him up the stairs in a rush. Relief washed over her to see the bathroom there had been remodeled completely.

"Come on. Let's get you warmed up."

She had managed to figure this out at the farmhouse, so she turned the knobs properly. The large walk-in shower wasn't as massive, but the Jacuzzi-style bathtub had been rather tempting.

Shaking that from her thoughts, she doubled down on caring for the still silent Remi. The stream of water grew warmer under her fingers as Remi stared at himself in the mirror.

"Am I dead too?"

"No, you're very much alive… for now." Pulling him into the shower, she pulled his glasses off and placed them gently on the vanity. "Come on, big guy. You need to warm up."

Back in the shower under the warm water, she began washing the mud from his face and hair. He smiled at her, wiping her mud-covered cheek. Before she could say to stop, his lips locked with hers. He deepened the kiss and began undoing the back laces of her wedding dress. Her wanton desire surfaced in an instant, her fingers desperate to unbutton his shirt. At last, the muddy clothes thumped onto the shower floor.

His hands gripped her ass, bringing her wet, naked body against his. She could feel his cock growing hard between them, and for once, she was the warm one. She licked into his mouth, wanting to play with his tongue, explore his body, hear him moan like he had before…

Thunder roared somewhere outside, and they paused, looking at one another.

"For a ghost, you're pretty hot." Remi's blue lips were gone, the shivering ceased.

"For a groom, you're pretty brave," she retorted.

He laughed and began kissing her neck. "You think the owner will mind if we spend our honeymoon night here?"

"As a previous tenant, I'm sure I can convince him that it's purely for personal preference," she cooed, enjoying the way his hands explored her body. "So, are you really trying to make love to a dead girl?"

"Everything I know about the living says you're not-so-dead." Chills rattled her as his kisses trailed across her collarbone.

Hot hands squeezed her breasts, then he licked and suckled her nipples, tasting one then the next. Satisfied with his sampling, his hands flowed down her torso, finally dipping between her thighs. She leaned into him, still sensitive from the session on the desk. A finger rolled over her clit, and all the pleasure flooded through her. Her shoulders shook, and she slid her hand down his body. She gripped his hard cock, her pussy throbbing with need.

Fuck this foreplay...

"W-wait," she said out loud. Swallowing her fear, she prepared herself for what she wanted to voice. "Not yet. I want you on the bed."

Again, he tilted his head as a sparkle came to his eyes. "Me on the bed?"

"Yes. I want to..." She cleared her throat, reaching behind him to cut off the water, "...be in charge."

He nodded his head, mulling it over a moment. "I can get on board with that idea."

A grin stretched across her face as she pulled him along. Toweling off, they ventured through the upstairs hallway naked. Jenifer stopped before a door, and her giggles stopped. Her chest ached as she ran her hand over it. At last, she turned the old knob and pushed the door open. The bedroom inside looked...

"Wait, why...?" She lost her words, pushing inside the room and looking all around.

"Was this your room?" Remi strutted in behind her.

"More like..." Taking in the room, she found no detail missed or unpreserved. "It *is* my room. Someone kept it the same for... I don't even know how many years."

"Well, if the picture downstairs is accurate... it's pushing almost two hundred years," offered Remi.

Jenifer covered her mouth. "I'm a cradle robber."

Remi lost it, breaking into an explosion of laughter.

A letter drew her attention, the paper resting on the bed, her name clear across the top:

To Jenifer van Winkle,
May you find a way to sleep upon your bed again with the right
groom of your choosing.
Your great, great nephew,
Timothy van Winkle

"Wait, who got you into this?" Jenifer spun, showing Remi the letter.

"Timmy... do you think he knew something?" Remi marveled, a half-grin on his face.

"He must've known something because..." She looked down at her pale, curvy body. "I am very much back alive again."

Remi dropped the letter and kissed her again. He pushed her back until he backed her into the bed. Again, his groped her breasts, but she pulled him away. Baffled, he furrowed his brow. Gripping his shoulders, she switched where they stood. When she managed to circle him with the bed behind him, she shoved him down. He sat, a look of excitement growing on his face. Pushing him onto his back, she crawled on top of him, kissing him. Sucking on his tongue, she wanted to be in charge of this next session. Her knee had stopped hurting, bending easily once more, and she wouldn't let this opportunity be missed. She caught his tongue in her teeth when he ventured. Releasing him, she let him retreat a little.

"Good." She gripped his cock and stroked the length of his shaft. "Because I now own this."

Remi's eyes widened, and he fell silent.

Crap, did I overstep? I just... I just want to show him how much I enjoy him and want to please him. What if I'm being too much?

"Am I being too aggressive?" she asked.

"You did sign the paperwork to own it." He gripped her breasts. "Does that mean I own these now?"

She laughed. "Maybe?"

His voice deepened, his hands pulled her into him, and his lips tickled at her ear. "Look—be aggressive. I don't mind. Be creative."

The tension in her shoulders relaxed. "Then I'll take my time."

Remi's body tensed a little under her, his cock pushing into her palm where she still gripped him. Releasing him, she grabbed his wrists and pinned them above his head. Her fingers trailed down his arms, and he shuddered under her. Leaning in, she kissed him once more before nibbling on an ear. Another shudder and he tensed, his cock growing harder between their bodies. She began sucking on his neck, and he shifted. She could see he enjoyed every touch she gave him.

"Oh, this is a new venture for me," he gruffed, leaning his head to give her more room.

She sucked long and hard, leaving a hickey by the time she released. Venturing slow and agonizing downward, she relished leaving the marked trail. Tiny bursts of purple and red fireworks blossomed across his neck, down his chest, and snaked down his torso. She licked and sucked, kissing and worshipping his body as if daring to gobble him up. He moaned, covering his eyes with a forearm.

With a grin, she ran her tongue from base to tip across the underbelly of his dick. He grunted, the precum dripping down the side. Her tongue circled the mushroomed tip, and his body tensed. She had slid back off the bed some, running her hands along the inside of his thighs and squeezing. Again, she taunted him with long, sultry licks on all sides of his cock until at last, she began kissing his taut skin. She teased him with her lips, licks of her tongue, and the subtle sucking as if she aimed to French kiss his dick. A moan escaped him, his toes curling.

Squeezing his thigh, she rested her lips around the tip of his cock, tongue circling. She mimicked the speed that he had used for her clit. Remi took a deep breath and held it. Another squeeze of his thigh, and an audible sound of pleasure escaped his lips as the breath broke free. She wanted to hear him, wanted to make him beg for her to stop, only for her to continue until he exploded over and over again. His dick jumped, every finished rotation enhancing the tension in his body.

Like they say about marriage: What's his is hers, and what's hers is hers.

11

Definition of Luck

The heat of Jenifer's lips against the tip of his dick made him ache. His balls drew in, the agonizing desire to thrust further into the depths of her mouth was driving him crazy. Granted, the sexual torture and build had been amazing. Never had a woman blessed his body like she had. The way she made love to all of him was exhilarating. Her tongue circled the end of his dick, and he tightened his fist. He had to fight the urge to take over. Never had he wanted to release so badly in his life, yet he still wanted more of her play.

I want to cum so badly, but I don't want this to end.

At last, her lips slid down to the base of his shaft. His body shuddered, on fire with the electrifying pleasure it brought him. She sucked long and hard, tongue wiggling under his shaft in the wet heat of her mouth. As slowly as she had taken all of him in, she rose up and off with a pop of her lips. A grunt escaped him, his balls tightening. The heat of her finger started to massage them as her lips slid back down his hardened length. This time she pushed him to the back of her throat, rocking her head back before sliding up and off again.

This feels amazing but agonizing all at once.

"You can't cum yet," she ordered. The heat of her breath on his wet cock made it jerk.

Her tongue licked the side, her play with his balls still unfolding. Another squeeze of his thigh made him grunt. In his mind, he wondered if he might just release without even being inside her at all. The French kissing of his cock started once more, and his toes curled. His body stiffened, the urge to release so hauntingly close that he whimpered.

Jenifer broke away, leaving a rush of cool air to slam into him. Before he could take his arm off his eyes to see where or what she intended to do next, she was back to kissing his neck. Her pussy, wet and hot, began grinding against his cock's length. Another groan escaped him as she repeated a snaking trail of hickeys down his chest. Remi didn't care. He wanted to know how rough and demanding she would be, how long she would dare to keep him lingering in this state of want and need for release.

Halfway down his torso, she sat up, straddling him and pinning his dick between them under her. Removing his forearm, Remi met her provocative glare. His eyes fell to her hands where she groped her breasts, the sight only increasing his arousal. He slid his hands over her thighs, but she reached down and stopped them. Taking his wrists, she pinned them against the bed at his side. A wild grin and mischief filled her face. Leaning down, she kissed him deeply. Her hips shifted, the tip of his cock lining up with her wet pussy.

Tilting his hips, he managed to slide just the tip in, and even at this shallow depth, she could tighten on him. He shifted further, but she matched it and kept him from sliding deeper inside. Grunting with frustration, his smile broke their kiss.

"Not yet. We will get to that later." The voracious tone in her voice made his heart race. "I want…" Her eyes fell to his lips. "I want to sit on your face."

Remi cleared his throat, enamored with the confession. "Oh boy."

Jenifer flinched. "Too much?"

"No." He shook his head. "A little uncouth and raunchy, but I'm into it."

She kissed him once more, sucking on his tongue before pulling away and letting go with a pop. "I'll make this next part well worth it for you."

His heart fluttered. *I might die a happy man with a hard-on and blue balls and I don't fucking care. Let's do this!*

She spun around, quick and calculating as her knees rested against his shoulders. Her fingers gripped his cock as she lowered her wet and swollen pussy to his lips. Remi decided to be just as aggressive as she had been with him. Fingers tightened on his dick, a yelp of pleasure escaping her as he licked between the folds to her bean and back again, eating her like a starved animal. She rewarded him by pulling his cock back into the warmth of her mouth, suckling and thrusting him in and out. They moaned into each other. Her drool dribbling hot across his balls had him fighting the urge to cum.

She rocked forward, deep throating his cock as she squeezed his balls. He sucked on her clit, and she moaned on his dick. He teased her swollen clit gently with his teeth while muffling her scream on his cock. Tilting his hips, he began thrusting in and out of her vocal attempts of peaking pleasure. Again, he wrapped lips around the pink pearl and sucked, hard and long. Another grunt, and she deep throated him. At last, his pleasure spilled forth.

He moaned into her pussy as he came. Her tongue wiggled, and she swallowed with each release, but she didn't stop. Lips suckling and sliding up and down his overly sensitive shaft sent him into a louder response. She began grinding on his face, and he licked her up, still moaning as she made his orgasm linger in agonizing height.

At any moment, his hard-on would be lost, but something about the way she licked his dick just made him stay so hard.

I've never lasted this hard after…

Thoughts fell apart as he came again.

Shit!

A fire of arousal made him both numb and sensitive all at once. It suddenly hit him, what she had said before…

"What if I told you I might know a way to speed things along?"

He licked her deeply, and she hummed on his cock. Faster and faster, her lips slid over the swollen shaft. Again, he came back to her clit, and she went deep down on his dick.

If she can keep me…

They both shuddered with the pleasure they bestowed upon one another. He wanted to release again, so soon, but he fought it back. At last, she broke away. Both panted as she turned, straddling his waist again. She lowered her pussy onto his dick. Her hands caressed his chest and torso, and he gripped her hips, shifting his hips to slide a little deeper. Leaning back on his thighs, she took one hand and began playing with herself.

OH she feels amazing…

The rocking on his hips added to how his cock rubbed inside her tight pussy.

"W-wait!" Remi paled. "Shouldn't we get a condom? Can a ghost get… pregnant?"

Jenifer paused. "Wanna find out?"

"Wow." Remi rubbed his eyes. "You're fearless."

Jenifer shrugged. "It seems I have a second chance at love, and life, and well…we are married."

Remi nodded, pondering her situation and his own. "You know we may not get the money."

"I've got a mansion?" she offered.

Remi looked around. "I suppose I can set up my home business here."

She laughed, leaning down to whisper in his ear. "And I look forward to haunting your cock."

He laughed. "And something tells me you mean that." Wrapping his arms around her, they kissed. "Seriously though, are we really going to see what happens?"

"Why the fuck not?" She kissed him again, deeper this time. *I've always wanted a kid… and who better to take this path with…?* "But we just met. I almost ran you over."

"You couldn't run me over," she corrected.

"But now you're saying you want to have a kid with me, a complete stranger?" He could see the frustration building on her face.

"You're right… we barely know…" She tried to pull away but found he hugged her tighter. "Look, let me go…"

He nuzzled her ear, his voice deep. "Beg me for my cock, like you did that first night."

She froze.

"Tell me how badly you want it," he continued as his cock throbbed inside her. "I never want this to end."

"Please…" Her hips grinded against him. "Please give it to me."

He kissed her neck. "Give what to you?"

"Please, Remi…" She tried to sit up, but he kept her body pressed against his. "Please cum inside me."

A smile curved his lips, his heart racing. *I don't think I've ever heard a woman beg for that, and I kind of like it.*

"Fuck me until you cum inside!" Her voice sent excited shivers through him. "I want to make babies with you."

He froze. "Wait, what?" *Did she just say…?*

"I want to make babies with you?" She tensed. "Was that too much?"

Laughter rolled out of him like thunder. "You kill me."

"I'm sorry. That was too awkward." Jenifer buried her face into his shoulder.

"No kidding," he chuckled. "Shall we try again?"

Lifting her face, she kissed him, her hands pressed against his cheeks. "I love you. If this is how you solve problems, I will follow you to the ends of the earth, Remi."

Sighing, he searched her eyes. "You know..." She was so close he could actually see her face clearly. "...I like that idea."

Yeah, we may have just met, but something in my gut says she's the one I've been hoping for. Maybe my luck finally caught up to me...

12

Raw Confessions

I love this man.

Jenifer kissed Remi, dipping her tongue between his lips. She rocked against him, regaining their lost sexual momentum. He still wouldn't allow her to sit up. She tried once more, but his large arms hugged her tighter, her breasts aching from their closeness. His knees lifted, and before she fathomed what he planned on doing, he began fucking her hard. Her body arched, allowing his cock deeper inside her. An orgasm exploded from her, and she tightened around his rock-hard cock.

With each thrust, she could feel the gush of her pussy. Remi began to moan, his dick swelling for a moment, adding to her rising orgasm. Her voice cried out, visceral in the moment as he pushed hard inside her. His cock jerked, the rush of hot cum filling her as she gasped. He slowed his rocking hips, teasing her like she had done with him before. They were both breathless with her still lying on top of him, neither willing to move.

He rubbed her back, and at last, inhaled a deep breath and released it, slowing his breathing. Jenifer cuddled against him, listening to his thudding heart. It sounded like the hooves of a horse trotting across a bridge. After a while, she sat up to find Remi fast asleep. Smiling, she eased away and folded her blanket over him. It didn't completely cover his haphazardly placed body, but it would keep him warm for the time being.

She tip-toed to the wardrobe, opening it to find an array of modern clothes. Again, a note pinned to a skirt made her smile:

Aunt Jeni,

Hope at least some of these tickle your fancy. There will be food downstairs, and a credit card in the far left drawer under the microwave.

Timmy

Looking back to the variety of clothing, she muttered, "What in the hell is a credit card and microwave?"

Remi rolled in his sleep, making the bed squeak. He had managed to burrito himself in the blanket now. Peering back into the wooden wardrobe, she grabbed a skirt and a rather skimpy tank top. She liked this new fashion, had seen it a few times on women driving by or even jogging down the road. Slipping them on, she was out the bedroom door and racing down the stairs.

My, these are so much more.. freeing! And they weigh nothing! No more hoops or corsets, no more lacing. It just pulls on and stretches as needed! How amazing clothes have become!

Tears filled her eyes as she stumbled to a stop in the kitchen. It was so different and grand. The white countertops sparkled, and the sink had a long gooseneck spout. She rushed to the deep sink and marveled over how many pans it could fit all at once.

I could hide dirty dishes in this—it's so deep!

Turning around, she saw many objects she hadn't encountered before. Large metal boxes of varying size caught her curiosity. This largest when opened was cold inside, much like the ice boxes her cousins kept certain times of the year. Food and milk were in strange boxes and containers with colors and writing. She shut that door. The next two seemed to do nothing but light up when the doors were opened.

How strange! Wait, is that... is that a chocolate cake? Oh, maybe later... First, I want to see what the other metal boxes have inside.

Shutting the door, she realized the box said *oven* but had no place for wood or coal.

These all just have racks, but I have no idea what for. I have so much to learn about a kitchen... I wonder if Remi can cook?

The other box said microwave, and she opened the drawer beneath it. Inside were menus and a tiny hard red rectangle with *Timothy van Winkle* embossed into it.

How does this work? Why would anyone want this?

"So this is a credit card..." She flipped it over and over, but it was beyond her. "I'll have to ask Remi how to use this later."

"JENIFER?" Remi voice made her drop the card and slam the drawer closed. "JENIFER!"

He's awake! That was a quick nap!

"IN HERE!" She walked to the entryway. "Remi?"

"WHERE ARE YOU!" His voice echoed through the house.

"Wow, you're loud." She blinked as he wandered butt-naked to the top of the stairwell.

"Yeah, my voice carries for miles." He shrugged, coming downstairs. "Or so I've been told by the neighbors."

"Oh! Oh no." She covered her mouth.

"What's wrong?" He rushed to her, grabbing her shoulders.

"You don't have any clothes." She tried not to laugh at the realization.

"Oh shit." He smirked. "But were you going to even give me the chance to put any on?"

She rolled her eyes and paused when her eyes caught on the old Victorian chair. "You know, that's a good point."

I've always wanted... could we? Why not? After all, this is technically our wedding day... Glancing at the clock, she corrected, *my wedding night.*

He followed her gaze. "Wow, it's already night, huh?" Sashaying past her, he called back. "You hungry? Whoa, check out this kitchen!"

Without any hesitation, Remi started opening and closing cabinets and more. He pulled various items out, laying them on the island counter. Jenifer watched with fascination as he conjured his magic before her. His twisting of knobs and retrieval items from all over left her in awe. He produced eggs without chasing chickens, a flame with no match, and even ingredients she hadn't seen him conjure. He chopped cheese, vegetables, and meat with speed and accuracy. Propping her chin up with her elbows, she watched the wonderous naked chef perform before her.

"Sorry I can't do bacon... or take advantage of those pork chops in there," he announced, mixing eggs. "I'm a little too exposed to risk grease popping and ruining both our night-time fun."

"What are you making, then?" she asked, watching as he added butter to the hot pan, rolling it around.

"Eh, a sort of Western omelet. They didn't have tomatoes or onions." Shrugging, he focused on the task at hand.

Jenifer's stomach grumbled, and her heart skipped a beat. *When was the last time I felt hungry?*

A plate with a perfectly made omelet slid into place, and she took in the glorious smell. The first bite of buttery, fluffy egg with a hint of green pepper and cheese fueled her desire to eat. By the time he finished making his own, joining her on the stool next to her, she had finished a good two-thirds. By the time she cleaned her plate, she realized he had watched her. Slowly, taking another bite of his own omelet, he smiled at her with a sparkle in his eyes.

"You're so damn cute." He snort-giggled and turned to his own meal. "I'll keep cooking for you as long as you keep enjoying my food like that. Deal?"

"Deal." She smiled, stretching with satisfaction. "Thank you. I feel much better."

He was nearing the end of his omelet. "So, I saw you staring at the clock. Was that some epic heirloom?"

Jenifer's face flushed. "I was staring at the chair."

"The chair?" He took one more bite before sliding the plate away.

"Well, besides being the last place I ever sat..." Her fingers balled some of her white cotton skirt to soothe her nervousness.

Remi narrowed his eyes at her. "Were you waiting on someone that day?"

Her eyes shot up to his, paling. "I was waiting on my brother to come get me for my wedding."

Eyes wide, Remi straightened. "Damn. Didn't make it pass the bridge, right?"

Jenifer nodded, her eyes falling across his naked body. "How can you sit there so casually naked like this?"

He shrugged. "What choice do I have? My clothes are in the shower upstairs and I wasn't going to try to walk down those stairs wrapped in that big ass quilt."

Shaking her head, she laughed. "Right."

"So the chair?" He circled back. "Was that all just the memory? I half-expected you to mention your mom or dad."

"N-no, but..." Once more, her face flushed. "I was thinking *we* could use the chair for *something.*"

He smirked, lifting an eyebrow. "Oh?"

"Never mind. I'm just being awkward." She turned away. *What the hell am I thinking? Why would he think this idea is sexy at all?*

The heat of his palm slipped up her leg and thigh. She turned on the stool, gasping as his fingers began rubbing between the folds of her pussy. He pressed his lips hard against hers. She deepened the kiss, and his fingers slid inside her. A moan escaped her lips, and she could feel his hard cock rub against her knee. The very idea had invoked a physical reaction.

He wants me like I want him. That desire to explore one another, to bring pleasure upon him in any way I can manage. I've never felt loved or love so strong for someone until I met him. Every moment self-sacrificing and unquestioning. How precious of a person you are, Remi.

13

Haunted House

He loved how her tongue forced its way into his mouth only to coax his own to be caught between her suckling lips. Abandoning his initial play, he knew she was wet and ready. He thought of her growing excitement at the thought of him and her... *on that chair? I think I can accommodate that little fantasy.*

Scooping her up in his arms, Remi stood up from the stool. Jenifer hung onto his neck, eagerness on her face. He stopped in front of the chair.

Crap. Do I put her in the chair or do I sit or...?

"You think I could still sit on it if you're sitting there?" It seemed she was trying to figure the logistics out as well.

"You mean my cock?" He let her down on her feet. "I don't know if I'm hard enough for that."

"I can fix that."

She pushed on his chest, and he fell into the chair. It was wide enough for her to spread his legs open, kneeling before him. The way her skirt flared out all around her only added to his rising desire.

Her warm palm and finger wrapped around his dick, rubbing and stroking. They locked eyes, and she smiled. Leaning in to where her breath washed over his cock sent a shudder through his shoulders. Her nipples were hard under the thin tank top. Licking his lips, he wanted to suckle them, to tease them between his teeth once more.

She blew a stream of air across the underbelly of his cock, still stroking him with her fingers. His eyes were back on her own, and she opened her plump lips. Goosebumps rolled over him as he watched her lick him from base to tip. It had felt so amazing earlier, but watching it now added a new layer of arousal. A second lick took his breath away, and his body tensed with provocative want. His fingers gripped the chair arms. Another lick, and he shifted to press his cock firmly against her tongue.

Fucking glasses... I need to invest in some damn contacts because I would pay good money for a less foggy version of what I am watching her do to my dick. Son of a bitch.

Her tongue circled the mushroom cap, and he groaned. With agonizing slowness, she slid her lips over and down the length of his cock. Before the tip hit the back of her throat, he gave a disapproving grunt. She made a pop as she let go and grinned. Wet with her saliva, her stroking fingers brought on greater pleasure. She twisted her hand, the tips of her fingers sliding across new places.

Fighting the urge to close his eyes, he watched her again take his cock into her mouth. She didn't rush any part of the blow job, and he wouldn't dare disrupt it. Every moment added to his pleasure, his blood rushing as he fought the urge to push deeper down her throat. He wanted to linger on this agonizing edge, savoring each passing moment, drowning in the way she toyed with him.

I could die a happy man...

Pulling away, she stood, clearly debating which way to face. He laughed, pulling her onto him so she faced his chest. Placing her hands on his shoulders, he was quick to have his hands under her skirt and pull her into position. She slid her knees forward, skin pressed against his thighs and into the back of the chair, and he ran his hands along her curves, piling the skirt at her waist. Her pussy was dripping wet as he guided himself inside.

"But the skirt..." She shifted in the chair for a better angle.

"Fuck me in your skirt," he told her.

She blinked, but he throbbed inside her, and she tightened in response. "As you wish, husband."

"I fucking love you."

She laughed, gripping his shoulders tight as she began to rock her hips slowly back and forth. "You feel so damn good."

Weaseling his hands out of the skirt, he watched the pleasure on her face with each tilt of her hips. He goaded her to change method, and at last, she bounced up and down. His cock hard inside her, she moved him in and out of her. She began moaning, arching her back as she closed her eyes, head tilted back. Pulling at her tank top, he freed a breast and latched onto her nipple. Hungry, he supported her angle, allowing her to rely on the strength of his arm to bring them both deeper pleasure.

He moaned into her breast, and her fingers gripped the back of his head, keeping him there suckling and teasing. She found a combination of rocking and bouncing, his cock growing harder with each thrust. Her skirt fluttered with each drop and rise, and all at once, they peaked together. Both moaned as her thighs hugged his hips. He pushed hard into her, panting, rocking into the last of the orgasm.

They relaxed, and she leaned back with a wondrous smile.

"Is that what you wanted?" he asked, hands running down her back.

"Yeah..." She bit her lip in thought before voicing the curiosity haunting her. "Where else can we have sex, you think?"

Remi's eyebrows raised high. "You want to go around having sex on furniture?"

She shrugged, batting her eyes at him. "Yeah, I kind of do."

With that, he lifted her off his lap and rose from the Victorian chair. Peering up the stairs then back to the kitchen, his mind raced. Looking back to Jenifer, he frowned. She was rubbing her knee, the swelling kneecap making it clear that he would have to be more mindful with the next spot for intercourse to unfold.

The bed is out of the question. Oh the counter top but... she may not want to bend that knee. Oh, I know!

Without warning, he chucked her over his shoulder. Up the stairs he went with her giggling the whole way. They reached the bedroom, and he put her back on her feet in front of the mirror-topped dresser. She glanced around with a confused expression. When he gestured for her to turn around, she saw him standing naked behind her.

"Your knee doesn't like to bend, right?" He smiled at her in the mirror.

"Right." Her breath caught as his hands snaked in front of her.

One traveled up and beneath her top to grope a breast. The other dove under the waistband of her skirt, sliding between her thighs to her already sensitive clit. She stiffened, and he moved them closer to the dresser. His breath poured over her shoulder, and goosebumps rippled across her skin. Her palms landed flat on the dresser as he played with her, massaging her breast. He loved being able to watch her face as he touched her.

"Is this an okay angle?" His hands retreated to her hips. "Your knee okay if...?"

"Fuck me."

"My pleasure." He smirked.

Pulling up the back of her skirt, he bunched it on top of her hips. The tip of his cock rubbed against the opening of her pussy. She bent over deeper, an arm on top of the dresser. It was more than enough for him to slip inside her pink folds. They moaned together as he slid inside her. His grip on her hips tightened, and he caught her gaze in the mirror.

He gave her a stern look. "Fast and hard this time, then you rest your knee. Got it?"

"Yes, sir."

He pulled back, watching his cock slide back like the hammer on a revolver. When they locked gazes in the mirror again, it was the last thing he saw. The heat spilled over him, the pleasure of his cock thrusting in and out, hard and fast. Her eyes clenched, Jenifer gripped the dresser, thighs bouncing against the lip of the dresser. The mirror wobbled, threatening to break free. Remi shoved forward, releasing with a groan. Her pussy tightened on him, a gush of wet heat soaking his thighs as the mirror cracked.

"Oh no!" Jenifer pulled up and away as the shards fell across the dresser. "That's bad luck!"

"If that means seven years of bad luck for me having you haunting my dick, is it really bad luck at all?" Remi marveled.

They laughed, the adrenaline keeping them going as he pulled her to the bed. Laying side-by-side, he pulled her into him. She smelled wonderful, like peach blossoms in spring. Fighting the weight of sleep, he let his daydreams fill his mind before he dared to voice them at last.

"I think I like the idea of making a mini-me or mini-Jen." He sighed.

"You promise to cook, right? I'll make the babies; you make the dinner." She held his arms around her.

"I'll cook everything but fish," he offered. "I'm allergic."

"Gross. I hate fish."

"My God, where have you been all my life?" he breathed.

"Stuck on a bridge waiting for you to come pick me up, apparently."

Epilogue

Two women raced up the muddy slope and fought one another to enter the old farmhouse. The television crew turned, catching the cat fight rolling into the receiving room where Bailey guffawed over the shrieking, wet duo. At last, the weight of the eyes in the room was enough to make them let go of one another's hair and make an attempt to straighten their drenched clothes.

Both had blonde pixie cuts, and the overdone makeup had a few of the crew whisper-wondering if they were siblings. They both peered around, but one stepped forward. Pointing a zebra-striped manicured finger, she came full force at Bailey.

"You! You're the agent in charge of my contract." She snatched the name tag on Bailey's lanyard, jerking the woman forward. "My stepfather put me up to this, and I expect to be treated as a guest of honor."

"K-Karen?" Blinking, Bailey jerked her tag back. "Where have you been? You were supposed to be here days ago."

"Well, my flight to Hawaii got cancelled, and I figured why not go through with this? At least I might become famous." She looked around and pointed at the emo-intern. "Are you Remi?"

"No," Bobby scoffed.

"Hey, bitch, Remi belongs to me." The other woman at last spoke up, the camera man still recording since the fight during their grand entrance.

"What?" Karen spun to shriek at Bailey. "You let him marry her? She was riding my ass all the way from Gainesville!"

"N-no." Bailey marveled over the squabbling women. "I don't even know who *she* is?"

"Bitch, I'm Monica."

Silence fell over the room. Thunder rumbled, and Monica heaved her double-D breasts, stretching the tiger-striped tank top to its limits. Eyebrows lifted around the room, everyone watching to see if the fabric might give way. A feral cat-like hiss erupted from her hot pink lips as she shoved past Karen. The producer's step-daughter lost her balance and landed in the arms of two stagehands who pushed the woman back to her feet for fear she might bite.

"Where is my Remi?" Monica backed Bailey against the wall. "I am here to take what is mine home! How dare he marry someone other than me!"

Bailey paled, then cleared her throat. "He's not here."

"Wait!" Karen joined Monica. "Isn't that the lame-ass home business douche I was supposed to marry for extra cash?"

"He married for money?" Everyone could see the whites of Monica's eyes. "But I have money!"

Clearing his throat, Bobby stepped into the open. "Like she said, he's long gone. We think he got washed away on the bridge."

"WHAT?" Monica spun on her stiletto heels with the grace of a pole dancer.

"His car was on fire. They said lightning hit it."

"Wow... talk about bad luck." Karen shuddered. "Poor bastard."

"They didn't find his body but..." Everyone paled, the silence this time eerie and unsettling as eyes darted away. Hail Marys started around the room as several crew members crossed themselves.

"What's the matter with all of you?" Karen walked up beside Monica, former anger subdued into curiosity.

"What the fuck happened to my Remi?" Monica's Boston accent had boiled to the surface.

Bobby waved for them to follow him upstairs. No one dared to follow the trio. He led them down the hall and into the master bedroom. On a desk was a small LED screen and desktop computer. He sat down, booting it up as the two glared at one another, claws out again. The window suddenly blew open, the rain and wind kicking up with the residual bands of the hurricane that had raged for days.

"Look, I would have been here sooner, but the bridge was out," Karen started, feeling the need to justify herself.

"We seriously think he and the ghost bride were washed away." The intern's words dropped like a stone.

"Ghost bride?" Monica scoffed, rolling her eyes. "You can't be serious."

"Look, this is the last footage we have of him." Bobby twisted back to the two women, their arms crossed and faces unamused. "They didn't know we had hidden cameras in some of the rooms. I swear to you, two people walked into this room that night. I saw her, touched her, hell—even wanted to have sex with that woman in white. None of us knew she was a ghost yet." He frowned, crossing his arms. "Bailey certainly has a signature clear as day on that marriage certificate she mailed out."

"Oh my... this is stupid." Karen started to walk out of the room. "First that whole Blue Lady ghost story, and now this. I am going home. Fuck this."

Bobby turned back to the computer, pulling up the video, and Karen paused, curious now. Both women leaned in. The frozen frame showed Remi in drenched clothes carrying an armful of toiletries and sweats. He seemed to be talking to someone or something as he marched in. There, floating in the middle of the screen, was a light orb. Monica practically climbed over the emo-intern to rewind the video, cranking up the volume as they watched the conversation play out with a single entity in the room. He had pushed the orb into the room.

"Alright!" Remi said loudly.

He closed the door and rushed to unload his arms onto the bed. The orb hovered close behind him for a moment before travelling to the door and back to him. Remi glanced over his shoulder and smiled, turning back to divide the items evenly as if for two people.

"There, I suppose you should use the shower first," he announced to the orb. "W-wait, what are—"

Static popped and clicked, a faint voice disrupted by the ruined audio.

"Look, we just met and..." Remi stumbled, looking at something as the orb brightened. At last, he whispered, "Dammit, you're gorgeous."

They could see Remi's breath in the air as a shudder shook his shoulders. His pants fell to the floor. He jolted in surprise, stopping by the bed. He sat in alarm, shaking his head as if agreeing to something. Pulling off his shirt, he muttered about his missing glasses. The video scrambled and ended with pops and a click.

"Wait, what happened?" Monica shook the mouse, rewinding the video to watch it again. "Where's the rest?"

"That's all we got. After that, not another hidden camera worked. We didn't check the footage until way after." He turned to look at Karen, who was on her way out the door.

"First, Mark Wilder, now this Remi guy..." Karen bitched. "Fuck this! I'm going home."

THE END

Beating it
WITH
Bloody Mary
Honey Cummings
Urban Legend Erotica Collection

 Table of Contents

Dedication

1

A Storm Was Coming

Mary couldn't remember how she ended up imprisoned inside this dark place or anything else about herself—not even her last name. *This blows.* Everywhere in the pitch-black abyss looked like stars sparkling, fading in and out without a pattern. Upon further inspection, Mary discovered candles and flashlights coming from behind pools of dark mirrors that held strange faces and unknown places. Each portal was a copy of the mirror on her side, whether a medicine cabinet, hand mirror, or even large wooden heirloom mirrors.

They come in waves; it's always dark as night on their side, and they are terrified out of their minds. No matter who they were or where they came from, they whispered the same thing from all directions as she stood in an endless space where she was neither dead nor living. *I suppose I was terrified when I used to dabble in the occult, too.*

"Bloody Mary, Bloody Mary, Bloody Mary."

Did I die and become Bloody Mary? Am I in some sort of Purgatory or... Her chest ached as she dropped to her knees. *Is this my personal Hell? Did I do something terrible? Why can't I remember?*

"Hell Mary, Hell Mary, Hell Mary."

Her heart throbbed inside her chest as she searched the mirrors of murmurs, all saying her name in one manner or another, some less dark than others. *I've been here for so long that I've lost track of time. Should I just give up entirely on the idea of escaping?*

"Mary Worth, Mary Worth, Mary Worth. Nothing is happening. Ugh."

Sometimes, they whispered it three times; other times, they performed the chant ten times. *Five. I think the number is five when it does something different.* Others squinted their eyes at the mirror, looking through her as she pushed on the glass and beat her fists against it in hopes something would change. Smells, warmth, and even a ripple in the mirror would hint something was happening on that fifth repeat of her name.

Please, tell me some of them can see me trapped in this dark tower of mirrors? At times, she would lock eyes, and for a fleeting moment, a look of recognition and fear would cross their faces before they ran away or the mirror dissolved like dust in the wind. In those moments, she tried to escape but found she couldn't even get a strand of hair to cross the glass of the mirror.

Flopping onto her back, Mary huffed. *I'm so overdressed for this bullshit.* She fought with the red skirts of what looked more like a prom dress than a dress for a gala or cocktail party. Her halter top fit snugly enough not to slip easily down her torso, but it left little protection from the chill that crept through this wall-less prison. *I'm so bored.* She glanced over at a mirror; the bluish glow emanating from it made her arch a brow. A flick of a finger brought the mirror closer. *At least I mastered that trick. Before, I was walking a mile to get to one.*

A broad-shouldered man was beating on a door while holding a glowing rectangle. "Hey! Don't do this," he roared. "You can't lock me in here all night!"

Propping up on her elbows, she snorted to herself. *Is that a smartphone? I suppose that counts as a flashlight.* She bit her lip in thought. *He hasn't said my name, so why can I hear and see him?*

"Come on! I know hazing is outdated, but this is still hazing guys!" He flopped his back against the door and slid to the floor. "At least I have my cell phone," he mumbled.

"Cell phone?" Mary lurched forward to sit fully. "Since when did they stop looking like glowing, building bricks? How long have I fucking been here for him to say it's a mere cellphone? I mean, when I was there, it was cell phone and the smart phone. And what was it? Ah, yes, the iPhone and Omnia?" She called the mirror even closer, squinting her eyes into the darkness in hopes of getting a better look. "Man, why do I have to watch technology improve with no means to play with it?"

A loud huff escaped the man as he glared down at his phone, occasionally tapping his thumb on it. He looked Latino, with hazel eyes, a five o'clock shadow, and a bald-fade haircut. A strong jawline led her eyes to his pronounced Adam's apple and collarbone that peaked out of his wide-neck, raglan shirt. The sleeves were pushed up to his elbows, exposing strong forearms and angular wrist bones. The clean-cut college boy dripped of masculinity.

"Hello, sir." Mary held the edges of the old, vintage, body mirror, her body warming with arousal at the eye candy before her. "But he hasn't said my name or the chant? Well, who am I not to take advantage of this moment and enjoy myself for once." She bit her lip, contemplating the mischievous deeds and desires stirring at her core. "I've been inadvertently summoned countless times by women named Mary being fucked within sight of a mirror. I mean, it's not like he can see me." Hissing, she continued to think out loud. "Does this make me some kind of creepy pervert? I just need some visuals to get off..."

Knocking on the closet door made them both jolt. "We need to hear you say it, CJ!" someone shouted.

"Fine." Exasperated, CJ mumbled something quickly under his breath.

"LOUDER!" The cackling from the unseen group annoyed Mary as much as it did CJ. "And you better be in front of the mirror."

"You better let me out of this closet after this," growled CJ as he looked around the room.

She could have sworn their eyes met, and it made her face flush. He shuffled closer, and she held her breath as if he might discover her and her naughty thoughts. Reaching out, he gripped the mirror in the same place she held it. A warm sensation hit her hands, and she let go, gasping. *What the hell was that? Is he some sort of wizard?* Glaring at the mirror, his eyes had lost hers, and a pang of regret ached in her chest. In fact, she swore she could feel the heat of his body through the magic of the mirror, and her body throbbed with want.

I must be beyond horny to be so sensitive to his every look and touch. To feel the heat of a man in my arms again... Licking her lips, she pulled her skirt up, hands trailing up her inner thighs as she began to play with herself. *I'm doing it. Even if he sees me for a moment, it's not like he knows I'm a real person desperate to cum.* Her pussy slick with anticipation, she circled her pink pearl. *Oh, I'm more than ready...* A jolt of pleasure shot through her, and his eyes locked on hers. *It's been so long.* She held her breath. *Don't look away... I'm so into this moment... Please don't look away.* Her fingers slid back down, dipping inside, and she inhaled swiftly with a wave of pleasure.

"Bloody Mary." His voice was deep, and his eyes were on her as he spoke her name. "Bloody Mary."

Mary inhaled deeply as she retreated to her clit, circling ever faster. "That's it, baby." He licked his lips, clearing his throat. "Keep saying my name." She exhaled as she began to edge on the verge of an orgasm. "Oh, how I wish we could hook up right here and now."

"Bloody Mary," he called to her, his voice low and provocative. "Bloody Mary."

Her fingers dipped inside her flower, and she hummed. *So close... don't stop... one more time...* she pleaded in silence, eyelids heavy as she retreated once more, circling as she inhaled. Each movement was more sensitive than the last. The electric shock of pleasure made her flinch and shake. The scent of cologne filled the air, sending a shiver through her body. *It's almost as if he can touch me. Please touch me...* She closed her eyes as the peak of her orgasm teasingly teetered just out of reach. *So close...*

"Bloody Mary." The deep roll of his voice made her inhale.

"Fuck, yes!" she exclaimed as she climaxed, dipping her fingers deep into her pussy, stroking fast and hard.

His hands passed through the mirror's threshold, and he fell toward her. "What the fuck!" he shouted.

The weight and feel of him on top of her added to her climax, and she crested higher. "Fuck me!" she squealed in ecstasy.

Her thighs attempted to close but found a man's hot torso between them. Wide-eyed, she glared up at him, and in her lust, gripped his shirt and pulled him closer. He didn't refuse; as their lips met, she deepened the kiss. As if caught in her spell, she could hear him unbuckling and unzipping. The heat of his hand rubbing her swollen pussy made her grind against his fingers, and he moaned in her lips, tongues entangled. He pulled away, biting her lip before freeing his hard cock from his pants. Both panted with erotic excitement.

"Who are you?" He had come to his senses and tried to retreat, but her ankles locked behind him.

"Does it matter?" With her heart pounding, her mind raced with how to keep him there. *I can't let this chance pass me.* "Fuck me. I want you so badly. Please, fuck me."

"I don't know who you are..." She tugged him closer, wrapping her thighs tightly around his hard planes. "But you're not gonna let me leave." A haphazard smirk crossed his face, and at last, naughty desires flashed in his eyes. "I'm CJ; I assume you're Mary?" he offered.

"Fuck me, CJ," she demanded, earning a growl in response as he contemplated the offer.

"Please tell me your name is Mary." CJ's eyes snaked down her body before resting on the apex of her thighs where his hands slid, slow and hot to her throbbing desire. "So wet…"

"You summoned me; now give me what I want," she commanded.

"I thought you took souls," he snorted. His fingers slid over her opening before dipping his long, thick fingers inside her channel.

Her face flushed, and she snarked, "Well, the Victorians thought this was soul-taking, so let's die a little tonight."

"You have no idea how lucrative that sounds to an English major with a Victorian Era history understudy." CJ sucked on a cheek with a look of wonder on his face. "Who are you?"

"Don't tell anyone, but I'm really into nerds." Turning her head away, her commanding attitude began to falter. *Shit, I can't.* Squeezing her eyes shut, she cursed herself. *Fuck, fuck, fuck! He's going to leave before I even get his cock inside me!*

2

Beyond the Limit of Their Bond

The girl was pale, almost glowing in the darkness of the closet. CJ Galdur struggled to make out his surroundings, but he couldn't tear his eyes away from the lustful beauty he found himself on top of. *Am I still in the closet? Is this the plan: get the new fraternity brother laid? I'm game for that. She's fucking gorgeous and ready to go!* Black tendrils of hair fanned out, framing her flushed cheeks and deep red lips. Her dark eyes and alluring voice cut through him. She had gotten him hard instantly. *How did I not notice her in the closet with me? What kind of girl is willing to bang the new guy and be ready...*

He grabbed her chin, turning her eyes back to his. "I want your eyes on me, Mary."

He pressed the top of his cock against her opening and her breath caught, thighs squeezing him in anticipation. Slowly, he rocked his hips forward, and he watched her arch along with him. The strapless red dress in the dark closet made her look like a long-forgotten deity of desire. Her pussy tightened around his hard shaft as he pushed deeper inside her wet heat until he was buried to his hilt. A moan escaped her as she rocked against him, pulsing and throbbing, edging him closer to an orgasm.

Leaning down and kissing her neck, he whispered, "I wasn't expecting to take the flyers[1] today..."

She retorted, "And I wasn't expecting the town bull to wreck my china shop today."

They paused and chuckled over it before he shook his head, meeting her gaze. "Who are you?"

"Doesn't matter." Mary squeezed her channel tight around his cock, swaying her hips and making him shudder. "Now, give me a bit of your soul, would you kindly?"

Locking lips, she suckled on his tongue as he began fucking her, slow and steady. Pulling back just far enough for the ridge of his cap to catch the muscles at her opening, CJ teased her by hovering there. At last, agonizingly slowly, he slid deep into her, hips connecting once more. He slid in and out, slowly still. Mary wiggled with frustration.

"Faster, harder," she pleaded.

"Patience," he admonished.

Weaving his arms under her, he managed to find the top latch and zipper at the back of her dress. The heat of her hands slid under his shirt, gliding over the ripples of his ribs before clawing at his back. Ramming hard and fast inside her, he tugged the dress down to expose her breasts and mocha-colored areolas. Mary arched, nails scratching across his shoulder blades in reply. She moaned as her legs shook. Her honey dripped between them with each motion, spurring him on to keep her exploding.

---

[1] Figure of speech meaning to take a chance against the odds, or make a choice without knowing the outcome

Biting Mary's lip, CJ sucked it playfully as if teasing her about where he aimed to be next. She wiggled on his hard cock as he kissed down her porcelain neck, white as snow, leaving red and purple blossoms leading downward until he reached her nipple. Lips wrapped around the bud as the tip of his tongue circled. CJ snaked a hand between her legs, finding her clit with his thumb. She bucked in reply, and he let go of her swollen nipple.

"Keep that up and we might really blow off the groundsills," he mocked with another circle and buck.

"Shit, I shouldn't have tossed off before..." Her breath caught as his cock jumped inside her.

His smile widened. "You started without me? How long have they had you in this closet?"

"I don't want to talk about it." Her thighs squeezed as she tightened around his throbbing member inside her. "Fuck me until we die, you nerd."

"As you wish, Bloody Mary," he cooed, leaning down to suckle on the other nipple.

Circling his thumb on her clit, he could feel her drawing ever closer to another orgasm. She kept trying to say something but couldn't; she tightened and jolted as he played with her more aggressively. Catching her nipple in his teeth, he tugged and pinched. A gush and pulsing teamed with her cry. He had set her orgasm into full bloom, reaching a new height. Riding his hands up her legs, he found her hips hidden deep in the red curtains of the dress and began hammering her, hard and fast. She arched until she lifted off the ground, lifting her knees for deeper penetration. As her nails dug deep into his back, he pulled out, stroking as he came across her red dress and breasts.

CJ moaned. His eyes stayed on her as he came, cum sparkling across her body underneath him. "Sorry, not ready for basket making." He gave a coy smile as he continued the exchange of dated terms.

She threw her hand over her face, chuckling. "And this is my only dress... so that's going to be interesting."

CJ leaned back and knelt between her open legs. "If that's the case, I owe you a dress. That was ... amazing."

She frowned. She opened her mouth to say something but clamped shut fast. Frustrated by the sudden sour shift, he began rubbing between her swollen, hot petals. She gasped and gripped his wrist in alarm. His fingertips played with her hardened pearl and teased the weeping gash.

"Don't... I don't think, oh!" she gasped, stopping her words.

Her strength didn't stop him from dipping two fingers inside, stroking. A visceral scream escaped her, and her knees clamped hard into his ribs as she came again. Her orgasm, violent and sudden, exploded with a gush of fluid as she came. Not satisfied, CJ didn't stop until her voice hit a new pitch and a fountain exploded forth. Her fingers tight on his wrist, she stared up, wide-eyed and panting.

"What did you do to me?" She marveled over what he had summoned forth. "Th-that's a first. So many firsts, but that..."

"If you misbehave and get sad, I'll have to do it again to teach you a lesson," he warned, hazel eyes glowing in the abyss as he licked his fingers. "You understand?"

"Oh, you're something else." She looked at her dress, now wet and cum-stained, and smirked. "Something to remember you by?"

"Maybe, but..." Tucking himself away, he spun around and began searching the floor. "I want your number to take you out on a proper date." He found his phone by the door and unlocked it to see several missed calls and messages. "Damn, didn't even notice everyone blowing it up." Spinning around, he found himself alone. "M-Mary?"

He was met with silence as he stared at his reflection in the mirror; cum was splattered across the glass. *What the fuck?* Crawling back, he looked behind it and felt all around the closet in a panic. *Where the hell did she go? Don't tell me there's a door over here.*

Nothing. His heart thudded hard in his chest, and he read the texts he had missed.

[FratBoss: Where the fuck r u?] Friday, October 13, 11:33 a.m.

[Mark: How da fuck u get out of a locked closet?] Saturday, October 14, 1:12 a.m.

[FratBoss: Not cool man. Where did u go?] Saturday, October 14, 2:45 a.m.

[Timmah: Dude. Call me when you get back. We need to talk.] Saturday, October 14, 3:33 a.m.

[Unknown: Hey this is Geo. Frat Boss is looking for you. Call him at 321-555-1234 in case you don't got his number bro] Saturday, October 14, 2:41 p.m.

[Mark: I'm in a situation. Heard you ghosted the fraternity after haze. We'll talk when I get back to normal. I'm with Tim trying to figure out what the fuck he did to me.] Sunday, October 15, 7:23 p.m.

[Timmah: Look, don't do anything too crazy until I get back. I fucked up man, the hazing for you and Mark, it backfired. Please tell me you're alive.] Sunday, October 15, 8:37 p.m.

[School: You were reported absent today.] Monday, October 16, 7:48 a.m.

[FratBoss: It's been 2 days. Plz call me ASAP.] Monday, October 16, 9:45 a.m.

He swallowed; time didn't make sense anymore. "Was I in this closet whacking off to the mirror for three days? What the fuck did they slip in my fucking drink?"

[CJ: What the fuck did you put in my drink]
[FratBoss: Where r u?]

CJ stood and tried to open the closet, but it remained lock.

[CJ: Still in the closet, asshole]

He heard a huge scuffle, and the door swung open. Everyone was dumbfounded as they looked at one another. *What the hell is going on?* Relief filled their faces, and they all started to laugh; the fraternity leader and a professional student of almost twenty years, Jason, patted him on his shoulder. CJ furrowed his brow, looking back to the closet and to his phone. *It's almost completely dead at three percent, yet I had a full charge when I went in here.* His stomach knotted.

"Man, that's a damn good prank," reassured Jason. "You didn't mention you were a magician; that's impressive."

CJ looked over them, not sure what to say. "No one slipped something in my drink, did they? Acid? Peyote? Shrooms?"

There was another exchange of visibly confused faces.

"No, man," Geo spoke up, throwing his hands up. "They would shut the whole fraternity down and kick us out of school over that."

CJ scrolled through his phone and asked, "Where's Timmy? Wasn't he the one that set this up?"

"You know," hummed Jason, looking overly thoughtful. "When did that short bastard haul ass on us?"

"He said something about Mark," answered CJ. "The last guy that just joined the frat, right?"

"Oh, shit, Marky-Mark?" Geo waved a hand. "He swapped the Lady in Blue Ghost Challenge days and figured it would cheer the poor guy up. His girl got caught fucking an AbraXus Tasker College kicker, so he set him up for a wild weekend."

Maybe that's it. They just hook us up with one-night stands, thought CJ.

"Wasn't that this weekend?" Jason arched a brow.

CJ pushed through them, tapping on his cell phone and ignoring anything else they had to offer. *If Timmy set this up, he must know her. I could not care less for these asshats.*

[CJ: I need Mary's number. Now.]

[Timmah: Who the hell is Mary? I don't currently know anyone named Mary. Did she mention me?]

Covering his mouth, CJ glared at himself in the hallway mirror. *Was it a dream?* Lifting his shirt, he could see the scratches, and a shudder rolled over him. *Who the hell is Mary? And how do I find her?*

If Love is Perfect

Tugging up her dress, Mary muttered curses under her breath. "My legs are like a newborn deer, and I'm a wreck." Smirking, she raised her eyebrows high and confessed, "At least I got laid. That hasn't happened ever since…" her voice trailed off. *All I know is, I've been here.*

Wiggling her body, she shimmied the dress until it slid up, covering her breasts. Looking down, she scoffed. *I'm still … sticky. Great. I should have locked my ankles harder so he would have cum some place less … messy. It's not like a ghost woman can get knocked up. I mean, if I am Bloody Mary, right? But I don't have any other dress or clothes. Fuck my life.*

Reaching behind her, Mary groaned. Her arms stretched behind, doing battle with the open flaps of her gown. She couldn't get the zipper all the way up, let alone latch it. *Are you kidding me? Am I going to face the next few decades holding this dress up? Had to pick a halter top, didn't you, Mary? Straps aren't sexy, and this has easy off and on features. My ass!* Frustrated, she tucked the skirt between her legs to sop up the wetness that had dribbled down them. *Maybe I can get him back here to help me out...*

"Who was that magical man?" Looking at the twinkling mirrors that spanned across the darkness, she noticed one brighter than the rest. "Is... is that daylight?" She flicked a finger, and it shot across the room and paused to float before her. "You got to be fucking kidding me?"

The reflection was indeed daylight, and much to her delight, CJ stood on the other side of the pool. He lifted his shirt, exposing the marks she had left behind in her ecstasy. A smile crested her face, and he smiled in unison. *I guess we both left a little something to remember each other by. Shame he didn't take me with him.* Her heart broke as he walked out of view. *Maybe one day, we can...* The pain made her drop back to the floor, clutching her disheveled skirt.

Looking down at her dress Mary cringed. *Ah, how am I going to shower here? I'm just a cum-covered apparition in the mirror now. Gross.* She frowned before making herself laugh. *How ridiculous is this whole situation?* Her anxiety tightened in her chest and throat again, and she shook her head. *Think about something else,* she demanded to herself.

"Time passes fast over there, doesn't it? I've seen faces age in a matter of weeks. Is it that time has no meaning anymore and weeks were really years? I have no idea if it's been a few hours or days since we..." Her heart leapt to her throat, and she fought to hold back the tears. "How easily will you forget me, mystery man who entered this place and left as soon as you wished? Hmmm, CJ?"

With a wave of her hand, she called forth an assortment of mirrors. *If I can only track him. He's at least interesting enough, no? Will he call my name again? Even then, will I hear it among a thousand others?* Giving chase to him proved difficult. Ignoring the echoes and mutters of those trying to summon her, she searched for him and his voice among the waves of glittering pools. Candles came and went like fluttering fireflies. Flashlights beamed like lighthouses that had lost their purpose and no longer functioned to salvage the lost souls at sea or warn of rocky shores.

"This is pointless," she murmured in defeat.

Waving her arm, the mirrors soared away, and Mary began her aimless march. *Where the hell are my shoes?* The dress started sliding down, and she yanked it up. *Ugh, this marble floor is cold, and that old carpet that appears on occasion is gross. Blegh.* Turning at random, the mirrors grew in size as she clenched her teeth. *There must be more portals to look through, more to this place than I realize. If he can travel here and leave, maybe I just need to find the mirror I came through.* Another tug of the dress and she stumbled to a stop, spinning to look at all the mirrors behind her. A flash of the Terracotta Army came to mind, and she scoffed.

"How did I get here?" she shouted, but her voice didn't even echo in the emptiness. "I WANT THE FUCK OUT," she screeched, straining her voice to the point of breaking.

Closing her eyes, she searched her memories. A song played from a nearby mirror, though a new decade had passed since she last heard it. *That's right, I've heard this song. I loved this song.* Adjusting the skirts, she sat down with her elbows on her thighs and propped her face on her hands. Holding onto the nostalgic sensation working itself into knots at her core, she pushed to uncover the fuzzy flashbacks lingering just out of reach. *That's right, that night, at the dance...*

"Mary, I thought you were coming with Jason?" A voice from her past shook her awake.

Opening her eyes, she found herself in front of a mirror, lipstick in hand. "W-wait..." Blinking, she stared at her reflection and dropped the bright red stick. "I'm..."

Startled, she watched as lipstick smudged the snow-white sink and turned to find herself in a public restroom. *I've seen this place before.* Outside the doors, she could hear the familiar song, yet behind her, the entire wall was covered by a massive mirror. A shudder raced over her body. Her heart leapt, and she backed up against the bathroom stalls. Someone shrieked in the stall behind her.

"Damnit, Mary! That scared me!" A toilet flushed, and a blonde-haired girl with green eyes frowned as she stepped out from the stall. "So, Jason... he finally ditch you?"

"I..." Shuffling out of her way, she arrived at the sink and frowned at the lipstick. "Sorry, I'm not ... myself?" Mary locked eyes with her reflection, and it flashed as if seeing herself in the abyss. "I don't know what the fuck is happening right now."

"Look, sorry I didn't say anything about it, but you know how the debutants are around here." The girl scoffed, washing her hands. "Man, why'd you drop the lipstick? I wanted to put that shade on."

Mary shook her head, bolting out of the bathroom into the crowd of party goers. Clutching her chest, she spun in the crowd, lost in the roar of music and her beating heart. A disco ball spun overhead; lights of all colors scattered over the crowd, everyone dressed like they were attending a high school prom. Every girl wore a fluffy skirt or heavy dress—popular in the late 80s or early 90s. Pushing through people, Mary made it to a buffet table. An assortment of alcohol took up most of the real estate, and she leaned on it.

Was it a dream? Or did someone slip something to me? Slapping her cheeks, she stared at the banner on the table: "Party like it's 1999."

"Is that you, Mary?" A male voice made her heart flutter. She turned, hoping for CJ but found a stranger. "Where's Jason? I thought you two..."

"N-not here," she stuttered. Mary tucked a lock of hair behind her ear, and her eyes darted down to her now clean dress. "I'm sorry; I must be going."

"Uh oh." He gripped her arm before she could leave. "Did he finally break up with you?"

Shit, I can't remember ... anything. Tears welled up in her eyes from frustration. "I need to sit down; I'm not feeling so great."

"Look, I mean, we all knew." He let go, and she darted back through the crowd.

Why don't I remember these people? What year is it? Where am I? Shoving out double doors, she found herself alone in a hallway. *There are no lockers, so this isn't a high school.* Walking down the hall, she searched the posters and flyers for clues. *There!* She doubled back to a flyer. *2013. These have events for 2013 and college dorm news and more. I'm a college student. But is this the present or past? Does CJ even exist?*

"Mary." The voice startled her, and she twisted to face him. "I thought you left?" He was handsome, and her heart fluttered at the man before her—blue eyes, blonde hair, and tanned skin, all packaged in a tuxedo. "Nevermind that," he deflected, glancing down and away. "Look, if I knew you were coming, we, well, I would have..."

"Jason." His name fell from her lips as a wall of bitter emotions exploded in her core. "I don't care anymore."

"Excuse me?" He met her gaze, knitting his brow in confusion. "Mary, I know you're confused about why I broke it off with you yesterday, but—"

Her chest stung, and she cut him off. "But nothing! I've already forgotten you, and it's not like you've come looking for me." Mary clamped her lips closed. *He doesn't know I've been trapped. This is just a memory in a mirror. He probably just thinks I left to save face or dropped out and ghosted everyone.*

"I see." Jason's tone softened, and he turned his back to her. "Sorry, I saw you rush out here and thought it was because you saw me. I was mistaken. Look, I'll see you at the after party at our frat house." And with that, he stomped off, shoving through the double doors back into the party.

I wasn't important enough for you to even remember when I went missing, she mouthed to herself as a tear slid down her cheek. *I want someone to at least remember me and sincerely miss me.*

The hallway lights started to flicker, and the room grew darker. Closing her eyes, Mary steeled herself for her return to the abyss of starlight-by-mirror. The music had allowed her to relive a moment, faded and long gone. The hurried whispers of those calling her name replaced it as the mirror dissipated, lost to the void once more. Goosebumps rolled over her as she began to walk aimlessly again. Her bare feet slapped against the black marble. Emotions were goading her to go someplace—anywhere new—as she paced meaninglessly. Again, she tugged her dress back up on her hips; the back had unzipped again, and though she tried once more, she was still unable to reach the top.

A smile crept across her face as her body buzzed with wanton desire. *You know, maybe CJ might miss me? At least for a fleeting moment, I wasn't alone anymore...*

4

If Hate is Perfect

Staring into the rearview mirror, CJ found himself waiting. *For who? What exactly...* Ripping his eyes away, he drummed his fingers on the steering wheel. *Why can't I forget about Mary?*

It had been weeks since his sexual rendezvous with the mysterious lady in the mirror. Chills rolled over him, and he shuddered them off. His mind wandered back to her soft skin, the rustling of her red dress, and the sound of her voice, still sharp. When he closed his eyes, he could still feel the heat of her lips and the warmth of her thighs pressing on him. She haunted his dreams, and he woke cold and covered in sweat. Even with the top down on his convertible Corvette and the hot sun bearing down on him, he couldn't stop shivering from a combination of excitement and fear. Nothing seemed to cut through the unease that knotted his gut about what he wouldn't allow himself to consider.

What and who she might actually be is... The flirty and lust-loving side of him had died that night when he crossed back from the world on the other side of the mirror. *Was it all an illusion? Did I have a mental break down? But the scratches, the kiss, the sex...* A

202

heat washed over him, and he cleared his throat, shaking his head. *If I keep circling back like this, I'm going to be at full salute,* he jeered at himself and stared across the street.

"Hey, baby!" A petite, busty girl sashayed up to the car with her posse of debutants hot on her heels. "Sorry, it took me a little while to finish shopping with the girls." They giggled in unison as she flicked a strand of short, red hair from her eyes. "See you later, ladies." She swayed her hips until she was at the passenger door and reprimanded, "Babe, the door?"

"It's unlocked, Chelsea," he drawled.

"Babe..." she lowered her voice, sneering, "the girls are watching."

"They're always watching," he deadpanned as she looked back at her posse with a nervous laugh. "You're not even carrying anything, and you called me to come get you, so here I am."

Giving him a disapproving glare, Chelsea jerked open the car door and slammed it behind her. "You're embarrassing me."

Whispers and gossip erupted, but he put the car in drive and squealed down the street. Whatever he saw in her before was lost. It had been an empty relationship—always one sided with her side being the only one benefitting from their relationship. His thoughts drifted as she jabbered on about nothing of importance. CJ didn't say a word to Chelsea as she carried on the conversation about her newly dyed red hair, the upcoming annual frat and sorority gala, what she expected him to do for her, and how embarrassing it was that he couldn't at least *open the damn car door* for her. Relief washed over him as they pulled in front of her driveway—a rental property he assumed Daddy's money paid for since she didn't have a card in her wallet that carried her own name.

"I'm sorry, are you mad at me?" Chelsea cooed, leaning over to kiss his cheek. "I didn't mean to get so mad at you, baby. How about you come inside..." she said, shifting to a sultry voice and whispering in his ear, "the house and me." The mood swing was knee-jerking to him as she continued pawing at him. "I'll make it up to you if you make it up to me." She bit teasingly now, nibbling and licking his ear.

"No, just got something on my mind." CJ stole another glance at the rearview mirror. *Nothing.* She bit harder as if demanding a reaction against his will. "Chelsea, stop." Her hand slid over his thigh and snaked toward his crotch. "I said stop." He pushed her off and glared at her. "I don't think—"

"What's your problem?" Chelsea snapped, crossing her arms. "What did they do to you during their hazing ritual? Did they not have a warden or chaplain? I mean, at least a marshal present? Maybe I should have a word with Jason."

"What the hell does Jason have to do with our relationship?" Shaking his head, CJ locked eyes with her. "Every time you seem unhappy with me or something I'm unwilling to do, you threaten to see him as if he's in charge of every decision I make. What does my fraternity president have to do with our relationship?"

"Look, I'm trying to be the best girlfriend, but if this keeps up CJ, we can't be together." She tsked and opened the car door. "I have a reputation to keep. At least your frat boss gets that; I don't know what I was thinking settling with you. Rumors are going to start getting around, and you know how I feel about gossip."

"You mean you want to be the one dealing out the gossip," he corrected. "Not on the receiving end. I don't give a shit what they think. This isn't fucking high school."

Chelsea rolled her eyes, and her scowl deepened. "I hate to tell you, but without me, you'd be nothing. Don't forget we have a gala; I expect you to spare no expense."

"Yeah, I got you. I'll be your little cheese boy one last time," he spat in reply. "But after that, I'm done putting on airs for the debutants who you worship so dearly. You can go get cash from your little fuck boy Jason from now on."

They glared at each other for a moment as her mouth opened and closed like a fish with no voice. At last, she marched off, almost falling when one of her heels caught the crack between the two concrete slabs of the sidewalk. CJ's temper burned as he peeled out into the road and headed home.

What relationship? he thought bitterly. *We both came from money, and it has been more of an arranged relationship, for what? Gossip? Sure, it's been fun fooling around, but now, it's more trouble than it's worth. Besides, I think I've fallen for Mary. Whoever she is, she must be an English major. History or anthropology minor, at the very least?* He pushed the garage button, and it started to open as he pulled up the driveway. *She caught all those references so maybe a minor in Victorian Era culture? Literature?*

Putting the Corvette in park, CJ leaned on the steering wheel in defeat. The garage went dark as the door closed; the hot, stale air reminded him of the closet all those weeks ago. *Dammit, just thinking about it...* He puffed out his cheeks as his pants tightened from the rise of his cock. *Fuck it.* He marched for his bathroom, tossing clothes off as he made his way through the house. Slamming the water knob, the shower sputtered to life. The cold splashes made him flinch but did nothing to quell the arousal and heat of lust building from his core.

Leaning into the water, eyes tight, he began stroking his hard dick. Flashes of her red dress and the way her pale body blossomed out from the folds of the skirt made him moan. Licking his lips, his thumb rolled over the tip of his shaft as he thought about the kiss they had shared. The water grew warmer at last, and his balls tightened.

So close... Edging, at the cusp of an orgasm, a moan escaped him. He muttered naughty desires, stroking faster and firmer. *She was so wet...* He let his mind wander back to how her hot, tight pussy squeezed around his cock as he entered her. His dick throbbed as the tight, tingling sensation began to build. *That's it... just a little more.* He moaned again as he drew near the edge. A sharp ache cut through him before he could release, his body betraying him.

"Fuck me." He slammed the knob and shut the water off.

Frustration filled him as he marched angrily into his bedroom, water dripping off his chin and body. He froze. Slowly turning, he focused his attention on the mirrored wall. Arching a brow, another wave of provocation beckoned him and his cock, making him throb with desire once more. Licking his teeth, he stared up at the ceiling, hesitant to let himself act upon the lustful wants of his body and mind.

"What the hell do I have to lose?" CJ smirked, allowing himself to catch his own devilish expression. *I mean, I'm just beating it with Bloody Mary. It's not like anyone is watching me, and, even then, I wouldn't mind an audience.* A shudder of exhilaration fluttered over him. *Even sexier if she can see me...*

A chill of excitement crawled up his spine as he approached. Leaning an arm on the mirror, he let the tip of his cock touch and rub the cool glass of the mirror's surface. Closing his eyes, he tilted his hips, so the underside rode up the glass, and by the third tilt, it began to slide on precum. Edging closer, he feared rushing it. The mirror was warm from his efforts, almost vibrating as pleasure rolled through him. Muscles through his body tightened.

"Mary," he moaned, daring to reach down and begin stroking, pressing his cock firmer onto the mirror. "Bloody Mary."

Eyelids heavy, he stared past himself, deep into the depths of the abyss where a haze of red looked watery in the rise of his ecstasy. He could smell her perfume. Moaning as his arousal teetered on the edge again, he didn't want to peak just yet. *Just a little longer.* His reflection seemed to have dissipated as he rubbed the shaft up the glass before retreating. Rolling a thumb over the weeping tip of his cock, he glanced down to see the tip pressed against its mirrored doppelganger. *Let me linger on the edge, let me see her before...* Thoughts of her rolled forward. *The way her legs wrapped around me and how she rocked, making me catch my breath.* The pleasure of the head sliding against the glass left him wanting. *I just want to see...*

5

Stainless Bride of Stainless King

"**B**loody Mary." His voice cut through the overwhelming storm of mirrors and people calling to her.

"CJ, I found you, but…" Mary paused a moment, fearing that time had lurched forward in this endless eternity where she couldn't grasp if she lived in the past, present, or future. "Please, let me have this much."

"Bloody Mary." Again, the provocative way he spoke her name sent goosebumps across her skin.

She waved the mirror to her. The room was dark behind him. Droplets of water beaded down his body in rivulets. He seemed of the same age, but she couldn't tell in the lack of light. His forehead leaned against the mirror, and he stood naked before her. Steam painted the glass, disappearing only to reappear with each labored breath. The muscles in his body were taut as he edged closer to an orgasm; the muscles in his forearm flexed as he stroked his cock, pressing it against the glass.

"Oh, say it one more time for me." Pressing against the glass, she could feel the heat of his body through it and wished either of them could push through the cold, hard threshold that kept them divided by nothing more than ill-fated magic. "Five times, my love. Once more and perhaps one of us can touch the other like that night."

"So close," he muttered, rubbing against the mirror with the tip of his cock, slick with precum as he moaned.

Mary's fingers slid between her thighs, rubbing the folds of her pussy. The tip of her finger found her clit before riding her pink crevasse to dive into the wet depths. Pulling back her honey across the pink jewel, she began to pleasure herself alongside him. *If I can't fuck him, I'll gladly play with myself as I watch him cum across my mirror.* His eyes shut as she waited, agonizing over wanting him to call her name for a fifth and final time. He bit his lip and repositioned in front of her—palms overhead and body flat against the mirror as he rubbed his cock against the glass, enjoying the sensation. She inhaled swiftly as CJ fucked the mirror with thoughts of her in his mind and on his lips.

"Open your eyes and call my name, please." Pleading, she drank him in before letting her own dress drop to the floor. "My Adonis, let us lose a little more of our souls together again." Mary knelt before him, the glass a cruel reminder she couldn't escape this prison.

A moan escaped him, and he murmured her name at last, "My Mary."

The mirror rippled, and his cock pushed through like a clear edition of a gloryhole. Hungry to play, to touch, Mary took his cock into her hand. Her tongue teasing and licking the crown made his eyes pop open in time to watch her take all of him into her mouth. His cock bumped the back of her throat, and his body twitched. Palms crumbled into fists against the mirror overhead and he bit his lip as she pulled out his length until her lips popped. Locking eyes with him, she rolled her tongue once more over the edge of his crown, and his cock throbbed in reply.

"This is unfair," he whined.

Pulling slowly off his cock, tongue wiggling firmly against the underside, her lips popped once more before meeting his gaze. "Unfair. This time only your cock came through."

"Tell me I'm just dreaming about a gloryhole with the woman haunting my dreams." He weighed her expression before letting his eyes dip down and back up her naked body as she knelt in a pool of red fabric.

"It's no dream." Her tongue circled the tip of his cock, and he inhaled swiftly. "Does it feel real?"

Flustered, face flushed, CJ confessed, "I haven't been able to orgasm since we met. To be honest, I was afraid that I had made you up and..." He stopped and redirected his intent, "So, if you could lend me a hand?" He arched a brow and smirked. "Perhaps we can help one another out once more."

"Another round of the little death, then?" Mary ran her tongue across his cock's belly from hilt to tip.

"I will give you as many deaths as you please," he cooed, pressing himself against the magical glass barrier that separated them.

Mary's heart fluttered, her eyes locked with his as she took him into her mouth once more, slow and agonizing. *Payback for how slow he teased me last time.* He was swollen and hard; the corners of her mouth ached from the thick girth of his cock. *Oh, to think he gave this to me once before.* Again, he bumped the back of her throat, and she shook her head. A moaned escaped him, tilting his head back, enjoying the heat of her mouth. *Slow. I want him to teeter as I agonize and haunt him.* She rode her lips slowly to the crest, only to slide back to repeat the motion. Each deep-throated wiggle made him moan louder as his cock throbbed.

"So close," he breathed.

Mary's hand slid down her abdomen between her straddled thighs. Dipping her fingers in and out, she slurped and pumped his staff. Rolling a finger over her pink bud, she moaned, and he thudded against the glass as if bucking from the wave of pleasure her voice brought. As her finger circled her clit, slick and ever faster, she started to peak. Another lustful moan erupted from her as she too bucked, pulling his cock deeper between her lips. Hollowing her cheeks, she pressed forward until the barrier allowed him no deeper. His cock throbbed, jerking once before the heat of his cum filled her mouth, and she swallowed. CJ tilted his head back, moaning as her tongue wiggled and suckled; she swallowed each spurt as she dipped her fingers within herself. She teased him, agonizing as she continued to play by licking his length until he banged on the glass.

"No more," he pleaded between pants.

Releasing him, she wiped her mouth, and a smile crossed her face. "Begging me to stop?"

"Come out," he demanded.

A frowned soured her mood. "I'm trapped," she announced.

"How can you leave?" CJ pushed against the glass. "Is this ... magic? A curse?" He stepped back, looking the mirror over, and when he pushed back, not even his cock could cross the barrier again. "How did you get there in the first place?"

"I don't know." She stood and turned away from him. "If I knew, I wouldn't still be here."

"Tell me, are you visiting me through the mirrors from your room? Where do you live? Can I come to you?" CJ leaned hard against the mirror, his breath fogging the barrier once more. "I want to visit you again, if you'll allow me."

"I ... don't know where I am. This strange place has no end to darkness or mirrors." She dipped her legs into her dress, tugging it up on her hips. "But I would love more visits from you. Someone who sees me as a woman and not a phantom in the mirror."

"If I call your name, will you appear for me?" She spun to see the hungry expression on his face and her breath caught. "How many times shall I say it? Three? Ten?"

"Five." Mary marched closer and leaned against the barrier, the heat of his body still radiating through. "Call my name five times, no less, no more, and I should appear. I should be able to hear you call for me through a mirror of your choice."

"What if I want to touch you?" He raised a palm to the mirror, and both marveled as it passed through where he had been denied just a moment ago. "Is there a trick to this? Something I must do?"

"I don't understand how or why?" Mary hesitated to touch his arm, but without warning, he quickly grabbed her wrist and pulled until her palm locked with the barrier. "See, I cannot cross. You are the first to do so in all the time I've been here. Perhaps I'm nothing more than a phantom after all. With no body to leave the mirror with."

"I wish you could feel how hard and fast my heart beats when I see you, every time I even think of you." His leaned his forehead on the glass, and she placed her own against the barrier, so they could stare into one another's eyes. "Do you remember how you got here?" He released his grip on her wrist, so he could cup her face. "How can I free you?"

"If I could remember... I wish I knew." Tears welled in her eyes.

"Mary, do you have a last name? Maybe I can search for information, proof of your existence," he offered.

"My name..." The memory broke loose, and for the first time, she remembered. *I have a last name!* "Emrys!"

"As in Merlin?" he mused.

"*O Merlin, do ye love me?*" Mary murmured a quote from "Idylls of the King." Some part of her missing life flooded forward; she had once indulged in old texts and poems about magic and knights in the library's archives. "*Great Master, do ye love me?*"

"Who are wise in love, love most, say least." CJ's reply was quick and concise as his thumb glided over her bottom lip. *"To what request for what strange boon?"*

The room and barrier shuddered, and Mary was quick to shove his hand across the barrier. "Go!" she commanded as his mirror became nothing more than darkness. "Is this what it was like, I wonder." She turned back to the abyss of floating lights and reflections with a heavy sigh. "Is this the tower Merlin was imprisoned within when Vivien lost her temple in the old stories?"

6

The Mortal Dream That Never Yet Was Mine

CJ was on a mission. His professor did a double take as he rushed down the steps, following him all the way to his office. CJ stuck his foot out to keep the door from slamming shut. Furrowing his brow, they glared at one another in a mute argument. The plump old man snorted, shoving his glasses up and pushing the door for reassurance. CJ's arm thudded on the wood, and his muscles flexed as he pushed it open a little more, earning a rumbling sound from the older man.

"What is the meaning of this, Mr. Galdur!" erupted the Professor, his face red with the rise of his blood pressure as he defeatedly let CJ enter. "This is rather uncouth of you."

"I need to know more about Merlin," demanded CJ, shutting the door behind him. "You're the only one I know who might be able to point me in the right direction."

"Why the sudden interest, my boy?" Clearing his throat, the professor dropped a stack of folders onto his desk, drumming his fingers on a stack of books as he measured CJ. "I mean, besides the old poems, there's not much else to be taught."

"I mean…" CJ paused, searching his thoughts before speaking again, "Merlin was caught in Vivien's tower, so I need to know if or when he escaped?"

The professor narrowed his eyes before he asked, slowly and calculating, "And what makes you think I know the answer to such a quandary?"

"Well, Professor Gawain, I'm pretty sure besides Old English I and II, you've also taught History on Medieval Times, and let's not forget the Arthurian Legends and Lore courses for the Anthropology Department." CJ smirked as the red in Professor Gawain's face returned. "Surely, of all the professors in this college, you are the most well-versed in this."

"You caught me, but you still didn't answer my question." Flopping into his chair, he opened a drawer to produce two shot glasses and an ancient bottle of liquor. "How about we do this shot for shot. We ask, we answer, and we take a shot."

"Fine." CJ took the freshly poured shot. "It's because I met a girl." He chugged it back, and it burned. "What is this stuff?"

Professor Gawain chuckled, pouring his glass. "It's the Holy Grail!" He took a shot and teased, "Your turn again. What does Merlin have to do with a girl?"

CJ watched him fill his cup and remarked, "She shares the same last name. Wasn't his name Myriddin Emrys?" He took his shot, squinting as it only added to the fire in his gut.

"Yes, it is." Professor Gawain giggled as he threw back a shot and exclaimed, "Do you know the origin of your last name?"

"No." CJ took a seat, inhaling deeply before downing his third round. "Ugh, what is this?"

"The Holy Grail, my son!" Gawain pulled his glasses off and refilled the shot glasses once more. "To Galdur and Emrys finding their way back once more!" he cheered, raising the glass high to CJ before sucking it back. "Where did you meet this girl?"

CJ covered his mouth and mumbled through his hand, "In a mirror in the closet." A look of surprise struck his face as he met Gawain's shiny-eyed glare. "What did you put in my glass?"

"Drink first," demanded Gawain. "Go on!" Swallowing, CJ didn't break his stare as he took another shot. "I told you, the Holy Grail. You're wasting questions on the same answers, Chadwick J. Galdur." Another round of shots and refilling of glasses followed. "Tell me, does she cross the barrier or do you? This is vital, so answer in earnest."

As if it were a belch rolling to the surface, CJ blurted the answer. "I can sometimes cross into the mirror." He covered his mouth and jolted to his feet. "Fuck!" The world tilted, and he sat back down. "What did—" CJ stopped, his mind reeling as he calmed just enough to think of a more profitable question. "Who are you, really?"

"Ah, now we're asking the right questions, but you need to drink before I can reply." Gawain slid the glass over.

"R-Right. Drink. We ask, we answer, and we inebriate." Reluctantly, CJ drank it.

"I am Gawain!" he announced; laughter filled the room as his cheeks were rosy with liquor. "Knight of the Round Table, King-Consort to Queen Florie of Escavalon in the Fairylands, Finder of Vivien's tower and the last quest of Merlin!" Another shot down, and he exhaled. "Do you love her?"

"Yes," CJ didn't flinch at his own reply. "It's why I need to know how to get her out of there. Do you know how to get Mary out of the mirror?" CJ poured both shots this time, taking his down and slamming the cup.

"The great proof of your love," Gawain answered. "It's as simple as that." He tried to pour more, but the bottle was rendered empty now. "Shoot, she's decided we've had enough." He motioned to the shot. "Did you want it?"

The buzz came on strong and hard, but there was a warming sense of elation as CJ snarked, "You didn't drink."

Cackling erupted from Gawain, and he took the last shot. He added, "We should do this again!"

"I don't know, Professor." CJ slurred his words as he wobbled to his feet. "I'm done drinking with you. When I sober up, we need to talk."

"You should get with Timmy. He might know more." He put the items back into the drawer. "Besides, I can't believe you can stand."

"I need to get home." CJ stumbled out of the office and called Chelsea. "Chelsea, you owe me. Come and get me, bitch."

"Are you, are you drunk?" Chelsea sounded breathless. "Where are you?"

"English hallway?" CJ staggered into the hall, holding his throbbing head as he weaved his way to the bathroom. "I'm in the first-floor men's bathroom." He hung up as she shrieked something. *As many times I've been her chauffeur, she can at least return the favor for once.*

He pushed through the bathroom doors and made his way to the middle sink. He leaned on the counter and wrenched the faucet on; desperately, he splashed cool water on his face and body. Sweat poured over him as his whole body vibrated with the aftermath of the strange liquor. Frustration fueled him.

I don't want to go to the damn gala with Chelsea, he confessed to himself at last. *I don't even love her.* He was quick to unbutton and pull off his shirt as his body temperature continued to rise. *Is it the alcohol, or am I burning a fever?* Shaking his head, he looked into the mirror. Biting a lip, he searched beyond him, hoping to see a flash of lips or red or anything from the world he had slid into twice now.

Heaving a heavy sigh, he placed a hand against the glass. "I'm going to figure this out, Mary." He scoffed to himself, shaking his head as the world tilted and wobbled. "Damn, this shit is strong."

He tried another round of splashing, struggling to knock the heat down and sober up. He was astonished at how, despite the heat in his core, he didn't feel sick or even the slightest sense of nausea. Cursing Gawain under his breath didn't do anything to relieve his throbbing skull.

When I asked him who he was... Squinting at his reflection, a wave of confusion baffled him. *Did he say he was a Knight of the Round Table? As in the Knight Gawain in the stories?* Shaking his head, he tried recalling the information only to find the moment fading as if it was a fleeting memory. *I'm never drinking the Holy Grail ever again.*

"What the hell is wrong with me?" CJ turned the water off. *If I call her, would she...* "Mary Emrys, Mary Emrys." His heart fluttered. *Is it okay to summon her here and now?*

The door slammed open, and he spun to see Chelsea march in with a look of pure rage written across her face. "Why is your shirt off?" She came closer and made a disgusted face. "And why are you sweaty and smell of booze?"

"I drank the Holy Grail with the Knight Gawain," he mused, still feeling he could tell no lies.

"What did you drink?" Chelsea crossed her arms and corrected him. "You mean Professor Gawain?"

"Holy Grail. The knight and I took turns taking shots," he giggled. *I sound like a crazy person, but it's the truth, isn't it? That really just happened!*

"Why would you drink with that fat fuck?" she snarled.

"Hey, he's a king-consort to a queen fairy. And a nice guy," CJ slurred, the Holy Grail still rolling the words out without warning. "Not like you understand that there's more to life than your reputation."

"Look, we need to get you home. You need to forget everything that just happened and get back to ... normal." She grabbed his shirt and shoved it into his chest. "Put on your shirt."

"No," he replied. "I'm hot."

"God, what a big ego you have," she retorted.

"Wow. You're so shallow." Blinking, CJ snorted. "No, like I'm overheating. Why are you so vain? Can't a person express they have a fever using the word *HOT*," he enunciated awkwardly.

Chelsea huffed and rolled her eyes. "Just put your shirt on."

"No," he insisted. "I'm HOT," he repeated.

"Fine." A smile twisted her lips, and she shoved him against the counter, his back to the mirror. "How about..." she spoke slowly as she unbuckled his belt and unfastened his pants, "we have a little fun?"

"No," he said harshly, gripping her wrist to stop her. "No means no, CHEL-SEA," he slurred, wobbling.

"Oh, come on, CJ. Why call me out here?" The anger shifted to sultry in her face and voice, making him flinch. "I know you like the idea of fucking in public. You're already undressed. Why else would you call me?"

"Because I needed a ride?" he answered, regretting having made the call.

Chelsea ran her hands up the ripples of his torso until she hooked them behind his neck. "Come on, baby. I've always wanted to fuck someone in the men's bathroom."

Dryly, he echoed, "*Someone*?" Squinting his eyes, he hooked a finger and pulled her turtleneck down to reveal a fresh hickey. "Maybe you should ask whoever left these to help you fulfill that wish. Jason, perhaps?"

Clapping a hand over it, she shoved away and hissed, "And who left the scratches on your back, huh?"

"Mary Emrys," he spoke without hesitation and bit his tongue. *I wasn't going to confess, but the alcohol is still forcing answers out of me. I mean, I thought I was slipped something, not that I cheated on her. Wait. Let's be honest here. We broke up a month before that anyway, or did she forget? I already knew she was sleeping around on me before the hazing.*

"Oh, yeah? Jason's old fling, huh?" Chelsea puffed herself up. "So, you'd rather be with leftovers who dropped out than with someone like myself."

"Wait, you know who she is?" CJ's chest ached and his heart raced. *This is the answer I need! Do Chelsea and Jason know something? Did they know Mary when she was... was...*

"Fuck me and I might tell you more?" Sucking on a cheek, her eyes dropped to the tightness in his pants. "I mean, I should at least get one more round before we end this, no?"

"Bitch, my dick isn't a merry-go-round ride," he retorted.

"So, it's her and not me now?" The scowl returned, and she marched away, crossing her arms as she spun to face him and reprimand him again. "Huh? Some bitch that you're not man enough to bring around or openly date? As I see it, you want your cake and eat it too!"

"Her name is Mary!" Every nerve in his body tightened, and he couldn't contain it anymore. *If we're going to air my dirty laundry, she's got more, and I'm done dealing with debutant bullshit.* "Since we're being so honest. We broke up months ago because you were cheating on me, and now you call me out. I texted you the week you didn't pick up or reply that this was over. Since then, you seem to be pretending we're still a thing. It's over, Chelsea. It's been over for weeks!"

Chelsea cocked her arm back, ready to slap him as she came marching back. CJ gripped the counter with his hands, white-knuckled and ready to take the hit. Warm hands glided over his shoulders, and Chelsea stopped, stumbling back. She pointed, words lost, as she backed away toward the door. CJ glanced down, and relief filled him as he recognized Mary's arms.

"He's mine now!" Mary's voice sounded ominous as it resonated through the mirrors all at once.

Chelsea released a blood-curdling scream and rushed out, shrieking like a banshee. Heaving a sigh, CJ tilted his head back to see her hovering over him. Her eyes were solid black for a moment before she blinked and looked down at him in surprise.

"Am I..." She pushed against the glass and managed to pull herself out of the mirror a little further. "Am I coming out of the mirror? Oh my God, I'm out! I'm coming out, but I'm stuck," she grunted.

CJ turned to get a better view. "I think so?" Her head, shoulders, and breasts were free as she pushed and wiggled. "Are you stuck?"

She reached for him, and he grabbed her arms. "Ready?" With a nod, he tugged her, but she didn't move, and the mirror wouldn't bend or give. "I think that's as far as you're going to get. Maybe it's like the other day when I couldn't get all of me through the mirror like I had that first time."

Her face became distraught. Tears were falling ever faster, and she began to panic. CJ's heart was breaking. *There must be a way to free her from the mirror.*

7

Have Ye Found Your Voice

This can't be it. Mary's thoughts spiraled around the possibility of traversing back into the real world. Panic filled her as she wondered, *Will I be denied fully escaping the abyss? Why even let me do this much if I can't get any farther?* CJ had left her arms aching, but neither of them could make the mirror bend or budge. He rushed over to lock the bathroom door.

"In case someone comes by," he explained as his eyes dipped to her breasts and his eyebrows flicked high, "and sees what I see."

His words earned a laugh, despite her tears. "You unzipped my dress, and I can't..." she choked on her words as her panic broke. Sniffling, she said, "It slipped off when I rushed forward to save you from... from... Chelsea." The name rolled from her memory, and she began wiping the tears from her face. "I think ... I know her," she said, unsure of the reason behind it.

"Yeah, I was a little surprised too." He squeezed between two sinks to get closer to where she protruded from the glass. "Apparently, she's banging your ex-boyfriend, Jason?"

"Jason." CJ's hands slid across the glass before tickling her ribs where the mirror had stopped her. "Jason dumped me before the gala, but I don't remember what happened after that." She giggled as fingers glided up her ribs. "Stop, that tickles."

"Well, you stopped crying, which matters more," he murmured as he continued gliding his hands up her torso to cup and grope her breasts. "Does this tickle?" He blew across her nipple, and the heat of his breath made it rise slightly.

"Y-yes." She palmed his forehead but failed to shove him back. "What on earth do you think you're doing?"

"Having some fun with the woman I love." He wrapped his lips around her nipple and suckled long and hard.

A gasp and shriek escaped her. "CJ!" Pushing on his shoulders, she couldn't move him as his tongue flicked and circled. "Oh, this isn't fair!"

His lips popped off her breast, and he smirked up at her. "Why is that? I mean, I owe you from last time." He blew circles around the other nipple and added, "This seems like the perfect time to return the gesture."

"B-b-b-but my hands!" she exclaimed as he took the nipple into his mouth, repeating the motion before releasing her once more.

"Yes? What about your hands?" He arched his brow playfully.

"They're out there," she announced.

"And?" He returned to the other nipple, licking and kissing it passionately.

"I can't get off," she said frustrated.

Moving to the other breast, he replied, "Then this should help for when you can."

Hot lips kissed her other nipple. Hissing as she sucked air between her teeth, his playfulness made her loins ache with desire. From the angle she hung out of the mirror, it was impossible to twist or turn to escape his onslaught. Teeth nibbled at her, and she shrieked once more. At last, she gripped the hair on the back of his head, forcing him to tilt his face up and look her in the eyes. His grin sent goosebumps over her. His tongue snaked out of his lips, and the tip lapped at her nipple. She jerked him back out of reach, and he smirked.

Sucking on a cheek, she warned, "Gentle..."

On the other side of the mirror, her body was heating up and growing wet. Everything throbbed with sexual desire to be touched, licked, and fucked. His hands massaged her breast in anticipation.

"Are you sure you want gentle?" he teased.

"I command you to be gentle," she announced.

"Yes, mistress." He narrowed his eyes.

Slowly, she guided him back to her breast as he lapped out for the nipple with his tongue. She kept him too far to suckle or nibble just yet. His eyes remained fixated on her as the tip of his tongue toyed with the erect nipple. *He sends my body into a frenzy at just a glance. How I wish he was licking my clit this way.* Leading him closer, he gave her breast gentle kisses and sucked softly. Another wave of arousal rolled through and pimpled her skin.

A little closer, he tried to nibble, but she jerked him back again. "I said *gentle.*"

"Forgive me, mistress," he muttered as his pants tightened.

"Again, do it right," she demanded, leading him to the other breast.

She hummed as the hot velvet of his tongue ran across her areola before circling her nipple. She pulled him closer, her fingers still interlocked with tresses of his hair as his lips wrapped around her nipple. She moaned as the pleasure made her body buzz. Slowly teasing her, he began to suck and flick. Her body flinched; her loins throbbed with the rise of wanting to go further.

Oh, how I want him to fuck me right now. She bit her lip, moaning as she pressed him harder into her breast.

He suckled harder, deeper, yet slow and agonizing with unpredictable taps and strokes of his tongue. His hand massaged her other breast as his mouth remained latched to her. Taking the other nipple between a finger and thumb, he pinched and tugged. She gasped and whimpered. Wiggling her hips, all she could do was close her thighs tight together in a failed attempt to satisfy the aching desire that lay out of reach. A warm trickle snaked down a leg—her body signaling it was ready and wet for what it anticipated to happen next. Teeth teased her once more, and she shrieked. Releasing her grip on him, she pushed on the mirror in hopes of moving further out—still nothing, not even a millimeter.

CJ moaned into her soft flesh, and her heart thudded fast and hard. *I want to cum so badly. If I could just play with myself. I have never wanted a dick inside me so desperately in my life. What the hell!* His actions evolved, becoming rougher and more tantalizing. In reflex, she jerked her legs, knees knocking into the mirror and unable to push him away once more as he swapped breasts once again. He kissed and licked her breasts as if he were making out with them, and it drove her wild.

The sound of a zipper brought her attention elsewhere as he pulled free his hardened length. *I'm not the only one who wants to fully fuck.* He moaned into her breast once more as he stroked his cock. Pulling away, his free hand slid over her collarbone and gripped her neck. She stiffened as he cast a dangerous glare.

"I want to fuck you so bad right now," he confessed.

"I'm so wet and ready." His fingers tightened as he hummed, precum dripping from the tip of his dick. "I want to bend over for you so badly."

"Keep talking." His hand let go, massaging a breast again. "I'm almost … there," he panted.

Licking her teeth, she cooed, "Are you going to be a good boy and cum for me."

"Yes, mistress," he hissed and grunted, edging closer to a climax.

"Next time, I want that dirty mouth licking my pussy," she confessed.

"Yes, mistress," another grunt as he squeezed her breast tight.

She moaned, eyes dropping to watch him stroke himself faster. "I want to watch you cum."

"I'll cum for you," he reassured breathlessly.

"You better if you want this again..." She pulled the hand off her breast and wrapped her lips around two of his fingers.

A moan escaped him as she suckled on them, wiggling her tongue against them. "Fuck me," he muttered.

She deep throated them, fingertips knocking on the back of her throat. His body went taut and flinched. Her eyes stayed on his stroking until, at last, a stream of cum shot against the mirror. Three more spurts followed as he grunted. His breathing was loud and heavy as he pulled his fingers free from her lips with a pop. They searched one another's expression until their eyes opened in alarm. Mary was moving!

"Shit, you're sliding back in," he interjected.

Panic washed over her. Pushing her hands against the mirror only made them sink in, and she was unable to pull them back out. The abyss started to swallow her back in—slowly but frighteningly picking up speed. Her breasts were sinking into the mirror, and CJ cupped her face. Their lips locked, and he deepened the kiss. The pressure behind it sent her heart aflutter. He kissed her cheek and neck before at last whispering in her ear.

"I promise, I will find a way to get you out of there." With that, he suckled hard and long on her neck.

"Please help me," she said with a quavering voice as her anxiety tightened in her throat.

"I will." He kissed her lips once more before the mirror stole her away.

8

Ride, Ride, and Scream Until Ye Wake

CJ drummed his fingers on the steering wheel. In the dark garage, his mind just kept spinning in circles. He couldn't get the look of Mary's fearful expression out of his memory. When he lost her in the mirror and failed to call her out again, he had felt dread like no other. After cleaning up his mess, he had raced back to Gawain's classroom to find him gone. He called Chelsea, but she refused to acknowledge what had happened. She acted like he had never asked her to come get him, pretending she didn't see a naked woman in the form of an old friend crawl out of the mirror. More unnerving was that no one seemed to care Mary had gone missing.

Scoffing, he pulled out his cell phone. He scrolled through the history, needing to see it again for reassurance. He confirmed he indeed had called her earlier today. *Is she playing dumb or is there some other magic unfolding here? Could it be people aren't supposed*

226

to remember seeing her in the mirror? He flipped through his texts and paused over his last message from Timmy, fellow frat brother and part-time bellhop out of New Jersey.

[Timmah: Who the hell is Mary?]

CJ's eyes searched the air as he thought for a moment. *He was the one that planned my hazing. Plus, he's majoring in magic and occult history. Maybe he did something or at least knows something I can do to help her.*

[CJ: The girl I met in the closet when you asshats hazed me.]
Waiting, he could see the message flip to "read"; a reply was being actively written.
[Timmah: So, in the closet you met someone named Mary? Did Jason put a girl in there? I told him that was a dick move since you're dating Chelsea. Sorry I wasn't there to supervise.]
[CJ: I broke up with Chelsea months ago. Jason knows that. He was part of the reason why. No, they didn't put a girl in there.]

He waited a moment, but no reply came, so he pressed further.

[CJ: Look. Something weird happened. Aren't you majoring in occult and magic?]
[Timmah: Did they slip acid in your drink?]
[CJ: No.]
[Timmah: Wait, which closet?]
[CJ: The one next to the basement door, under the stairs.]

The phone started to ring.
"You met Bloody Mary?" Timmy blurted as CJ answered.
"How'd you know?" CJ swallowed.

"I bought the mirror because it belonged to someone who got sucked in or was rumored to fall into it." Clearing his throat, Timmy lowered his voice. "So, did you find out who she is? How long has she been stuck in there?"

"Well, that's the weird part." Leaning back into the driver seat, he sat in his driveway, wondering how to even start. *How do I explain something I still can't understand?* "It's Jason's ex-girlfriend."

"The one who went missing?" Timmy seemed alarmed. "Are you sure?"

"Yeah, I mean, Chelsea saw her the last time she appeared," answered CJ as he furrowed his brow. "But now, she acts like it never happened. Mary said they were friends, so it seems—"

"Wait. How many times have you seen her?" CJ could hear Timmy shuffling through a desk drawer. "She keeps reappearing for you. How many times?"

"Um, three times, I think?" CJ's face heated from the memories.

"Just an apparition in the mirror who you can talk to?" The drawer slammed, and a chair squeaked as Timmy called out to someone. "You two stay here, I have to head back to campus."

"Not like I can go far without her anyway," a familiar male voice grumbled.

"Is that Mark?" asked CJ. "Where the hell has he been?"

"Long story." Timmy circled back and pressured for an answer. "Can you communicate with her?"

"About that, I, um..." CJ choked, coughing a few times before blurting his confession, "I fucked her the first time."

"You what?" The phone fell silent for a long while. "And what about the other times?" Timmy asked slowly and calculating.

"We talk and touch and, well, cross in or out of the mirror but only partially." CJ groaned and added, "I sound like a lunatic."

"No, you don't," Timmy reassured him. "So have you been visiting the mirror in the closet to look for her?"

"No." CJ was offended at the idea. "I call her name five times, and she appears in a mirror sometimes."

There was silence again as the sound of a car started. He couldn't make out the conversation; clearly, Timmy's hand was over the phone. A woman's voice fussed, and before long, another door shut and the engine revved. The familiar delayed connection of a hands-free system caught the last bit clearly.

"Fine, but it's dangerous," relented Timmy.

CJ's nerves tightened, and he added, "Look, I don't know what is happening, but it's crazy and honestly..." CJ shuddered as Mary's face came to mind once more. "I want to help her escape that place."

"Okay, if you're willing, I might be able to pull this together." Timmy sighed, and after another long pause, he started to divulge information. "The mirror in the closet is the one Jason pushed her into."

"Jason?" Scoffing, CJ retorted, "You make it sound as if Jason purposely put her in that mirror." The long pause that followed made his stomach twist. "C'mon, Tim. Someone can't just curse someone into the mirror."

"They can... and have." Timmy inhaled deeply. "How much do you know about Merlin and his mistress, Vivien?"

"Gawain already talked to me about that," mumbled CJ.

"Oh. So, he actually revealed—" Timmy stopped and changed what he intended to say. "Look, CJ, Jason isn't who and what you think he is."

"He's a scumbag," CJ announced flatly.

"Agreed, but we're talking about something not ... normal ... or even human," Timmy suggested.

"What part of this conversation is fucking normal," announced CJ.

"What if I told you he was a changeling?" Timmy offered. "Do you know what that is?"

CJ struggled for words before he blurted, "As in a child swapping fairy?"

"See, for an English major, you know your stuff," commended Timmy. "Sometimes it happens as a newborn, and the stronger ones can completely replace teenagers in most cases. But the ones you have to watch out for are those who steal the likeness of grown-ass people, including owning their life, not just their looks."

"Jason's a changeling?" CJ furrowed his brown, struggling to process the idea.

"And not any changeling," warned Timmy. "He can hide a person anywhere. Normally, they just misplace you in our world or send you to live out your days in the fairy realm where you turn fae and at least gain some powers, but he's a dark changeling." Tim hesitated as if trying to put the words together. "As crazy as this may sound, they can put people into a dark realm, a mirror realm, where they age more slowly and can watch the outside realm from windows or mirrors. On occasion, if there's magic or a strong enough connection, they can contact someone on the outside, but it's rare."

CJ listened, hand over his mouth. *Magic? Realms? Fae? Jason's a fucking changeling? What the hell is happening here? Did Professor Gawain slip me LSD?*

"Which brings me back to Merlin and Vivien." Timmy cleared his throat.

"What does that have to do with them?" CJ shook his head and spoke louder, "What does any of this have to do with me?"

"Vivien used the magic from a dark changeling to trap Merlin in the tower," declared Timmy. "Mary, the one in the mirror who Jason hid away, her last name is Emrys. The same as Merlin." Timmy spoke slowly and seriously. "And then we have Vivien Galdur."

"Mary is Merlin, and I'm..." CJ leaned back in the driver seat, rubbing his forehead.

"Right, so here's where it really gets weird..." Timmy sounded like he was tiptoeing now with the information.

"What a damn minute," growled CJ. "How do you know all of this shit about me, Jason, fucking Bloody Mary?"

There was a long hush before Timmy sighed and relented, "You wouldn't even believe me if I told you."

"Try me," CJ pressed. "I want answers for it all."

"Fine. Listen, if you do love her, there's a chance we can break her out, but..." Timmy groaned as if pained. "I like to fuck with people and trick them, but not completely destroy lives. In the end, I just want some good entertainment. I mean, I can't help it. It's in my nature."

"What's the problem?" demanded CJ. "Spit it out already."

"You need to figure out how to get into the mirror realm. Not just your dick, but all of you. It's going to be a dangerous move," Timmy forewarned.

"Yeah, because I can get stuck in there," CJ confirmed.

"No, because there is ancient magic teamed with fae magic. Jason has some control just as Vivien did. Possibly, you do too?" Timmy seemed unsure. "And she must love you back. The confession goes both ways, and I don't know how much that old adage of true love plays into this. I'm completely guessing, CJ."

"There has to be a way to make sure we can leave there once we reach her," CJ insisted.

"The mirror in the closet is the original." Timmy hummed in thought, working out the possibilities in his mind. He announced, "I suspected it was a magical heirloom when I first found it. To think, it could be the portal Vivien used and kept in the forest. Anyway, if you find that specific mirror, you can pull her out. Maybe if I can get there in time, I can lend you a hand with the magic. If Jason comes for you, play dumb—you know nothing. If he gets even a hint or suspicion that you know he's not human, he'll slit your throat."

"In that case, I'm counting on you." CJ ended the call. *I've got a plan, but I need to think this through.*

9

Know Ye the Stranger Woman

Panting, Mary's body buzzed with elation despite the over-whelming feeling of crushing dread. She could still feel the cold of the mirror swallowing her, overshadowing the heat of the moment. *The way he clung to me when he realized it was taking me back...* The look on his face only added to the pang in her chest. *I'm not the only one feeling broken that I couldn't completely crossover.*

Everywhere his lips and tongue had teased left behind heat not even the cold mirror could snuff out, driving her arousal to an aching like no other. *I don't want to cry anymore. Please, just take this pain away. Don't let the pleasure still haunting me be extinguished.* Lying back on the floor in the darkness, her hands slid between her thighs. *I'll cling onto what good vibes I have in this shit moment.* Mirrors twinkled all around like flickering candles.

I want to feel... A finger slid between the swollen folds of her pussy, rubbing across the slick opening. *...alive!* Her breath caught and her touch revived what he had set in motion. With ease, her finger slipped inside, hot and wet; she ached with desire. *Oh, how I wish I could feel his cock inside me again. I want him to fuck me.* Stroking in and out, her pussy tightened on her fingers, and she whimpered in frustration.

Eyes shut tight, she focused on recalling those first moments with CJ—the heat of his body and torso caught between her thighs. The lingering memories made her arch as she bit her lip. Her finger glided out and up to circle her clit. A moan escaped her as her body tensed, the tingling of her arousal increasing. Skin pimpled in anticipation and groping her own breast, she clung to the feeling of his tongue on her nipples.

So close... Her fingers stroked in and out once more. She imagined the heat of his hands running up her legs, lips on her own, and even his voice as he—

Mary, Mary. CJ's voice filled her ears.

Again, she returned to circling her pink jewel. "Call my name again," she pleaded.

Mary... Louder, she heard the voice and a fist pounding on a mirror, lost in the sea of the abyss. *Mary... cum...* His voice faded as she peaked.

Her muscles tightened as she sat up, sucking in air, eyes wide open from the exhilaration of the violent release. Fingers dove inside to feel how her pussy tightened in her orgasm. At last, she cried out as she egged the orgasm on until she peaked higher, squirting from the stimulus of it all. Breathlessly, she came to a stop and looked all around at the twinkling of glass in the silent space. Creasing her forehead, she finally gathered the thoughts to express the sudden confusion.

"It's quiet." The unease tightened in her chest as a chill crossed her body, skin dimpling once more. "Since the moment I woke up here, it's never been this quiet." She gathered her dress and slipped it on, tugging it up as she glanced around. "Why are all the mirrors so far away and no one's calling my name?" Her heart began racing, the dryness in her mouth adding to her building fear. "Does that mean I can't even hear CJ?"

"That's right," a familiar male voice replied within the darkness. "He can't call you, you can't hear him, and I can make this permanent if you don't behave, Mary."

Chills snaked up her spine, bristling the hairs on her arms. "Jason."

He stepped out from behind an old, wooden-framed mirror in the distance, much like the one she recalled seeing CJ in that first time. "What are you doing here?" Her stomach knotted. "You did this to me, didn't you?"

"I had a reputation to keep, and if you would have stayed home from the gala that night and not caused a fucking scene..." he snarled as his eyes went solid black and his skin sparkled like shimmering water. "It's not easy for my kind to blend in, and had I known you were a cambion—"

"A what?" she chirped, confused. "A cambion? What in the hell is that?"

"Don't be coy with me." He snorted in frustration, agitated as he ran a hand through his hair. "I thought you were human, and ever since I slept with you I just can't—"

"Fuck you!" She gave him a baffled expression and exclaimed, "I'm human! You're the fucking creature who threw me into a mirror-filled hell hole!"

Jason gave a disgusted expression, curling his lip to reveal a fang. "Are you telling me you don't even know what you are? *A chrebair chuilig.* You flea-ridden woodcock." He muttered something in another language before sneering at Mary once again. "You're an insult to your lineage."

"What the fuck..." Mary was shocked over the insult to injury. "I'm trapped here, and you show up just to patronize me? Why? Because you can?"

Snorting, he closed the gap between them in an instant; she had no time to react until it was too late. His fingers wrapped tightly around her throat, and his soulless eyes burned away her anger until fear sent her body trembling. She could barely keep her toes on the ground as she pulled at his arm. *This is it; I'm dying here.* Tears welled in her eyes, and she let her arms fall to her sides in defeat. Closing her eyes tight, she thought bitterly, *At least I'll leave here if I die.*

He gave another disgusted hiss as he dropped her to the floor. "Please, I don't have enough clout to stand trial if I kill you, even if you're only cambion. They'd strip me of my title and far worse."

Coughing and sputtering, she croaked, "What the hell is a cambion?"

Exasperated, he knelt before her and held her chin, forcing her to meet his gaze. "I suppose I owe you this much. Half human, half incubus, or in this case, succubus." Releasing her, he paced away toward that singular and specific antique mirror. "Surely, an old English geek like yourself recalls tales of Merlin being a cambion? Granted, there are no books here to keep you entertained."

She swallowed hard and took a deep breath. Mary demanded, "Why have you come here?"

"To warn you." He turned back to face her, running his fingers through his hair again. "Stop reaching out to CJ … or else."

"Or else what?" Mary threw out her arms. "You'll throw him in here?"

Jason scoffed, laughing before he answered, "And give you a chance to gain power, so you both can break out of here? I think not." He ran a finger across his throat. "I'll kill your human fuck boy in a heartbeat."

Rage and fear fought against one another inside her for a fleeting moment before the anger drove her to shout. "And what if you're wrong about him, too?"

"Excuse me?" Jason furrowed his brow.

"What if you're wrong?" Mary pulled herself to her feet, tugging the dress up before balling her fists at her sides. She yelled, "He's not human either!"

Rage was written on his face, his fangs gritting.

"If you think I reached out to him, you're wrong!" *Shit, what am I doing? Won't this put a target on CJ?* Biting her lip, she didn't want to spin it further. "Whatever you are, you're shit at recognizing others, so be sure before you act." *That's it, plant enough self-doubt and just maybe...* "Whatever the hell you are, you can't be that powerful if me fucking another guy riles you up."

Again, he was at her throat. "Listen, wench, pissing off a dark changeling is a dangerous matter." Letting her go, Jason marched for the mirror. "Fucking succubi and their pheromones that keep their mates coming back. Never again." And with that, he disappeared into the mirror before it faded away into the dark.

10

Who Pounced Her Quarry and Slew It

CJ paced in his bedroom, mind spiraling with everything Timmy had told him. Some of it made obscure sense, while other answers left him baffled. All he could confidently confirm was he had magic, she had magic, and magic had caused the fiasco of her being trapped in a mirror for years. *I knew Jason was a dick, but shit.*

Glancing down at his phone, he wondered if he should call Timmy again or even his professor to pry further. His stomach turned, and he shook his head at both ideas. *Timmy is on his way back; I can wait. As for the other, I don't think I can handle another round of the Holy Grail.* He marched to the mirror and pounded his fist against it.

"Where are you, Mary?" He searched his own eyes. "Why haven't you heard me? Or replied?"

Pulling off it, he walked away holding his mouth. *Did it somehow end our connection? If so, is there a way to get it back? Is it possible I broke it somehow? Or does she not want to see me?* He twisted, crossing his arms as he stared in frustration at his reflection in the mirror.

"What happened to you, Mary?" A scowl crossed his face, but again, he didn't see the world that once lay just under his reflection and gaze like before. "Why can't I get in or, at the very least, see it?"

Suddenly his reflection smiled and placed its hands on their hips. "What's the matter, CJ?" The deep voice resonated in the mirror. "Did you lose something?"

CJ's heart leapt to his throat, and he struggled to swallow it. He took a few steps back until his legs pressed against his bed. *So, he can pass through the mirrors, but do I let him know I know who he is? No, Timmy said play dumb if he comes after me.*

"It's all a dream," cooed the black-eyed version of himself in the mirror, waving a hand in a grand gesture. "The stress has eaten away at you. Pull yourself together," it reassured.

Are you kidding me? CJ sat on his bed, balling fistfuls of his comforter as he stared wide-eyed. *Magic is a terrifying thing, but how is this any different from how he's manipulated me outside of this?* He could feel a calm starting to take over as his fear dissipated at each suggestion the doppelganger offered to him.

"The gala is a big event, and let's be honest, the hazing ritual went too far," it offered. "Clearly, someone slipped something into your drink. Surely, if you ask Jason, he'll confirm it."

CJ covered his mouth and mumbled, "What the fuck."

"Now, pull yourself together. Chelsea needs you to take her to the gala tonight," it demanded. "Don't disappoint Jason and the fraternity. They need you to make an appearance and keep your shit together." It pounded the mirror with its palms, making CJ flinch. "As for Mary," it warned with a hiss, "forget she ever existed. It's the best for you. Don't you want your life back?"

The mirror shattered into a million pieces. Tiny shards bounced and rained down on the floor, some of them tapping against his shoes. Rage filled CJ. *Who the fuck does he think he is? How is this any different from a jealous, dickhead ex-boyfriend showing up and trashing my room? Fuck this. I'm not scared. I'm not afraid of being cursed into the mirror realm with her if that's how this ends. Before that, I'll make it clear I intend to fight back. Two can play at the game of manipulation. Let's make him let his guard down.*

A grin flashed across his face as he stood. Glass crunched under his shoes as he went to the closet to pull out the tuxedo he had intended to wear. *You want me at the gala, Jason? Fine. But you're going to regret it.*

[CJ: Hey Jason. Did you ever figure out if someone slipped something in my drink?]

[FratBoss: Oh! Hey man! You feeling, ok? Yeah, we found out who did it and reported him. You still coming to the gala?]

Ha! CJ marched for the bathroom. *Eager to see if you convinced me? Does this mean you can't force anyone to do your bidding? Or am I somehow immune?*

[CJ: In that case, I'm relieved.]
[FratBoss: Me too. So, the gala...?]
[CJ: I'll let Chelsea know I'll pick her up. Getting ready. You said you had some plans for after the gala?]
[FratBoss: Yeah. I'll explain when you get there. It's an after-party celebration at our frat house and Chelsea's sorority is joining.]

CJ froze. *That's a little weird. Why keep that secret?* Every nerve tightened as he started the shower and waited for the hot water. *Something's not right.*

[CJ: Hey Tim. What's your ETA?]

[Timmah: Uh, well Mark and his girl came so a few hours out. Meet at the gala?]

[CJ: Ok. What does our fraternity and Chelsea's sorority have in common?]

[Timmah: Huh? That's rather specific.]

[CJ: Jason's up to something. Not sure where I fall but I got a bad feeling about tonight.]

[Timmah: I'll make some calls.]

Tossing his phone on the vanity, he shed his clothes and slid under the water. Heat and steam enveloped him, but his mind couldn't let go of thoughts of Mary. Licking his lips, the taste of her skin and the soft warmth of her breasts came rushing back. A groan rolled from him, starting deep in his gut before he let it audibly escape his lips. His hand slipped down his abdomen and he started to stroke his cock slow and steady. He grew stiffer with each round, the tingling and arousal growing.

"Mary..." Each tug grew firmer as he came to a full hard-on. "Mary..." He muttered with eyes shut as streams of water raced down his body. "Mary..." A moan escaped as he curled his toes. "Mary..." Muscles grew taut, and he braced his other arm against the shower wall as he began to peak. "Mary..." he moaned her name, leaning his head back as he came. "Mary..." Her name left his lips like a sigh of relief.

Finishing, his body buzzed from thoughts and memories of her. Drying off, he glanced at the tiny mirror, wondering if she had at least heard or seen him beyond the haze of steam across the glass. The alarm on his phone startled him, and he shut it off. *This is it. The gala. I'll destroy you if it's the last thing I do in the world of the living, Jason.* He pulled on his tuxedo with practiced skill and paused before sliding his tie to his collar.

He caught a look at himself in the mirror and grinned. "Fuck this."

Leaving the tie loose, he unbuttoned the jacket and top buttons on his white shirt. Pulling the cufflinks back out, he tossed them onto the vanity.

Leaning onto the counter, he smirked. "Just you wait, Mary. I'm coming for you."

Marching away, he texted Chelsea.

[CJ: You better be out front when I drive up or I'm not stopping.]

11

Arriving at a Time of Golden Rest

None of the mirrors were answering to her. She could hear murmurs but nothing as clear as before. *Fuck you, Jason.* Running from one place to the next, the mirrors were just out of reach before shooting far away. Lungs starting to sting, she leaned on her knees as sweat dripped from her chin. *How could he do this to me?* She sunk to her knees and fought back the tears threatening to spill forth.

"That asshole doesn't deserve my despair." She sniffled, wiping her cheek. "I guess it's all up to CJ to rescue me. But I'm just some apparition in a mirror. I heard Jason talk him into believing that I'm just a drug-induced hallucination a moment ago. I mean, that makes more sense than the truth."

More tears fell, and she wiped to no avail to keep them from streaking down the length of her face. *How could I not realize I was sleeping with a monster? And worse, he broke it off with me to go out with my best friend Chelsea. I mean, what is so special about her?*

"Mary..." Her name sounded like a sigh.

"CJ?" One mirror stood out near where she sat. "Come, mirror." Much to her relief, it rushed to her call. "It's CJ, but the mirror is too fogged over. Can you hear me?" She hugged it. "I guess not. He really did cut my ability to communicate."

Looking around, the darkness had lost its beauty—now bare of all sparkling mirrors. The mirror in her arms buzzed with warmth despite the cold enveloping her in the absence of the vibrant magic and candlelight.

"Fuck this." CJ's voice came through clearly.

"CJ!" The mirror wiped clear now, she watched him make himself appear disheveled. "CJ! CAN YOU HEAR ME?" she shrieked into the mirror with no response from him. "Fuck! I can't do anything like this! What's happening?"

"Just you wait, Mary. I'm coming for you." He marched away, leaving her staring in disbelief.

"What does he mean he's coming for me?" Pulling to her feet, the mirror faded to nothing in her hands. "Shit! Where did he go?" She squinted her eyes all around, hoping for a glimmer or any sign. "Come on, there must be another. Something about him keeps breaking through. Come on, CJ, where are you?"

"I hope you're watching," CJ scoffed. "It's going to be quite the show."

A sparkle caught her eye, and she summoned the mirror. "Ah, a rearview mirror!" He was driving as she watched helplessly.

Every nerve tightened as he stopped to let Chelsea slide into the passenger seat. Her eyes glanced at the mirror for a moment before darting away and nudging it off herself. *She knows! Not in a I-saw-a-naked-mirror-ghost-grab-my-boyfriend way but more of a my-ex-bestie-is-watching-me-from-there-guilty way! What the hell are she and Jason planning on doing to CJ?*

Standing up, Mary looked around the abyss and began walking aimlessly like she had done so many times before. "Where was it? I kept shoes on this whole time until CJ came and when I was running a moment ago… Yes!" Carpet, old and torn, lay across the cold, black marble at her feet. "This must lead somewhere."

Swallowing her fear, she held the mirror tight and began to follow the runner. With the images upright, it seemed purposeful, and she presumed it led someplace important. *Where? Why haven't I found it or noticed before?* Pictures of kings, queens, knights, and wizards lay faded. In some places, it looked as if someone had burned holes or ripped out entire entities—at least their faces.

Looking at the mirror in hand, she couldn't hear anything. CJ glanced into it constantly, searching, and she knew it was for her. Inhaling deeply, she held her breath in hopes of keeping her emotions at bay. *I need to trust him. He's figured something out. Now, I need to keep calm and really see this place for the first time.*

Exhaling, she stumbled to a stop. The runner came to an end, and she stood in front of a large room lit by a fireplace. The hearth was massive, something worthy of a castle. The warm, wooden floor was soft to the touch as if well-maintained and waxed. Stacks of books and shelves with jars and more leather-bound tomes filled the three walls. Her heart skipped a beat, fluttering as she took it in.

"Fucking walls! And … and…" A blood-curdling scream escaped her. "Holy shit!"

She tripped on the carpet, falling back on her rump. In one of the high-backed chairs were two skeletons entangled with one another. She shook as she slid further back, at a loss for words. *What in the hell is this? Some fucking "A Rose for Emily" moment? Who are they? I mean, I suspected someone died here, but I wasn't hoping to fucking find them!*

A log popped in the fireplace, making her yelp before she turned back. "They're gone?" In a blink of an eye, the skeletons had vanished with nothing more than a piece of parchment in their place. "Where the hell am I? What's going on?"

The mirror in her hand dissipated, and she muttered curses under her breath. She sat, staring at the letter, too scared to move or even venture where death had embraced death. *Pull yourself together, Mary. This isn't Jason. It's too much like a dark romance or gothic romance vibe. Clearly, someone else was trapped here, waiting to be found.* Standing up, she whimpered to herself. *But why did it have to be me?*

Tiptoeing to the chair, she kept searching all around. *I swear if something pops out at me, I'm going to start swinging. It's not like I can run away.* The old, thick parchment was too dark to read so far from the fire. Huffing, she wandered closer to the fire, tugging her dress up once more in annoyance. At last, she could read the faint ink scrawled across it.

To our descendants who find themselves caught in my spell,

Beware of the dark changeling, for he seeks what I promised and denied him. You see, it was my magic I offered if he could help me ensnare my lover.

My pride and desire have brought an end to the love of my life, and soon after, I shall follow him to the depths of Hell, always there in his shadow for all eternity.

One day, the changeling will try to recreate the spell to syphon the magic. If you find yourself in such a situation, I bid you good luck.

You see, in my foolishness, the only way I made to break the spell is—

Ink had spilled across the page, and the last line only gave the writer's name.

Yours truly,
Vivien Galdur

"Of course, I can't see it." Balling it up, she threw it at the chair. "How fucked up that I have to pay for Merlin's mistress' tower. What kind of dumb luck is this?" she shouted, fists at her sides. "THIS SUCKS!" Her voice echoed throughout the room.

Looking at the other high-backed chair, she sat down. *Oh, to be able to sit in a real chair and have a warm fire.* Her eyelids grew heavy. *So tired.* Pulling her legs onto the chair, she hugged her knees as sleep weighed down on her. *At least I feel safe here. It reminds me of Grandma's house... I can remember being a kid... I remember the dance... it's like I'm a shattered mirror scattered across the floor...*

12

While All the Heathen Lay at Arthur's Feet

Pushing through the double doors and into the main event ballroom, CJ grimaced. All around were elegant gowns of all colors and types, but he failed to recall that it was intended to be a masquerade. *No one said anything about wearing a mask. I have a bad feeling about this.* Masked faces halted to face him; his exposed face sent murmurs all around the room. As soon as Chelsea pushed him aside to enter, they all snapped back, resuming what they had been doing.

He gripped her arm, forcing her to stay close to him. "Chelsea."

"I have nothing to say to you." She didn't even attempt to look at him. She wore a mask on her face; moments before in the car, she hadn't even let him know he would need one. "Let me go."

"What's really happening here?" he demanded. "The masks? Mary? Jason and you? What's supposed to happen at this gala with Mary and I being a central part?"

She yanked her arm back, her eyes dark within the mask, and she shoved him back a few steps. "Just play your part." She disappeared in the crowd.

"Fuck me." CJ wandered over to the appetizer table and popped a grape in his mouth. *She didn't even acknowledge how disheveled I look. Not a flinch, sneer, or anything. That means she doesn't care how I look as long as I'm here. Jason, what the hell are you planning to do with me tonight? Is this what they did to Mary? Is it because we are descendants of wizards or something?*

CJ continued to pick at the food in thought. *I mean, this whole thing seems off. The way she's at Jason's every beck and call and the pressure to join his frat house. Was I being manipulated well before Mary became involved? Is there a reason they are trying to do all this while Timmy is away, seeing he's an occult and magic expert?*

Then, he had an epiphany. Patting his pockets, he desperately searched for his cell phone. *Where the fuck is it?* A chill crept up his spine, and he raised his chin to meet Jason's gaze. In his hand, he wiggled CJ's cell phone. Chelsea stood behind him, turning her face away. *She always does that when she feels guilty and can't admit she's done something wrong. So, this is it. He's planning some magical event, and I'm the target. Does that mean everyone here is...*

Scanning the room, the gala seemed to take a dark turn. Baroque music filled the room, and he realized something was off about the dancing couples as they took turns, exchanging partners, and filling the space with tandem coordination straight out of a historical film. *There's no fucking way this many college brats mastered classical ballroom dancing overnight.* His heart pounded hard in his chest and nausea washed over him. *The whole place is in on it, and I'd bet not one of them are human.*

His gaze bounced from mask to mask. He saw irises in yellows and reds, glowing with cat-like pupils. Under them, crimson-painted lips covered their fangs. Looking closer, some even had misshapen ears. Their laughter at his impending doom began to fall on him in this fleeting moment. Rushing back a few steps, he bashed into the table. A three-tier tray of mini quiches toppled over with a loud clatter, sending him running out the door.

I need to escape! Behind him, he heard the rush of footsteps. *It's not just Jason after me!* Thoughts filled his mind. *Where do I even hide or go?* Turning a corner, a group was rounding the opposite end of the hall. He doubled back and took a different hallway. Tugging and pushing on doors, he pleaded, *Come on! One of these ... just one of these should be enough.* At last, a door pushed open, and he stumbled in. His heart stopped.

"Really? The women's restroom?" He turned to lock the door. "Fuck! No lock? What is up with this building!" Spinning, he stared wide-eyed at the frightened expression of his face in the mirror. "The mirror!" He rushed it, palms smacking against it. "If only I could go through it like that time before when no one could find me for a few days. Jason didn't even know where I went, so there's a chance." Looking at his reflection, he steeled himself. "I can do this. If I am a descendant of Vivien, then I can control the mirror world like Jason." Taking a few steps back, he glared at the mirror with new resolve. "Mary Emrys, Mary Emrys, Mary Emrys, Mary Emrys..." He paused, licking his lips before saying it for the fifth and final time. *Please let her or the magic hear me this time.* "Mary Emrys."

The smell of a fire burning met his nose, and he rushed forward. Hands shoved him from behind in his moment of wanting to slow down. *Shit! They found me!* Bracing to smack into the mirror, he tensed and closed his eyes. *Please let me in!* A rush of frigid air washed over him like a curtain before he slammed into a chair and fell to the ground with it. A woman's scream filled the air. He scrambled to his feet in time to see Mark, now translucent, nod and smash the mirror, so it would start to dissipate.

"M-Mark?" he sputtered. "MARK!"

"Closet!" Mark shouted as the last tendrils faded away.

CJ turned to the panting woman who held her chest, no longer able to keep her shrieking going. "M-Mary!"

She rushed to her feet. "CJ? But how? Did Jason…?"

"No." CJ patted himself down a moment as if checking that all of him had made it to the other side. "Where are we?"

"I don't know. Well, you're inside the mirror, but I just found this place," she confessed. "After that first time together, I lost track of my shoes and noticed a carpet. When I followed it, I found … walls," she offered. "Wait, how did you find me?"

"I called your name." CJ marveled over the space and the direction he had come, picking the chair up. "Could you not hear me?"

"No." Mary tugged on her dress. "I suspect it was Jason."

"Fucking Jason," CJ guffawed. "Dark changeling bullshit."

"A what?" Mary marched toward him, poking a finger into his chest. "You know what's happening? I want answers, CJ. Are you the reason why I'm here?"

CJ froze. "I don't even know anymore."

His gaze followed her arm up to her neck to the furrowed brow and scowling lips of red. *Mary is pissed. She has every right to be.* His heart fluttered as he searched her eyes, wondering how much she knew. *Does she know she's a descendant of Merlin? That I'm a descendant of Vivien? Does she know there's something magical and haunting about who we are? The irony of being here in this tower of mirrors like the original cast of some fairy tale. I might be just as obsessed about her as Vivien was over Merlin in the room…*

With a sigh, he pushed her arm down and pulled her into a full embrace. He whispered, "I'm so glad you're okay. I was worried he had done something to you after he cut us off from one another."

The tension released in her body as fingers clutched the back of his shirt, desperate to hold him closer. "Me too," she relented, choking back the sobs. "What is he? Why me? How was I supposed to know I'm some kind of monster."

CJ pulled back. "You? A monster?" He cupped her face, using his thumbs to push the tears away. "No, never," he reassured. *Fucking Jason. What did you say and do to her? Was imprisoning her here not good enough?*

"Jason said I'm a cambion." She abandoned the embrace and turned away. The back of her dress hung open as she pulled it up once more. "I don't know ... how and what," she said, pausing to swallow. "Look, I'm sort of half-blooded succubus or demon."

"Like Merlin. Yes, that makes sense," he consoled her in a soft tone. "Just like your ancestor. It's okay."

"Is it?" she inquired.

"What does it change?" he pressed.

"I'm sorry. If I had known it would cause anyone, especially you, so much distress..." Mary's words faltered, and the muscles in her back tensed.

"Distress?" he questioned, confused. "What kind of distress? I feel fine."

"Well, you know..." She was too afraid to finish and gazed over her shoulder. "The problem with..." She hesitated again. "Down there. Jason and you."

"You lost me." He tilted his head, baffled as he arched a brow. "What do you think you did to me? And Jason?"

"Well, Jason can't get it up since he slept with me, so I assume—"

"Oh, hell, no!" CJ blurted, rubbing his forehead. "Is this why he has you here? Because he's got limp dick? Holy fuck..." The idea blew his mind, and he panicked to reply. "Look, it works perfectly fine without you. Granted..." His face flushed.

"It does?" She straightened her back, ears red with embarrassment and still too ashamed to turn to face him. "Are you sure it works without me?"

"Yes, it does!" he shouted, startling them both. "I mean, thinking about you turns me on, but I don't think that has to do with what you are. It's about how I feel ... about you." His words slowed, his shoulders dropping. *Just confess it. I mean, it seems silly to fall in love at first sight, but who in the hell else will I ever find who can go tit for tat with geeky references? This is worth an eternity of little deaths, and I'll gladly give her my soul if she wishes.* "I love you, Mary. It seems crazy. We barely know each other, but the chemistry and the way you look at me..."

Mary dared to peek over her shoulder at last. "You ... love me?" She asked skeptically. "Are you confessing that you love me? Some woman in the mirror?"

"I do," he confirmed. "I love you. Not an apparition, but the Victorian Era geek who was quick to tell Jason and his paranormal debutants to fuck themselves."

She looked away, once more clutching the front of her dress. "But what if it's all because of what I am? What if your feeling of love is from the demon side of me making you feel that way?"

CJ closed the gap between them, fingers tracing down the divot of her spine. "Then let me show you once more how much I mean it. Surely, you feel it as I do when we make love, when we kiss. Even now, you resist looking me in the eyes, knowing fully well you can't deny it either. Tell me you love me too, Mary."

Mary leaned into him, allowing the dress to slide to the floor. "Show me once more," she demanded. "Make me fall for you one more time, so I can be sure this isn't some delusion. My heart beats so fast thinking of you, and I don't know if it's affection or a false hope I can leave here," she confessed.

"Well, we're both stuck in here," he reassured her. "So, let's see what unfolds in this moment when we have all the time in the world."

13

With Dark Sweet Hints of Some Who Prized Him More

The heat from his hands glided over her hip and ribs. One hand ascended to grope a breast, the other descended to dive between her thighs. She leaned into the hard planes of his torso as his finger glided over her clit and followed her channel to the weeping door that awaited him. *Is it okay to lose myself to passion? Am I allowed to fall too hard for a man I've only lusted after since the moment he fell into my world?*

His lips kissed at her neck as his finger slipped inside her. She lifted an arm, running her fingers through his hair. Tension and doubts lost hold as pleasure and desire took over. His finger retreated to her pink pearl and began slowly circling, making her loins ache and buzz with arousal. She felt his cock growing hard within his pants as he pressed it between her ass cheeks. He pinched her nipple, and she moaned in reply. He kissed his way up, suckling on her earlobe.

"Sit down in the chair," he demanded, letting her go.

Mary abandoned her dress on the floor and sat on the chair. Nervous, heart racing, she sat with thighs closed as she stared up at the amazing man before her. CJ pulled off the tie and dropped it. After shedding the jacket, he unbuttoned his shirt and tugged to unbuckle his pants. His fierce gaze locked onto her where she sat, naked and swallowed by the high-backed velveteen tufted chair. Swallowing, she watched with arousing anticipation as his shirt fluttered to the ground, and he wiggled out of his pants. Shoes clunked onto the wooden floor, and she found herself shivering at the sight of him. As CJ stroked his hard cock before her, the distance between them seemed agonizing. She marveled over him just as she had done the day she sucked his cock through the mirror.

"Now, I recall someone telling me that next time I'm to..." His gaze shifted, dropping to her thighs. "...lick her pussy."

Mary's face blushed, and she pressed her thighs tight together. "I was just talking dirty to help you," she insisted.

"Look, I take such requests very seriously." He knelt before her, hands hot on her thighs, squeezing them.

"CJ." Her heart fluttered as he pushed her legs apart with a devilish smirk on his face and a sparkle in his hazel eyes.

"Yes, mistress," he murmured, leaning in as his shoulder slid past her knees.

"I don't think I can handle this," she half-laughed.

"You shouldn't demand things you aren't prepared to take responsibility for." The heat of his breath rolled over her pussy, and her back straightened.

"I confess," she blurted.

He paused and looked up as she held her reddened face. "You're the first to ever stop me."

"I've been fingered plenty of times, but..." she choked on her works, legs squeezing him.

"*But?*" he echoed back to her, biting his lip as he arched a brow.

"I've never..." She covered her face and quickly said, "I've never been licked down there!"

CJ laughed a moment, enjoying how her whole body shivered and flushed. "Is that all?"

"Is that all?" she flustered. "This is something I've never experienced, and I don't know if I want to!"

"Oh, trust me. I'm honored to be your first on this one." His grin was wide, and he leaned back on his heels to give her some space, so he could really take in her full reaction. "I don't think I've ever had a woman say no, let alone need to discuss this beforehand." CJ chuckled.

"It's not funny," she pouted, peeking through her fingers. "I don't think I can handle it."

"Look, I'm telling you, you'll love this more than you can imagine." Now his face flushed, and he reasoned with her. "Men love blow jobs. It's different from being jerked off or fucking someone; it's something in between." He searched for the words. At last, he added, "It gives you a sense of domination and being spoiled in some lustful ways."

Her face found a deeper shade of red. "You really want to lick my pussy?" *He can't want to do this? I mean, his face being down there? I mean...*

CJ stood and leaned over her. His lips tickled at her ear as his hard cock pushed against her thigh. "Baby girl, I don't just want to lick it." His cock jumped, pressing harder against her thigh. "I want to taste and eat it like my favorite dessert." He pulled away to kneel once more. "Eyes on me," he demanded, kissing down her thigh.

She watched, shivers of provocation washing over her with each touch. He glanced up on occasion to make sure her eyes were on him. His lips worked up her inner thigh until the heat of his breath washed over her pussy. *My God, was I always this sensitive down there!* She braced herself as he hooked his arms under and around her legs and pulled her to the edge of the chair. She yelped, placing her hands on top of his shoulders.

"That won't be enough to stop me," he warned with a lustful growl.

The silken heat of his tongue slipped between her folds, and she held her breath. Her body arched, only giving his tongue a chance to lick stronger before the tip of it circled her clit. She squeaked, unsure how to express the new sensation tingling and buzzing through her like electric shock filled with bliss. He moaned into her pussy, and she exhaled. For a moment, she forgot how to breathe as his tongue licked and circled her clit. The pleasurable sensations were unlike anything she had experienced before. He stopped, meeting her wide-eyed glare as she remembered to inhale once more.

"Shall I continue?" He lapped out his tongue and flicked her clit, making her body jolt.

"Y-Yes," she stammered. "Don't stop, I want to—"

A shriek escaped her as his lips wrapped around her clit, sucking long and hard. Her hands fumbled, unsure what to do until, at last, fingers tangled with hair. She jerked him back, and he grinned up at her as she panted, trying to find her words and thoughts. The shot of pleasure overwhelming and addictive. *I want more but...*

"Gentle," she demanded, fingers gripping his hair tight.

"There she is," he cooed, licking his lips. "I was wondering where my mistress was."

A smirk crossed her face, the game with his suckling was back in play with higher stakes. She lowered him back between her thighs. *That's right, I'm in control here.* His tongue licked her opening, and she moaned, trying her best to keep her legs open as she allowed him to return to his fun. She reached above, gripping the top of the chair to fight the urge to pull him away. *I want to see how it feels to cum like this. To get off on his mouth while he—* His tongue pushed inside, and her breath caught once more. *I love the way the way he wiggles inside, tasting me before licking up to my clit.* She could hear how he sucked and smacked like eating a wet dessert.

The tingling buzz built up, and she rocked her hips against his face. He moaned, and her toes curled. Thighs shook as the oncoming orgasm edged closer. Her entire body was on fire with delight and desire like nothing she had ever experienced. Again, his tongue dove inside her, and she gasped. A hand released her thigh, and his tongue returned to circling her clit. She glared down in time to catch his gaze. Fingers slipped in, stroking hard and fast. Before she could gather herself, his lips wrapped around her clit, sucking hard and flicking it violently. She bucked. *Holy hell, I've been missing out!* A squeal of pleasure escaped her as she came. He pulled back, his finger replacing his tongue as she squirted, hard and wet.

14

The People Called Him Wizard

CJ didn't give her a moment of reprieve. He rammed his hard cock inside her drenched, tight pussy. She cried out in ecstasy as he fucked her, keeping her orgasm exploding as he groaned. Her pussy was hot and on fire in the moment, and she pulled him down to her. Their lips pressed together, opening for one another. His cock jumped as her tongue met his, moaning as she tasted herself. As he pounded her, she broke off the kiss, tilting her head back. He bit his lip. *Hold out a little longer. I don't want to cum just yet. I want to see her in the throes of passion a little longer.*

Pulling out, he started to kiss his way down her body. Suckling on a nipple, his fingers dipped in and out of her. The sounds of her breath hitching goaded him to keep going—to not let a moment of his lustful conquest waiver. *She will know the depths of my love for her.* Another cry escaped her as he made her cum yet again. The onslaught would be something she would never forget. *To be able to be the first to give her this much pleasure.* His heart fluttered as he let go of her nipple with a pop.

Once more, he knelt between her thighs and licked her pussy. She inhaled swiftly as her body lurched forward and arched. He was hungry to give her all the pleasure he could fathom. She grinded against his tongue, and he moaned into her. Legs shuddered in reply. Suckling on her swollen pink pearl, he thrusted fingers in and out of her pulsing channel. Her thighs and his face were slick with his efforts, egging him on as he pounded her.

Looking up, she arched her body, her fingers were white-knuckled where they gripped the chair. "Cum again for me," he commanded. "Cum for me." Another hitch to her breath, and he used his other hand to rub her jewel. "Be a good girl now," he cooed, moaning as his fingers pleased and teased her. "Cum for me, Mary."

"Fuck!" she shouted before bucking once more. "Fuck me! Fuck me right now!"

"I am," he teased.

"I want—" Her breath caught, and she moaned as she orgasmed again, panting. "I want your cock," she breathed.

He retreated, standing as he stroked his cock. "You sure you're ready for this."

"Yes, please." She lay haphazardly across the chair, trying to catch her breath. "I've never wanted a cock inside me so badly in all my life."

"Don't I need to cum for you to show I don't need you?" He smirked, watching her thighs close and rub against one another—a sign she was still riding out her last orgasm. "Prove to you I'm not in distress?"

"Don't you dare," she guffawed, her breasts heaving up and down with her heavy breathing. "I believe you. I just want you to fuck me so badly. I want you inside me," she pleaded.

"Ah, then you're ready for the next thing you asked of me." Wiping his mouth, he motioned for her to flip around. "As I recall, you also promised you would bend over for me."

A smile spread across her face, and she shook her head. "You're a ridiculous lover."

Legs wobbling, she managed to turn herself, knees against the edge of the chair while her palms sunk into the seat cushion. CJ's hands gripped her hips firmly. His heart fluttered seeing how her body curved in and out, the way her spine led his gaze to the mess of hair, and how she peeked over her shoulder at him. He rocked his hips forward, rubbing his cock against the wet heat of her pussy, the flesh swollen and throbbing from his efforts. He bit his lip, thinking before he decided to speak up.

"Look, I don't know if I can pull out in time if we do this." He rocked slow, his cock riding against her opening and growing slicker with each pass. "You're so tight and wet, it's going to take everything I have not to be a two-pump chump," he laughed. "Never in my life," he muttered to himself.

"I want you to cum inside," she confessed.

His heart leapt to his throat. "Um, but if that happens, what if—"

"You love me, right?" She swallowed and rocked her on hips to slide across his cock.

"Y-Yes." He squinted his eyes.

"I..." She searched his face. "It's not the orgasms talking." They smirked at one another. "I love you, CJ. Like I can see settling with you and—"

Reaching down, he guided his cock inside her. "Fucking amazing."

She arched as a shriek escaped her lips. His rock-hard shaft pushed deeper inside her with each swift thrust. Her breasts bounced with each knock on his hilt. They both began to moan, his balls slapping against her with each forward thrust.

"Fuck!" she shrieked. "CJ! Cum for me!"

He groaned, pushing hard into her. Her pussy convulsed, tightened on his shaft, and he lost it. He came hard, letting his own cry of pleasure escape. His cock bumped and jolted with each spurt as she throbbed with her own orgasm. *I've never peaked at the same time as my lover before...* He tried to retreat, but both jolted, and he froze. *Shit. I'm too sensitive to move just yet. Holy hell.*

Swallowing, she stuttered, "That was amazing."

"Yeah, yeah it was," he agreed, "but I can't move."

She shook her head, laughing a little before agreeing. "Me neither."

Panting, he repeated, "I love you, Mary Emrys."

"And I love you, CJ," she breathed.

The sound of someone falling brought their eyes back to the fireplace. The wooden mirror from the closet was beside it, and Timmy waited with a change of clothes for them in his hands.

"What the fuck?" CJ marveled, scooping Mary into his arms to shield her. "How the hell did you get in here?"

"Ah, about that." Timmy laid the clothes on the opposite chair and turned away, though he could still see CJ in the mirror. "You've been missing for a month, so I came to make sure you weren't ... lost?" he offered, smirking. "But I see you had other plans."

"What about Jason?" CJ used a foot to slide his tuxedo jacket over to cover Mary.

"He's been dealt with." Timmy motioned with a hand. "It seems the gala was an unsanctioned fae ritual meant to drain the magic from a wizard or magic holder. Highly illegal. When Sir Gawain appeared, everyone scattered." Clearing his throat, he then revealed, "And thanks to a ragtag crew of a wraith, poltergeist, and pukwudgie, Jason was arrested by the fairyland officials."

"What's a pukwudgie?" whispered Mary.

"No fucking clue," replied CJ before speaking louder. "Thank you, but if you don't mind, can we get dressed before leaving."

"Oh! Certainly, by all means." Timmy smirked. "We pukwudgie just like a little harmless fun, so I'm glad to see this ended well like I intended. The mirror is safe, and the magic is now yours to control, CJ. Use it wisely, heir to Vivien's magic."

"Thanks..." He watched as Timmy left through the mirror.

"So, the mirror is yours?" Mary gave him an unsteady gaze.

"Like you, I had no clue until all this started to happen." He kissed the top of her head. "I guess we get to discover more about this together, my little cambion who craves the little death."

She hugged him. "Thank you for breaking the curse."

"Someone had to end the blood feud between Merlin and Vivien." He rubbed the back of his neck, brow high. "Who knew we could fuck our way to a solution."

She punched his arm, grabbing the clothes. "You need to fill me in on the details. For now, I want the fuck out of this mirror."

"Good point."

Epilogue

Jason sat in a mirrored cube. He had been caught doing ill to another magical being—something that never sat well with many ruling bodies. *At least I didn't get caught by the Yetis. I would have been torn limb from limb.* Sitting on the prison bed that made up half the cell space, he balled his fists. *Who knew CJ would figure out he could summon and control the mirror. Damn you, Vivien. You conniving harlot!* All he could do was stare down the reflection of himself—a melted version of Jason's face thanks to being disconnected from the human world.

"You can't do this to me!" he shouted, knowing the wardens could indeed hear him. "A changeling must be connected to the human world or it risks dying!" he warned.

"You act like we don't know that," Gawain chuckled, appearing in the reflection. "Listen, we thought long and hard, no pun intended, about this, and we determined a great means of keeping you connected."

"What's taking so long, old man," Jason sneered as an eye drooped further. "I'm melting already. My death will be nearing in a matter of hours. Granted, it beats staying here," he spat.

"Patience. These matters take time." Clearing his throat, he continued his explanation, "We needed permission, and it took some convincing. Someone closer or connected to you works best, no?"

"Convincing? From whom?" Jason gave a disgusted look. "I don't want to be visited by anyone! Unless... Did Chelsea offer?"

"Lord no, we are still hunting for that one," grunted Gawain in annoyance.

"I will not let just anyone see me this way." Jason stood, tapping on the mirror in anger.

"Well, we couldn't have you shifting to be their doppelganger to escape either," agreed Gawain. "But considering your love for mirrors..."

Jason's scowl faltered, and his eyes widened. "You wouldn't?"

"Look, there are fae in prison who would love access to something like this." Gawain smirked. "Consider it a means to ... make serving your *hard* time here a little more ... pleasurable. It will keep you from becoming a complete puddle on the floor."

"You can't do this to me!" Jason beat on the mirror.

The reflection shifted, and he found himself staring down from a ceiling mirror onto a bed. As the couple came into focus, he recognized them immediately: *Mary and CJ.* Dread filled him as they stared up at the mirror with a hint of hesitation across their faces. They looked to one another, whispering. Jason paled. He could hear them loud and clear.

"Are we sure about this?" Mary furrowed her brow.

"Look, the guy will die without it." CJ tried to not laugh. "I think he fucking deserves it. How many times did you watch someone fuck in view of a mirror while stuck there?"

Mary winced, shaking her head. "Don't remind me."

"As I see it, we're showing him mercy," offered CJ.

"NO!" screeched Jason, his voice breaking as his melted parts started to slip back into place. "ANYTHING BUT THIS!"

"Well, I guess it's not like he hasn't seen me naked or in the throes of passion," she reasoned to herself.

"That's the spirit," cooed CJ, tossing the covers to the side to reveal they were already naked.

"CJ!" Mary glanced up at the mirror, face blushing. "He's watching, isn't he?"

"Who fucking cares?" Her face and body flushed red. "Have I told you how good you look in red," he moaned into her neck. "Let me show him how to treat the girl of one's dreams."

Mary laughed, cupping CJ's face. "Is this when you confess you like other people watching you get off?"

"What can I say," he nuzzled into her ear and whispered, "It's quite the turn on when I do it with you in front of the mirror."

"Don't you mean Jason," she added flatly.

"That's just the bonus." He rolled her flat on her back, straddling her. "Now, where shall I begin?" His fingers slid across her lips. "With a kiss? Or perhaps..." He paused as he crawled backward and groped her breasts. "Nipples? No, no I want to hear you scream loud enough to shake the mirrors."

Pushing her thighs apart, he bowed his head between them as pounding on the mirror egged him on.

THE END

Idylls of the King, Merlin and Vivien

A storm was coming, but the winds were still,
And in the wild woods of Broceliande,
Before an oak, so hollow, huge and old
It looked a tower of ivied masonwork,
At Merlin's feet the wily Vivien lay.

For he that always bare in bitter grudge
The slights of Arthur and his Table, Mark
The Cornish King, had heard a wandering voice,
A minstrel of Caerleon by strong storm
Blown into shelter at Tintagil, say
That out of naked knightlike purity
Sir Lancelot worshipt no unmarried girl
But the great Queen herself, fought in her name,
Sware by her—vows like theirs, that high in heaven
Love most, but neither marry, nor are given
In marriage, angels of our Lord's report.

He ceased, and then—for Vivien sweetly said
(She sat beside the banquet nearest Mark)

"And is the fair example followed, Sir,
In Arthur's household?"—answered innocently:

Ay, by some few—ay, truly—youths that hold
It more beseems the perfect virgin knight
To worship woman as true wife beyond
All hopes of gaining, than as maiden girl.
They place their pride in Lancelot and the Queen.
So passionate for an utter purity
Beyond the limit of their bond, are these,
For Arthur bound them not to singleness.
Brave hearts and clean! and yet—God guide them—young."

Then Mark was half in heart to hurl his cup
Straight at the speaker, but forebore: he rose
To leave the hall, and, Vivien following him,
Turned to her: "Here are snakes within the grass;
And you methinks, O Vivien, save ye fear
The monkish manhood, and the mask of pure
Worn by this court, can stir them till they sting."

And Vivien answered, smiling scornfully,
"Why fear? because that fostered at *thy* court
I savour of thy—virtues? fear them? no.
As Love, if Love be perfect, casts out fear,
So Hate, if Hate be perfect, casts out fear.
My father died in battle against the King,
My mother on his corpse in open field;
She bore me there, for born from death was I
Among the dead and sown upon the wind—
And then on thee! and shown the truth betimes,
That old true filth, and bottom of the well,
Where Truth is hidden. Gracious lessons thine

And maxims of the mud! 'This Arthur pure!
Great Nature through the flesh herself hath made
Gives him the lie! There is no being pure,
My cherub; saith not Holy Writ the same?'—
If I were Arthur, I would have thy blood.
Thy blessing, stainless King! I bring thee back,
When I have ferreted out their burrowings,
The hearts of all this Order in mine hand—
Ay—so that fate and craft and folly close,
Perchance, one curl of Arthur's golden beard.
To me this narrow grizzled fork of thine
Is cleaner-fashioned—Well, I loved thee first,
That warps the wit."

Loud laughed the graceless Mark.
But Vivien, into Camelot stealing, lodged
Low in the city, and on a festal day
When Guinevere was crossing the great hall
Cast herself down, knelt to the Queen, and wailed.

Why kneel ye there? What evil have ye wrought?
Rise!" and the damsel bidden rise arose
And stood with folded hands and downward eyes
Of glancing corner, and all meekly said,
"None wrought, but suffered much, an orphan maid!
My father died in battle for thy King,
My mother on his corpse—in open field,
The sad sea-sounding wastes of Lyonnesse—
Poor wretch—no friend!—and now by Mark the King
For that small charm of feature mine, pursued—
If any such be mine—I fly to thee.
Save, save me thou—Woman of women—thine
The wreath of beauty, thine the crown of power,

Be thine the balm of pity, O Heaven's own white
Earth-angel, stainless bride of stainless King—
Help, for he follows! take me to thyself!
O yield me shelter for mine innocency
Among thy maidens!"

Here her slow sweet eyes
Fear-tremulous, but humbly hopeful, rose
Fixt on her hearer's, while the Queen who stood
All glittering like May sunshine on May leaves
In green and gold, and plumed with green replied,
"Peace, child! of overpraise and overblame
We choose the last. Our noble Arthur, him
Ye scarce can overpraise, will hear and know.
Nay—we believe all evil of thy Mark—
Well, we shall test thee farther; but this hour
We ride a-hawking with Sir Lancelot.
He hath given us a fair falcon which he trained;
We go to prove it. Bide ye here the while."

She past; and Vivien murmured after Go!
I bide the while." Then through the portal-arch
Peering askance, and muttering broke-wise,
As one that labours with an evil dream,
Beheld the Queen and Lancelot get to horse.

Is that the Lancelot? goodly—ay, but gaunt:
Courteous—amends for gauntness—takes her hand—
That glance of theirs, but for the street, had been
A clinging kiss—how hand lingers in hand!
Let go at last! —they ride away—to hawk
For waterfowl. Royaller game is mine.
For such a supersensual sensual bond

As that gray cricket chirpt of at our hearth—
Touch flax with flame—a glance will serve—the liars!
Ah little rat that borest in the dyke
Thy hole by night to let the boundless deep
Down upon far-off cities while they dance—
Or dream—of thee they dreamed not—nor of me
These—ay, but each of either: ride, and dream
The mortal dream that never yet was mine—
Ride, ride and dream until ye wake—to me!
Then, narrow court and lubber King, farewell!
For Lancelot will be gracious to the rat,
And our wise Queen, if knowing that I know,
Will hate, loathe, fear—but honour me the more."

Yet while they rode together down the plain,
Their talk was all of training, terms of art,
Diet and seeling, jesses, leash and lure.
"She is too noble" he said "to check at pies,
Nor will she rake: there is no baseness in her."
Here when the Queen demanded as by chance
"Know ye the stranger woman?" "Let her be,"
Said Lancelot and unhooded casting off
The goodly falcon free; she towered; her bells,
Tone under tone, shrilled; and they lifted up
Their eager faces, wondering at the strength,
Boldness and royal knighthood of the bird
Who pounced her quarry and slew it. Many a time
As once—of old—among the flowers—they rode.

But Vivien half-forgotten of the Queen
Among her damsels broidering sat, heard, watched
And whispered: through the peaceful court she crept
And whispered: then as Arthur in the highest

Leavened the world, so Vivien in the lowest,
Arriving at a time of golden rest,
And sowing one ill hint from ear to ear,
While all the heathen lay at Arthur's feet,
And no quest came, but all was joust and play,
Leavened his hall. They heard and let her be.

Thereafter as an enemy that has left
Death in the living waters, and withdrawn,
The wily Vivien stole from Arthur's court.

She hated all the knights, and heard in thought
Their lavish comment when her name was named.
For once, when Arthur walking all alone,
Vext at a rumour issued from herself
Of some corruption crept among his knights,
Had met her, Vivien, being greeted fair,
Would fain have wrought upon his cloudy mood
With reverent eyes mock-loyal, shaken voice,
And fluttered adoration, and at last
With dark sweet hints of some who prized him more
Than who should prize him most; at which the King
Had gazed upon her blankly and gone by:
But one had watched, and had not held his peace:
It made the laughter of an afternoon
That Vivien should attempt the blameless King.
And after that, she set herself to gain
Him, the most famous man of all those times,
Merlin, who knew the range of all their arts,
Had built the King his havens, ships, and halls,
Was also Bard, and knew the starry heavens;
The people called him Wizard; whom at first
She played about with slight and sprightly talk,

And vivid smiles, and faintly-venomed points
Of slander, glancing here and grazing there;
And yielding to his kindlier moods, the Seer
Would watch her at her petulance, and play,
Even when they seemed unloveable, and laugh
As those that watch a kitten; thus he grew
Tolerant of what he half disdained, and she,
Perceiving that she was but half disdained,
Began to break her sports with graver fits,
Turn red or pale, would often when they met
Sigh fully, or all-silent gaze upon him
With such a fixt devotion, that the old man,
Though doubtful, felt the flattery, and at times
Would flatter his own wish in age for love,
And half believe her true: for thus at times
He wavered; but that other clung to him,
Fixt in her will, and so the seasons went.

Then fell on Merlin a great melancholy;
He walked with dreams and darkness, and he found
A doom that ever poised itself to fall,
An ever-moaning battle in the mist,
World-war of dying flesh against the life,
Death in all life and lying in all love,
The meanest having power upon the highest,
And the high purpose broken by the worm.

So leaving Arthur's court he gained the beach;
There found a little boat, and stept into it;
And Vivien followed, but he marked her not.
She took the helm and he the sail; the boat
Drave with a sudden wind across the deeps
And touching Breton sands, they disembarked.

And then she followed Merlin all the way,
Even to the wild woods of Broceliande.
For Merlin once had told her of a charm,
The which if any wrought on anyone
With woven paces and with waving arms,
The man so wrought on ever seemed to lie
Closed in the four walls of a hollow tower,
From which was no escape for evermore;
And none could find that man for evermore,
Nor could he see but him who wrought the charm
Coming and going, and he lay as dead
And lost to life and use and name and fame.
And Vivien ever sought to work the charm
Upon the great Enchanter of the Time,
As fancying that her glory would be great
According to his greatness whom she quenched.

There lay she all her length and kissed his feet,
As if in deepest reverence and in love.
A twist of gold was round her hair; a robe
Of samite without price, that more exprest
Than hid her, clung about her lissome limbs,
In colour like the satin-shining palm
On sallows in the windy gleams of March:
And while she kissed them, crying, "Trample me,
Dear feet, that I have followed through the world,
And I will pay you worship; tread me down
And I will kiss you for it;" he was mute:
So dark a forethought rolled about his brain,
As on a dull day in an Ocean cave
The blind wave feeling round his long sea-hall
In silence: wherefore, when she lifted up
A face of sad appeal, and spake and said,

"O Merlin, do ye love me?" and again,
"O Merlin, do ye love me?" and once more,
"Great Master, do ye love me?" he was mute.
And lissome Vivien, holding by his heel,
Writhed toward him, slided up his knee and sat,
Behind his ankle twined her hollow feet
Together, curved an arm about his neck,
Clung like a snake; and letting her left hand
Droop from his mighty shoulder, as a leaf,
Made with her right a comb of pearl to part
The lists of such a beard as youth gone out
Had left in ashes: then he spoke and said,
Not looking at her, "Who are wise in love
Love most, say least," and Vivien answered quick,
"I saw the little elf-god eyeless once
In Arthur's arras hall at Camelot:
But neither eyes nor tongue—O stupid child!
Yet you are wise who say it; let me think
Silence is wisdom: I am silent then,
And ask no kiss;" then adding all at once,
"And lo, I clothe myself with wisdom," drew
The vast and shaggy mantle of his beard
Across her neck and bosom to her knee,
And called herself a gilded summer fly
Caught in a great old tyrant spider's web,
Who meant to eat her up in that wild wood
Without one word. So Vivien called herself,
But rather seemed a lovely baleful star
Veiled in gray vapour; till he sadly smiled:
"To what request for what strange boon," he said,
"Are these your pretty tricks and fooleries,
O Vivien, the preamble? yet my thanks,
For these have broken up my melancholy."

And Vivien answered smiling saucily,
"What, O my Master, have ye found your voice?
I bid the stranger welcome. Thanks at last!
But yesterday you never opened lip,
Except indeed to drink: no cup had we:
In mine own lady palms I culled the spring
That gathered trickling dropwise from the cleft,
And made a pretty cup of both my hands
And offered you it kneeling: then you drank
And knew no more, nor gave me one poor word;
O no more thanks than might a goat have given
With no more sign of reverence than a beard.
And when we halted at that other well,
And I was faint to swooning, and you lay
Foot-gilt with all the blossom-dust of those
Deep meadows we had traversed, did you know
That Vivien bathed your feet before her own?
And yet no thanks: and all through this wild wood
And all this morning when I fondled you:
Boon, ay, there was a boon, one not so strange—
How had I wronged you? surely ye are wise,
But such a silence is more wise than kind."

And Merlin locked his hand in hers and said:
"O did ye never lie upon the shore,
And watch the curled white of the coming wave
Glassed in the slippery sand before it breaks?
Even such a wave, but not so pleasurable,
Dark in the glass of some presageful mood,
Had I for three days seen, ready to fall.
And then I rose and fled from Arthur's court
To break the mood. You followed me unasked;
And when I looked, and saw you following still,

My mind involved yourself the nearest thing
In that mind-mist: for shall I tell you truth?
You seemed that wave about to break upon me
And sweep me from my hold upon the world,
My use and name and fame. Your pardon, child.
Your pretty sports have brightened all again.
And ask your boon, for boon I owe you thrice,
Once for wrong done you by confusion, next
For thanks it seems till now neglected, last
For these your dainty gambols: wherefore ask;
And take this boon so strange and not so strange."

And Vivien answered smiling mournfully:
"O not so strange as my long asking it,
Not yet so strange as you yourself are strange,
Nor half so strange as that dark mood of yours.
I ever feared ye were not wholly mine;
And see, yourself have owned ye did me wrong.
The people call you prophet: let it be:
But not of those that can expound themselves.
Take Vivien for expounder; she will call
That three-days-long presageful gloom of yours
No presage, but the same mistrustful mood
That makes you seem less noble than yourself,
Whenever I have asked this very boon,
Now asked again: for see you not, dear love,
That such a mood as that, which lately gloomed
Your fancy when ye saw me following you,
Must make me fear still more you are not mine,
Must make me yearn still more to prove you mine,
And make me wish still more to learn this charm
Of woven paces and of waving hands,
As proof of trust. O Merlin, teach it me.

The charm so taught will charm us both to rest.
For, grant me some slight power upon your fate,
I, feeling that you felt me worthy trust,
Should rest and let you rest, knowing you mine.
And therefore be as great as ye are named.
Not muffled round with selfish reticence.
How hard you look and how denyingly!
O, if you think this wickedness in me,
That I should prove it on you unawares,
That makes me passing wrathful; then our bond
Had best be loosed for ever: but think or not,
By Heaven that hears I tell you the clean truth,
As clean as blood of babes, as white as milk:
O Merlin, may this earth, if ever I,
If these unwitty wandering wits of mine,
Even in the jumbled rubbish of a dream,
Have tript on such conjectural treachery—
May this hard earth cleave to the Nadir hell
Down, down, and close again, and nip me flat,
If I be such a traitress. Yield my boon,
Till which I scarce can yield you all I am;
And grant my re-reiterated wish,
The great proof of your love: because I think,
However wise, ye hardly know me yet."

And Merlin loosed his hand from hers and said,
"I never was less wise, however wise,
Too curious Vivien, though you talk of trust,
Than when I told you first of such a charm.
Yea, if ye talk of trust I tell you this,
Too much I trusted when I told you that,
And stirred this vice in you which ruined man
Through woman the first hour; for howsoe'er

In children a great curiousness be well,
Who have to learn themselves and all the world,
In you, that are no child, for still I find
Your face is practised when I spell the lines,
I call it, —well, I will not call it vice:
But since you name yourself the summer fly,
I well could wish a cobweb for the gnat,
That settles, beaten back, and beaten back
Settles, till one could yield for weariness:
But since I will not yield to give you power
Upon my life and use and name and fame,
Why will ye never ask some other boon?
Yea, by God's rood, I trusted you too much."

And Vivien, like the tenderest-hearted maid
That ever bided tryst at village stile,
Made answer, either eyelid wet with tears:
"Nay, Master, be not wrathful with your maid;
 Caress her: let her feel herself forgiven
Who feels no heart to ask another boon.
I think ye hardly know the tender rhyme
Of 'trust me not at all or all in all.'
I heard the great Sir Lancelot sing it once,
And it shall answer for me. Listen to it.

In Love, if Love be Love, if Love be ours,
Faith and unfaith can ne'er be equal powers:
Unfaith in aught is want of faith in all.

It is the little rift within the lute,
That by and by will make the music mute,
And ever widening slowly silence all.

The little rift within the lover's lute
Or little pitted speck in garnered fruit,
That rotting inward slowly moulders all.

It is not worth the keeping: let it go:
But shall it? answer, darling, answer, no.
And trust me not at all or all in all.'

O Master, do ye love my tender rhyme?"

And Merlin looked and half believed her true,
So tender was her voice, so fair her face,
So sweetly gleamed her eyes behind her tears
Like sunlight on the plain behind a shower:
And yet he answered half indignantly:

Far other was the song that once I heard
By this huge oak, sung nearly where we sit:
For here we met, some ten or twelve of us,
To chase a creature that was current then
In these wild woods, the hart with golden horns.
It was the time when first the question rose
About the founding of a Table Round,
That was to be, for love of God and men
And noble deeds, the flower of all the world.
And each incited each to noble deeds.
And while we waited, one, the youngest of us,
We could not keep him silent, out he flashed,
And into such a song, such fire for fame,
Such trumpet-blowings in it, coming down
To such a stern and iron-clashing close,
That when he stopt we longed to hurl together,
And should have done it; but the beauteous beast

Scared by the noise upstarted at our feet,
And like a silver shadow slipt away
Through the dim land; and all day long we rode
Through the dim land against a rushing wind,
That glorious roundel echoing in our ears,
And chased the flashes of his golden horns
Until they vanished by the fairy well
That laughs at iron—as our warriors did—
Where children cast their pins and nails, and cry,
'Laugh, little well!' but touch it with a sword,
It buzzes fiercely round the point; and there
We lost him: such a noble song was that.
But, Vivien, when you sang me that sweet rhyme,
I felt as though you knew this cursèd charm,
Were proving it on me, and that I lay
And felt them slowly ebbing, name and fame."

And Vivien answered smiling mournfully:
"O mine have ebbed away for evermore,
And all through following you to this wild wood,
Because I saw you sad, to comfort you.
Lo now, what hearts have men! they never mount
As high as woman in her selfless mood.
And touching fame, howe'er ye scorn my song,
Take one verse more—the lady speaks it—this:

My name, once mine, now thine, is closelier mine,
For fame, could fame be mine, that fame were thine,
And shame, could shame be thine, that shame were mine.
So trust me not at all or all in all.'

Says she not well? and there is more—this rhyme
Is like the fair pearl-necklace of the Queen,

That burst in dancing, and the pearls were spilt;
Some lost, some stolen, some as relics kept.
But nevermore the same two sister pearls
Ran down the silken thread to kiss each other
On her white neck—so is it with this rhyme:
It lives dispersedly in many hands,
And every minstrel sings it differently;
'Man dreams of Fame while woman wakes to love.'
Yea! Love, though Love were of the grossest, carves
A portion from the solid present, eats
And uses, careless of the rest; but Fame,
The Fame that follows death is nothing to us;
And what is Fame in life but half-disfame,
And counterchanged with darkness? ye yourself
Know well that Envy calls you Devil's son,
And since ye seem the Master of all Art,
They fain would make you Master of all vice."

And Merlin locked his hand in hers and said,
"I once was looking for a magic weed,
And found a fair young squire who sat alone,
Had carved himself a knightly shield of wood,
And then was painting on it fancied arms,
Azure, an Eagle rising or, the Sun
In dexter chief; the scroll 'I follow fame.'
And speaking not, but leaning over him,
I took his brush and blotted out the bird,
And made a Gardner putting in a graff,
With this for motto, 'Rather use than fame.'
You should have seen him blush; but afterwards
He made a stalwart knight. O Vivien,
For you, methinks you think you love me well;
For me, I love you somewhat; rest: and Love

Should have some rest and pleasure in himself,
Not ever be too curious for a boon,
Too prurient for a proof against the grain
Of him ye say ye love: but Fame with men,
Being but ampler means to serve mankind,
Should have small rest or pleasure in herself,
But work as vassal to the larger love,
That dwarfs the petty love of one to one.
Use gave me Fame at first, and Fame again
Increasing gave me use. Lo, there my boon!
What other? for men sought to prove me vile,
Because I fain had given them greater wits:
And then did Envy call me Devil's son:
The sick weak beast seeking to help herself
By striking at her better, missed, and brought
Her own claw back, and wounded her own heart.
Sweet were the days when I was all unknown,
But when my name was lifted up, the storm
Brake on the mountain and I cared not for it.
Right well know I that Fame is half-disfame,
Yet needs must work my work. That other fame,
To one at least, who hath not children, vague,
The cackle of the unborn about the grave,
I cared not for it: a single misty star,
Which is the second in a line of stars
That seem a sword beneath a belt of three,
I never gazed upon it but I dreamt
Of some vast charm concluded in that star
To make fame nothing. Wherefore, if I fear,
Giving you power upon me through this charm,
That you might play me falsely, having power,
However well ye think ye love me now
(As sons of kings loving in pupilage

Have turned to tyrants when they came to power)
I rather dread the loss of use than fame;
If you—and not so much from wickedness,
As some wild turn of anger, or a mood
Of overstrained affection, it may be,
To keep me all to your own self, —or else
A sudden spurt of woman's jealousy,—
Should try this charm on whom ye say ye love."

And Vivien answered smiling as in wrath:
"Have I not sworn? I am not trusted. Good!
Well, hide it, hide it; I shall find it out;
And being found take heed of Vivien.
A woman and not trusted, doubtless I
Might feel some sudden turn of anger born
Of your misfaith; and your fine epithet
Is accurate too, for this full love of mine
Without the full heart back may merit well
Your term of overstrained. So used as I,
My daily wonder is, I love at all.
And as to woman's jealousy, O why not?
O to what end, except a jealous one,
And one to make me jealous if I love,
Was this fair charm invented by yourself?
I well believe that all about this world
Ye cage a buxom captive here and there,
Closed in the four walls of a hollow tower
From which is no escape for evermore."

Then the great Master merrily answered her:
"Full many a love in loving youth was mine;
I needed then no charm to keep them mine
But youth and love; and that full heart of yours

Whereof ye prattle, may now assure you mine;
So live uncharmed. For those who wrought it first,
The wrist is parted from the hand that waved,
The feet unmortised from their ankle-bones
Who paced it, ages back: but will ye hear
The legend as in guerdon for your rhyme?

There lived a king in the most Eastern East,
Less old than I, yet older, for my blood
Hath earnest in it of far springs to be.
A tawny pirate anchored in his port,
Whose bark had plundered twenty nameless isles;
And passing one, at the high peep of dawn,
He saw two cities in a thousand boats
All fighting for a woman on the sea.
And pushing his black craft among them all,
He lightly scattered theirs and brought her off,
With loss of half his people arrow-slain;
A maid so smooth, so white, so wonderful,
They said a light came from her when she moved:
And since the pirate would not yield her up,
The King impaled him for his piracy;
Then made her Queen: but those isle-nurtured eyes
Waged such unwilling though successful war
On all the youth, they sickened; councils thinned,
And armies waned, for magnet-like she drew
The rustiest iron of old fighters' hearts;
And beasts themselves would worship; camels knelt
Unbidden, and the brutes of mountain back
That carry kings in castles, bowed black knees
Of homage, ringing with their serpent hands,
To make her smile, her golden ankle-bells.
What wonder, being jealous, that he sent

His horns of proclamation out through all
The hundred under-kingdoms that he swayed
To find a wizard who might teach the King
Some charm, which being wrought upon the Queen
Might keep her all his own: to such a one
He promised more than ever king has given,
A league of mountain full of golden mines,
A province with a hundred miles of coast,
A palace and a princess, all for him:
But on all those who tried and failed, the King
Pronounced a dismal sentence, meaning by it
To keep the list low and pretenders back,
Or like a king, not to be trifled with—
Their heads should moulder on the city gates.
And many tried and failed, because the charm
Of nature in her overbore their own:
And many a wizard brow bleached on the walls:
And many weeks a troop of carrion crows
Hung like a cloud above the gateway towers."

And Vivien breaking in upon him, said:
"I sit and gather honey; yet, methinks,
Thy tongue has tript a little: ask thyself.
The lady never made *unwilling* war
With those fine eyes: she had her pleasure in it,
And made her good man jealous with good cause.
And lived there neither dame nor damsel then
Wroth at a lover's loss? were all as tame,
I mean, as noble, as the Queen was fair?
Not one to flirt a venom at her eyes,
Or pinch a murderous dust into her drink,
Or make her paler with a poisoned rose?
Well, those were not our days: but did they find

A wizard? Tell me, was he like to thee?

She ceased, and made her lithe arm round his neck
Tighten, and then drew back, and let her eyes
Speak for her, glowing on him, like a bride's
On her new lord, her own, the first of men.

He answered laughing, Nay, not like to me.
At last they found—his foragers for charms—
A little glassy-headed hairless man,
Who lived alone in a great wild on grass;
Read but one book, and ever reading grew
So grated down and filed away with thought,
So lean his eyes were monstrous; while the skin
Clung but to crate and basket, ribs and spine.
And since he kept his mind on one sole aim,
Nor ever touched fierce wine, nor tasted flesh,
Nor owned a sensual wish, to him the wall
That sunders ghosts and shadow-casting men
Became a crystal, and he saw them through it,
And heard their voices talk behind the wall,
And learnt their elemental secrets, powers
And forces; often o'er the sun's bright eye
Drew the vast eyelid of an inky cloud,
And lashed it at the base with slanting storm;
Or in the noon of mist and driving rain,
When the lake whitened and the pinewood roared,
And the cairned mountain was a shadow, sunned
The world to peace again: here was the man.
And so by force they dragged him to the King.
And then he taught the King to charm the Queen
In such-wise, that no man could see her more,
Nor saw she save the King, who wrought the charm,

Coming and going, and she lay as dead,
And lost all use of life: but when the King
Made proffer of the league of golden mines,
The province with a hundred miles of coast,
The palace and the princess, that old man
Went back to his old wild, and lived on grass,
And vanished, and his book came down to me."

And Vivien answered smiling saucily:
"Ye have the book: the charm is written in it:
Good: take my counsel: let me know it at once:
For keep it like a puzzle chest in chest,
With each chest locked and padlocked thirty-fold,
And whelm all this beneath as vast a mound
As after furious battle turfs the slain
On some wild down above the windy deep,
I yet should strike upon a sudden means
To dig, pick, open, find and read the charm:
Then, if I tried it, who should blame me then?"

And smiling as a master smiles at one
That is not of his school, nor any school
But that where blind and naked Ignorance
Delivers brawling judgments, unashamed,
On all things all day long, he anwered her:

Thou read the book, my pretty Vivien!
O ay, it is but twenty pages long,
But every page having an ample marge,
And every marge enclosing in the midst
A square of text that looks a little blot,
The text no larger than the limbs of fleas;
And every square of text an awful charm,

Writ in a language that has long gone by.
So long, that mountains have arisen since
With cities on their flanks—thou read the book!
And every margin scribbled, crost, and crammed
With comment, densest condensation, hard
To mind and eye; but the long sleepless nights
Of my long life have made it easy to me.
And none can read the text, not even I;
And none can read the comment but myself;
And in the comment did I find the charm.
O, the results are simple; a mere child
Might use it to the harm of anyone,
And never could undo it: ask no more:
For though you should not prove it upon me,
But keep the oath ye sware, ye might, perchance,
Assay it on some one of the Table Round,
And all because ye dream they babble of you."

And Vivien, frowning in true anger, said:
"What dare the full-fed liars say of me?
They ride abroad redressing human wrongs!
They sit with knife in meat and wine in horn!
They bound to holy vows of chastity!
Were I not woman, I could tell a tale.
But you are man, you well can understand
The shame that cannot be explained for shame.
Not one of all the drove should touch me: swine!"

Then answered Merlin careless of her words:
"You breathe but accusation vast and vague,
Spleen-born, I think, and proofless. If ye know,
Set up the charge ye know, to stand or fall!"

And Vivien answered frowning wrathfully:
"O ay, what say ye to Sir Valence, him
Whose kinsman left him watcher o'er his wife
And two fair babes, and went to distant lands;
Was one year gone, and on returning found
Not two but three? there lay the reckling, one
But one hour old! What said the happy sire?
A seven-months' babe had been a truer gift.
Those twelve sweet moons confused his fatherhood."

Then answered Merlin, Nay, I know the tale.
Sir Valence wedded with an outland dame:
Some cause had kept him sundered from his wife:
One child they had: it lived with her: she died:
His kinsman travelling on his own affair
Was charged by Valence to bring home the child.
He brought, not found it therefore: take the truth."

O ay,» said Vivien, overtrue a tale.
What say ye then to sweet Sir Sagramore,
That ardent man? 'to pluck the flower in season,'
So says the song, 'I trow it is no treason.'
O Master, shall we call him overquick
To crop his own sweet rose before the hour?"

And Merlin answered, Overquick art thou
To catch a loathly plume fallen from the wing
Of that foul bird of rapine whose whole prey
Is man's good name: he never wronged his bride.
I know the tale. An angry gust of wind
Puffed out his torch among the myriad-roomed
And many-corridored complexities
Of Arthur's palace: then he found a door,

And darkling felt the sculptured ornament
That wreathen round it made it seem his own;
And wearied out made for the couch and slept,
A stainless man beside a stainless maid;
And either slept, nor knew of other there;
Till the high dawn piercing the royal rose
In Arthur's casement glimmered chastely down,
Blushing upon them blushing, and at once
He rose without a word and parted from her:
But when the thing was blazed about the court,
The brute world howling forced them into bonds,
And as it chanced they are happy, being pure."

O ay,» said Vivien, that were likely too.
What say ye then to fair Sir Percivale
And of the horrid foulness that he wrought,
The saintly youth, the spotless lamb of Christ,
Or some black wether of St. Satan's fold.
What, in the precints of the chapel-yard,
Among the knightly brasses of the graves,
And by the cold Hic Jacets of the dead!"

And Merlin answered careless of her charge,
"A sober man is Percivale and pure;
But once in life was flustered with new wine,
Then paced for coolness in the chapel-yard;
Where one of Satan's shepherdesses caught
And meant to stamp him with her master's mark:
And that he sinned is not believable;
For, look upon his face! —but if he sinned,
The sin that practice burns into the blood,
And not the one dark hour which brings remorse,
Will brand us, after, of whose fold we be:

Or else were he, the holy king, whose hymns
Are chanted in the minster, worse than all.
But is your spleen frothed out, or have ye more?"

And Vivien answered frowning yet in wrath:
"O ay; what say ye to Sir Lancelot, friend
Traitor or true? that commerce with the Queen,
I ask you, is it clamoured by the child,
Or whispered in the corner? do ye know it?"

To which he answered sadly, Yea, I know it.
Sir Lancelot went ambassador, at first,
To fetch her, and she watched him from her walls.
A rumour runs, she took him for the King,
So fixt her fancy on him: let them be.
But have ye no one word of loyal praise
For Arthur, blameless King and stainless man?"

She answered with a low and chuckling laugh:
"Man! is he man at all, who knows and winks?
Sees what his fair bride is and does, and winks?
By which the good King means to blind himself,
And blinds himself and all the Table Round
To all the foulness that they work. Myself
Could call him (were it not for womanhood)
The pretty, popular name such manhood earns,
Could call him the main cause of all their crime;
Yea, were he not crowned King, coward, and fool."

Then Merlin to his own heart, loathing, said:
"O true and tender! O my liege and King!
O selfless man and stainless gentleman,
Who wouldst against thine own eye-witness fain

Have all men true and leal, all women pure;
How, in the mouths of base interpreters,
From over-fineness not intelligible
To things with every sense as false and foul
As the poached filth that floods the middle street,
Is thy white blamelessness accounted blame!"

But Vivien, deeming Merlin overborne
By instance, recommenced , and let her tongue
Rage like a fire among the noblest names,
Polluting, and imputing her whole self,
Defaming and defacing, till she left
Not even Lancelot brave, nor Galahad clean.

Her words had issue other than she willed.
He dragged his eyebrow bushes down, and made
A snowy penthouse for his hollow eyes,
And muttered in himself, "Tell *her* the charm!
So, if she had it, would she rail on me
To snare the next, and if she have it not
So will she rail. What did the wanton say?
'Not mount as high;' we scarce can sink as low:
For men at most differ as Heaven and earth,
But women, worst and best, as Heaven and Hell.
I know the Table Round, my friends of old;
All brave, and many generous, and some chaste.
She cloaks the scar of some repulse with lies;
I well believe she tempted them and failed,
Being so bitter: for fine plots may fail,
Though harlots paint their talk as well as face
With colours of the heart that are not theirs.
I will not let her know: nine tithes of times
Face-flatterer and backbiter are the same.

And they, sweet soul, that most impute a crime
Are pronest to it, and impute themselves,
Wanting the mental range; or low desire
Not to feel lowest makes them level all;
Yea, they would pare the mountain to the plain,
To leave an equal baseness; and in this
Are harlots like the crowd, that if they find
Some stain or blemish in a name of note,
Not grieving that their greatest are so small,
Inflate themselves with some insane delight,
And judge all nature from her feet of clay,
Without the will to lift their eyes, and see
Her godlike head crowned with spiritual fire,
And touching other worlds. I am weary of her."

He spoke in words part heard, in whispers part,
Half-suffocated in the hoary fell
And many-wintered fleece of throat and chin.
But Vivien, gathering somewhat of his mood,
And hearing "harlot" muttered twice or thrice,
Leapt from her session on his lap, and stood
Stiff as a viper frozen; loathsome sight,
How from the rosy lips of life and love,
Flashed the bare grinning skeleton of death!
White was her cheek; sharp breaths of anger puffed
Her fairy nostril out; her hand half-clenched
Went faltering sideways downward to her belt,
And feeling; had she found a dagger there
(For in a wink the false love turns to hate)
She would have stabbed him; but she found it not:
His eye was calm, and suddenly she took
To bitter weeping like a beaten child,
A long, long weeping, not consolable.

Then her false voice made way, broken with sobs:

O crueller than was ever told in tale,
Or sung in song! O vainly lavished love!
O cruel, there was nothing wild or strange,
Or seeming shameful—for what shame in love,
So love be true, and not as yours is—nothing
Poor Vivien had not done to win his trust
Who called her what he called her—all her crime,
All—all—the wish to prove him wholly hers."

She mused a little, and then clapt her hands
Together with a wailing shriek, and said:
"Stabbed through the heart's affections to the heart!
Seethed like the kid in its own mother's milk!
Killed with a word worse than a life of blows!
I thought that he was gentle, being great:
O God, that I had loved a smaller man!
I should have found in him a greater heart.
O, I, that flattering my true passion, saw
The knights, the court, the King, dark in your light,
Who loved to make men darker than they are,
Because of that high pleasure which I had
To seat you sole upon my pedestal
Of worship—I am answered, and henceforth
The course of life that seemed so flowery to me
With you for guide and master, only you,
Becomes the sea-cliff pathway broken short,
And ending in a ruin—nothing left,
But into some low cave to crawl, and there,
If the wolf spare me, weep my life away,
Killed with inutterable unkindliness."

She paused, she turned away, she hung her head,
The snake of gold slid from her hair, the braid
Slipt and uncoiled itself, she wept afresh,
And the dark wood grew darker toward the storm
In silence, while his anger slowly died
Within him, till he let his wisdom go
For ease of heart, and half believed her true:
Called her to shelter, in the hollow oak,
"Come from the storm," and having no reply,
Gazed at the heaving shoulder, and the face
Hand-hidden, as for utmost grief or shame;
Then thrice essayed, by tenderest-touching terms,
To sleek her ruffled peace of mind, in vain.
At last she let herself be conquered by him,
And as the cageling newly flown returns,
The seeming-injured simple-hearted thing
Came to her old perch back, and settled there.
There while she sat, half-falling from his knees,
Half-nestled at his heart, and since he saw
The slow tear creep from her closed eyelid yet,
About her, more in kindness than in love,
The gentle wizard cast a shielding arm.
But she dislinked herself at once and rose,
Her arms upon her breast across, and stood,
A virtuous gentlewoman deeply wronged,
Upright and flushed before him: then she said:

There must be now no passages of love
Betwixt us twain henceforward evermore;
Since, if I be what I am grossly called,
What should be granted which your own gross heart
Would reckon worth the taking? I will go.
In truth, but one thing now—better have died

Thrice than have asked it once—could make me stay—
That proof of trust—so often asked in vain!
How justly, after that vile term of yours,
I find with grief! I might believe you then,
Who knows? once more. Lo! what was once to me
Mere matter of the fancy, now hath grown
The vast necessity of heart and life.
Farewell; think gently of me, for I fear
My fate or folly, passing gayer youth
For one so old, must be to love thee still.
But ere I leave thee let me swear once more
That if I schemed against thy peace in this,
May yon just heaven, that darkens o'er me, send
One flash, that, missing all things else, may make
My scheming brain a cinder, if I lie."

Scarce had she ceased, when out of heaven a bolt
(For now the storm was close above them) struck,
Furrowing a giant oak, and javelining
With darted spikes and splinters of the wood
The dark earth round. He raised his eyes and saw
The tree that shone white-listed through the gloom.
But Vivien, fearing heaven had heard her oath,
And dazzled by the livid-flickering fork,
And deafened with the stammering cracks and claps
That followed, flying back and crying out,
"O Merlin, though you do not love me, save,
Yet save me!" clung to him and hugged him close;
And called him dear protector in her fright,
Nor yet forgot her practice in her fright,
But wrought upon his mood and hugged him close.
The pale blood of the wizard at her touch
Took gayer colours, like an opal warmed.

She blamed herself for telling hearsay tales:
She shook from fear, and for her fault she wept
Of petulancy; she called him lord and liege,
Her seer, her bard, her silver star of eve,
Her God, her Merlin, the one passionate love
Of her whole life; and ever overhead
Bellowed the tempest, and the rotten branch
Snapt in the rushing of the river-rain
Above them; and in change of glare and gloom
Her eyes and neck glittering went and came;
Till now the storm, its burst of passion spent,
Moaning and calling out of other lands,
Had left the ravaged woodland yet once more
To peace; and what should not have been had been,
For Merlin, overtalked and overworn,
Had yielded, told her all the charm, and slept.

Then, in one moment, she put forth the charm
Of woven paces and of waving hands,
And in the hollow oak he lay as dead,
And lost to life and use and name and fame.

Then crying I have made his glory mine,»
And shrieking out "O fool!" the harlot leapt
Adown the forest, and the thicket closed
Behind her, and the forest echoed "fool."

Honey Cummings

A passionate, award-winning author of Fantasy, Honey has turned her aim toward erotica. Blending everyday scenarios, and crafting them into steamy, blood-boiling moments for every shade of audience. Whether you want something short and hot, like a student-teacher hook up to the more paranormal flair, where Sleep with Sasquatch has unexpected bonus, look forward to erotic short stories, novellas, and hopefully a Trilogy in the future. Honey's debut erotic short landed at No. 3 in Urban Erotica and continues to satisfy readers time and time again. Be sure to leave her a review and let her know what you think!

amazon.com/Honey-Cummings/e/B07WFX5FDX
AuthorHoneyCummings.com
instagram.com/authorhoneycummings
twitter.com/HoneyCummings2
facebook.com/Author-Honey-Cummings-101408818012749

More Honey Cummings Books

Sleeping with Sasquatch
Cuddling with Chupacabra
Naked with New Jersey Devil
The Erotic Cryptid Collection

Laying with the Lady in Blue
Wanton Woman in White
Beating it with Bloody Mary
The Erotic Ghosts Collection

Beau and Professor Bestialora
The Goat's Gruff
Goldie and Her Three Beards
Pied Piper's Pipe
Princess Pea's Bed
Pinocchio and the Blow Up Doll
Jack's Beanstalk
Pulling Rapunzel's Hair
The Urban Erotica Fairy
Tale Collection

Curses & Crushes: KU short story

Queen's Incubus: YONDER webnovel

Writing as Valerie Willis

Cedric: The Demonic Knight
Romasanta: Father of Werewolves
The Oracle: Keeper of the Gaea's Gate
Artemis: Eye of Gaea
King Incubus: A New Reign
Queen Succubus: Holder of the Crown

Val's House of Musings: A Mixed Genre Short Story Collection

Writer's Bane: Research 101
Writer's Bane: Formatting

Writing MM Romance as VC Willis

The Prince's Priest
The Priest's Assassin
The Assassin's Saint

The Champion's Lord: YONDER webnovel
Champion's Love: KU short story

More books from 4 Horsemen Publications

Erotica

Ali Whippe
Office Hours
Tutoring Center
Athletics
Extra Credit
Financial Aid
Bound for Release
Fetish Circuit
Now You See Me
Sexual Playground
Swingers
Discovered
XTC College Series Collection

Aria Skylar
Twisted Eros
Seducing Dionysus

Chastity Veldt
Molly in Milwaukee
Irene in Indianapolis
Lydia in Louisville
Natasha in Nashville
Alyssa in Atlanta
Betty in Birmingham
Carrie on Campus
Jackie in Jacksonville
A Humorous Erotica Collection

Dalia Lance
My Home on Whore Island
Slumming It on Slut Street
Training of the Tramp
The Imperfect Perfection
Spring Break
72% Match
It Was Meant To Be... Or Whatever

Nick Savage
The Fairlane Incidents
The Fortunate Finn Fairlane
The Fragile Finn Fairlane
The Complete Package

LGBT Erotica

Dominic N. Ashen
Steel & Thunder
Storms & Sacrifice
Secrets & Spires
Arenas & Monsters
My Three Orc Dads: a Novella
Before the Storm: a Novella

Eskay Kabba
Hidden Love
Not So Hidden
Signs of Affection
Deeply Devoted to Him
Honest Love
A Plane and Simple Connection

Grayson Ace
How I Got Here
First Year Out of the Closet
You're Only a Top?
You're Only a Bottom?
I Think I'm a Serial Swiper
Lookin in All the Wrong Places
What Makes Me a Whore?
A Breach in Confidentiality
Back Door Pass
My European Adventure
An Unexpected Affair
Finding True Love
The Dr. Cage Chronicles

Leo Sparx
Before Alexander
Claiming Alexander
Taming Alexander
Saving Alexander
The Fall of the House of Otter
The Case of Armando

Robert Lewis
Someone to Love
Someone to Come Home To
Someone to Kiss

Discover more at
4HorsemenPublications.com